Cleansing Rain

Holly Ash

For Owen and Lily, the reasons I keep trying to make the world a better place and my sanity level is no longer what it use to be.

«« Chapter 1 »»

The edges of the microscope's eyepiece gently pressed on Zoe Antos's eyelids as she counted the shards of microplastic in the sample. Her team was testing a new formulation for their plastic decomposition project, a formulation she had developed. If they were successful, they would be one step closer to solving the plastic problem plaguing the oceans. The results she was seeing so far looked promising.

"Zoe, what are you still doing in the lab?"

Startled, Zoe whipped her head around, sending her brown ponytail over her shoulder. Her boss, Brett Klein, was leaning against the back wall, watching her with amusement. "I wanted to double-check the counts from this afternoon's samples before the weekend."

"You know we have a whole second shift of techs to do that."

"I know, I just wanted to see what the results were for myself."

"And?" Brett pushed off the wall and came over to look at her notes.

"It's the fastest rate of breakdown we've seen yet, though we're still not at a hundred percent decomposition."

"You'll get there." Brett picked up the clipboard to read it better. He picked up a pencil and make a quick note next to one of the lines — a data point he thought was significant. "Well, I'm taking off. The boys and I are heading up to the cottage to get it ready for the winter."

"And to give Kathy a weekend to herself." Zoe cocked an eyebrow at him.

"That too." Brett folded his arms and looked down at her, a fatherly expression on his face. "You really should wrap it up for the day too. Don't you have some big date night planned with Cole?"

"He has a late meeting, so I have plenty of time to finish and still make it to his place in time." Unlike the last two weeks, during which she had been so distracted by the experiment that she had completely forgotten to meet Cole at the restaurant. That man was a saint for putting up with her.

Brett laughed. They had been working together long enough for Zoe to know he didn't believe her. "If all of the lab supervisors here worked as hard as you do, we would have already solved all the earth's environmental problems."

Zoe rolled her eyes. "I'll see you on Monday." She would never finish on time if he kept distracting her. She turned back to the microscope, hearing Brett chuckle as he left.

It didn't take long before she got lost in her work again. She was on the last sample when her phone started to buzz in the pocket of her lab coat. Pulling it out, she saw a reminder on the screen that simply read, *You're going to be late.* Cole must have put it on her phone while she was in the shower that morning. She cleared the reminder and saw the time. If she didn't leave right now, she really was going to be late.

Zoe quickly cleaned up the samples, making sure everything was put away properly. She raced upstairs to her cube and barely slowed down to grab her jacket, purse, and computer bag, which she'd had the forethought to pack before heading down to the lab. By the time she reached the main level again, her jacket was on.

She dug through her purse, searching for her keys as she walked across the parking lot. Usually, she got them out before she left her desk, but she had forgotten in her hurry to get out the door. As her fingers enclosed the ridged metal of her apartment key, Zoe collided with something. The contents of her purse went flying across the asphalt as she stumbled back a few steps.

"I'm so sorry!" She didn't know the man she had run into; he had to be new to the facility. Green Tech Laboratories wasn't a huge operation, and Zoe recognized everyone who worked there, even if she was terrible at remembering all of their names. This man couldn't have been more than a few years older her — maybe he was working on a joint project with one of the local universities? The box he was holding had been knocked sideways, and half of its contents were strewn on the ground, mixed among the pens, notebooks, and lip gloss that normally lived in her purse. "Let me help you."

Zoe knelt and started to gather up the scattered papers. She wasn't trying to read the files, but the words "microplastics" and "decomposition rates" kept jumping out at her. These were files from her project. The reports were old, the research long outdated.

Why would anyone be reviewing this data when the project had progressed so far from what was in these files?

"I got it." The man snatched the files from her hand, shoved them back in the box, and took off across the parking lot. He was out of sight before she could fully comprehend what she'd seen.

Zoe gathered the rest of her pens from the ground while considering what to do. Something didn't feel right. She wasn't aware of anyone removing archived data in her five years working at Green Tech. Getting up, she headed back toward the building. Cole wouldn't be happy, but she couldn't ignore what she saw.

The security guard at the front desk looked up when she entered the lobby. "Hey, Zoe, did you forget something?"

"Hi, George." Zoe joined him. "It's probably nothing, but I ran into someone I didn't recognize in the parking lot, and he had a box of archived research from my department. I didn't authorize any document transfers — did Brett?" Maybe Brett had approved the transfer and forgotten to tell her. That might have been why he came to find her before leaving and had gotten distracted by the latest counts. It wouldn't be the first time something like that had happened.

George turned toward his computer. "What did the guy look like?"

"Ummm." Zoe closed her eyes and tried to picture him. "He had dark hair, almost a buzz cut, light tan skin. He might have been Middle Eastern? Probably in his mid-thirties, wearing a black leather jacket. Sound familiar?"

George shook his head and turned back to the computer. He clicked a few times, then grabbed his radio. "I need a gate check set up. Code 809."

His voice was calm and measured, very out of character for him. It put Zoe on edge. "Is everything okay?"

"The removal of any archived files requires authorization from the department head and the security chief. I don't have anything on file." George stood up and grabbed his jacket off the back of his chair. "Someone probably forgot to file their paperwork." He clipped his radio onto his belt. "Just to be safe, why don't you wait here while I do a quick check of the parking lot?"

Zoe sighed and took a seat on one of the lobby's brown leather chairs, pulling out her phone. She needed to let Cole know that she would be late . . . again. He was tied up in a meeting for at least another half hour, so she texted him: *Some kind of security issue going on at the lab. Will leave as soon as I get the all clear. Shouldn't take too long. Sorry. Be there as soon as I can.*

There — now he would know it wasn't her fault.

To her surprise, her phone vibrated with Cole's response. *R U Okay?* Zoe could almost picture him at the head of an overly large conference table on one of the upper floors of Wilborn Holdings, texting under the table while trying to slyly blow the hair out of his eyes. He had an appointment to get it cut on Sunday, though Zoe always preferred it a little long.

Zoe: *Yes, I'm sure it's nothing. Aren't you in a meeting???*

Cole: *I'm only here because Dad and Jackson were busy. My presence is just symbolic.*

Zoe: *It's your family's company. You're important too.*

Cole: *Only to you. How late do you think you're going to be? I made a reservation.*

Zoe: *IDK*

Cole: *I was looking forward to a night out.*

Zoe: *I know, I was too. I'll make it up to you.*

Cole: *How????*

Zoe: *I'll share my dessert with you.*

Zoe looked down at the ring on her left hand. The weight of it still felt foreign. Cole had proposed over breakfast last Sunday. She had asked him to pass the milk, and instead he'd handed her the ring box. It was a quiet simple proposal, unlike most things the Wilborns did, but to Zoe it was perfect.

Cole: *I was thinking something more personal. Like you could put on that outfit I like and have a little grown up fun.*

Zoe: *Focus on your meeting.*

Cole: *That's not a no.*

Zoe: *Get back to work.*

Cole: *Whoever schedules meetings for Friday afternoon should be forced to work the weekend. Maybe I'll put out a memo.*

Zoe: *You do that. I'll see you tonight. Love you.*

Cole: *Love you too. I'm looking forward to tonight. ;)*

With a chuckle, Zoe put her phone away. They had both been so busy lately, it would be nice to focus on actually being a couple again. They didn't have any social engagements that she knew of, so it would be an obligation-free weekend. She doubted she would have any issues convincing Cole to stay in with her.

"I couldn't find anything in the parking lot," George said as he came back into the lobby. "There's no reason for you to stay."

"Great." Zoe gathered up her purse and computer bag.

"Do you want me to walk you to your car?"

"No I'll be fine. See you Monday." She left the building, this time making sure she had her keys in her hand.

Halfway to her car, Zoe felt a presence behind her. A bead of sweat rolled down the back of her neck. This wasn't normal. She quickened her pace but couldn't seem to gain any distance. She was about to make a run for it when someone grabbed her arm and pressed what she assumed was a gun to her back. Zoe didn't need to look to know it was the same man she had run into before. Why hadn't she let George walk her to her car?

"Don't do anything stupid and I won't have to hurt you," he whispered in her ear, and a hysterical part of her wanted to laugh. That was something people said in movies, not in real life.

Her muscles tightened. "You can have whatever you want. Please, I don't want any trouble." Her voice was barely a whisper.

"It's too late for that. You're going to get me out of here, and then we can figure out how you're going to repay me for losing my files."

"Let me go and I'll call off the gate check. You can walk out of here without anyone suspecting a thing." Her voice was shaking so much it sounded like it belonged to another person.

"Right, 'cause I'm supposed to trust you." He increased the pressure of the gun on her back. "Which car is yours?"

Zoe tried to keep her hand from trembling as she pointed to her blue Chevy Bolt, which was plugged in at the back of the parking lot. There wasn't another car in the row. Most people had left an hour ago to make the most of one of the last nice weekends before winter. Why couldn't she have been one of them?

The man pushed her toward the car, never taking the gun off her back. Her legs fought her each step of the way, dragging as if there were weights strapped to her ankles. The man grabbed the keys from Zoe's hand and pushed her into the passenger seat. There was a moment when the gun wasn't pointed at her while he walked to the other side of the car, and part of her knew she should make a run for it—he probably wouldn't chase her now that he had the keys. But instead she just sat there, the disconnect between her brain and body growing with every passing moment.

Her captor turned in the driver's seat to face her. "If you give me away, you'll regret it." He put the gun in his jacket pocket and started the car. It only took a few seconds to reach the gate.

"Hey, Zoe," the female security guard said as Zoe rolled down her window. Zoe knew she was the second shift security chief, but she couldn't think of her name. "Isn't this your car?"

"Yeah, it is." Zoe tried to keep her voice as natural as she could. "But Stan has never driven an electric car, so I offered to let him take mine for a test drive." She glanced over at her captor, who looked at the guard with a perfect boy-next-door grin.

"There isn't a Stan on the employee roster." The second guard scrolled through something on his tablet, and Zoe's stomach flipped over. Had she already failed? Who would pay the price, her or the guards?

"He's a graduate student visiting from the U of M School of Natural Resources. I thought he signed in when he arrived this morning." The lie flew out of Zoe's mouth.

"I'll have to go back up to the office and grab the

visitor log."

Out of corner of her eye, Zoe saw her captor's muscles tense. She wondered how long it would take him to pull out the gun and shoot the guards. "Is that really necessary? We lost track of time in the lab, and now we're running late to meet Cole for dinner." She didn't like throwing Cole's name around, but she wasn't sure how much longer she could keep this up. If there was ever a time to play the dating-the-owner's-son card, it was now.

"The research Zoe's doing is really remarkable. I could have spent days in there if she'd let me," her captor said with a chuckle. Zoe did not like the casual way that he said her name, like they were friends.

"If you vouch for him, that's good enough for me," the female guard said.

No, no, no. It can't be good enough. Please don't let us leave, Zoe thought while she sat quietly and smiled until her cheeks hurt.

"If you could pop the trunk, we'll take a quick look and you guys can be on your way."

"Sure thing." Her captor reached down to the lever releasing the trunk and flashed the guard another award-winning smile. Zoe tried to mimic his calm demeanor, even though her insides were screaming.

She flinched at the soft bang of the closing trunk. "You guys are all set. Have a great weekend." Both guards stepped away from the car, and Zoe bit back the tears that formed as they pulled away from the lab.

They had only been driving for a few minutes when a ringing through the speakers interrupted the silence in the car. Zoe looked down at the car's touchscreen in horror; Cole was calling.

Within a second, the gun was pointed at her again.

The car swerved slightly as he cocked it. "Act normally and I won't have to use this."

Zoe choked back a sob and nodded. How was she going to talk to Cole normally with a loaded gun pointed at her? She took a deep breath as he hit a button on the steering wheel to answer the call.

"Hey." Her voice cracked.

"I'm leaving the office now. Are you on your way yet?" The sound of Cole's voice shot through her, and tears bubbled in her eyes again. She couldn't do this.

"Um, no. I'm still at the lab. Security hasn't given the all-clear yet." Zoe prayed he wouldn't notice the panic in her voice. She made the mistake of glancing over at the driver's seat. The gun was still pointed at her, and its owner watched her out of the corner of his eye.

Zoe fixed her sight on the road. She needed to focus if she was going to pull this off.

"Do you want me make some calls and see what's going on?" Cole asked.

"No, it's alright. I'm sure it's just routine and they'll let me leave soon." Her voice cracked again, more noticeably this time. She braced herself for a bullet, but nothing came.

"Zoe, is everything okay?"

"Yeah. It's just been a long week and I feel bad about missing date night again." At least that wasn't a lie. "How about you pick up some sushi from that place I like and we have date night at home? We won't have to worry about the food getting cold while you wait for me." She prayed Cole would understand what she couldn't tell him.

"Are you sure you're alright? It sounds like you're in your car. I thought you said you were still in the lab." There was a hint of panic in his voice that brought hope to her heart.

"It must be a bad connection or something." Her captor was getting antsy, his finger twitching over the trigger. "Look, I should let you go so you can call in the food. I love you, Cole."

The call ended before he could respond.

"Give me your phone," her captor growled. Zoe hesitated before fishing it out of her purse. It was in her hand one second and gone the next; she turned in time to see it shatter on the pavement behind them.

«‹«›»»

Cole did a U-turn the second the call ended, ignoring the honks from the other cars as he pressed his foot on the accelerator and raced toward Green Tech Laboratories. He tried to call Zoe back as he drove, but she wasn't picking up.

Something was wrong. Zoe hated sushi. She would never ask him to pick some up for dinner, and she certainly didn't have a sushi place she liked.

The parking lot was mostly empty when he pulled in. He glanced over at the row of charging stations where Zoe normally parked, but her car wasn't there.

"Where are you, Zoe?" he muttered under his breath. He nearly hit the security chief's car as he slammed on his breaks, jumped out of the car, and ran into the building, not caring that he was taking up three parking spaces.

"Where's Zoe?" Cole yelled as soon as he entered the lobby, startling the elderly security guard at the front desk. How had this guy managed to get a job in security?

"I'm sorry, Mr. Wilborn, my shift just started and I haven't seen her."

Cole slammed his hands down on the desk. "I called her twenty minutes ago and she told me she was here!" He didn't mean to yell, but his panic was starting to take control.

"Zoe left about an hour ago." The second shift security supervisor emerged from her office.

Cole swung around to face her. "Are you sure?"

"I searched her car myself before she left. She was with a visitor. She said they were running late to meet you for dinner."

The story didn't make any sense. Who was Zoe with? She had never sprung someone on him unexpected—she hated surprises of any kind. And she would never do something like that on date night.

"I need to see the security footage." Cole didn't wait to be invited back to the security office; there was no doubt the supervisor would follow him.

She sat down at the bank of computers and started to rewind the footage. "Okay, here they are at the security gate."

The video was in color ,but there was no sound. Cole was shocked to see Zoe wasn't in the driver's seat. She rarely let him drive her car, and there was no way she would let a stranger drive it. It was almost impossible to see her on the security video, but the man she was with looked completely at ease. Did Zoe know him? Had she lied because she was cheating on him?

Cole dashed the thought from his mind at once. There had to be more going on than what this video showed.

"Is there any footage of them getting in the car?" Maybe he would recognize who Zoe was with from a different angle?

"Let me see what I can find." She changed to a different camera and rewound until she found Zoe leaving the lobby, alone.

Cole watched in horror as a man approached her from behind. A flash of metal in his hand was visible right before he grabbed Zoe and pulled her against him. It was the same man driving her car.

Cole reached for the phone on the desk and dialed.

"9-1-1, what's your emergency?" The woman's voice on the other end of the line sounded disinterested.

"My fiancée's been kidnapped!"

"You can file a missing person's report at your local police station if she's been missing longer than twenty-four hours."

Cole's blood boiled with rage. "She's not missing. I'm looking at security footage of a man forcing her into a car at gunpoint."

That piqued some attention. "Sir, I'm going to need you to calm down and tell me your location."

"I'm at Green Tech Laboratories — the security supervisor will give you the details." Cole thrust the phone at the woman and strode out of the office. He couldn't stand around and wait; he needed to do something. Zoe was getting farther and farther away every second. He wanted her back. Now.

Cole pulled out his phone and called his dad. It only rang once.

"Cole? Is everything alright? Aren't you supposed to be out with Zoe?"

"Zoe's been kidnapped."

"Where are you?" his father asked with a proper sense of urgency in his voice.

"Green Tech."

"Stay there, I'm on my way." The line went dead.

««« Chapter 2 »»»

Zoe studied her kidnapper as they drove in silence. He was clutching the steering wheel so hard his knuckles were white. Was he nervous? He had seemed so sure of himself up to that point. His dark eyes were fixed on the road, but he seemed lost in thought, his lips twitching as if he were fighting the urge to talk to himself.

She couldn't take the silence any longer. Maybe if she could get him talking, keep him distracted, she could get away. "Cole's going to realize I lied to him and start looking for me soon."

He blinked a few times as if resetting his brain. "Is that supposed to scare me?" There was no emotion in his voice.

"Just let me go. I got you through the security gate at the lab, what else do you want from me?" He didn't answer. She decided to ask the one question she really wanted to know. "Are you going to kill me?"

He sighed. "That's entirely up to you."

"What does that even mean?"

"I need information from Green Tech. If you can help me get it, I'll let you live."

Zoe folded her arms. "And if I don't?"

He shrugged. "Like I said, it's entirely up to you."

She was going to die before this was over. There was no way she would help him. But Zoe did wonder what was so important at Green Tech that this man would go to these extremes to get it; nothing they were working on was particularly profitable. They were tackling global environmental issues. There wasn't a lot of money in that. It was something the Board liked to complain about whenever they came to the lab.

The man pulled into a grocery store parking lot, and Zoe's heart leaped in her chest. It was full of people stocking up for the weekend. All she needed to do was get someone's attention and she would be saved.

Her captor drove the car to the side lot. There weren't many people over there — Zoe assumed it was primarily employees using it. That meant she would have to make a bigger scene to get noticed. There were two people waiting next to an old Ford Tempo, the same type of car she drove in high school.

"Make one sound and it will be the last thing you do. Do you understand?" The gun had materialized again. All plans of escape quickly vanished from her mind, and Zoe nodded.

"Where the hell have you been, Ian? You were supposed to be here an hour ago," the woman standing next to the car said as soon as the driver's-side door opened.

Ian glanced back at Zoe, then stepped out of the car. "Iris, keep it down. Things at the lab didn't go as planned. We have a situation." He walked around the car to the passenger side, keeping his gun fixed on Zoe the whole time.

"What kind of situation?" Iris glanced at the car as Ian opened the door and pulled Zoe out. One hand flew to her mouth. "Jesus Christ."

"I did what I had to to get out of there." Ian didn't meet Iris's eyes. Was he afraid of this woman?

"This operation just got a lot more interesting." The man standing next to the car held his hand to Zoe. "I'm Blake."

Iris slapped his hand down. "You're an idiot." She got into the Tempo's passenger seat without another glance at Zoe.

"We need to get moving," said Ian. "I don't want to be out in the open when they start looking for her." He turned to Zoe. "You won't be needing this." He grabbed her purse out of her hands and tossed it in the back seat of the car, then reached down and grabbed her computer bag. "This, however, might be useful." He handed it to Blake. "Let's go."

Ian pushed her toward the waiting car, and she didn't fight him. Blake opened the rear passenger door and stood next to it like a chauffeur while Ian shoved her inside.

"Don't let her go anywhere." Ian pressed the gun flat against Blake's chest and slammed her door shut. Zoe watched him go back to her car and use his sleeve to wipe down the steering wheel and door handles. He left her keys conspicuously on the dashboard; he was probably hoping someone would steal it, sending the cops after the wrong person.

Blake got in the backseat with Zoe and leaned against the door with his foot up on the bench seat like they were out for a casual drive. His carefree demeanor made Zoe's skin crawl. She moved as far away from him as she could while Ian pulled the car out of the parking lot.

Zoe tried to pay attention to where they were going, but she had always been terrible with directions. She was pretty sure they were heading south, but she didn't recognize any landmarks or scenery. Ian took a lot of side roads, and she hadn't heard of any of the places on the few signs she saw.

After an hour of driving, the houses and businesses gave way to cornfields and patches of wooded area. Zoe stared out the window with a pained gaze. They hadn't seen another car on the road for a few miles. She shifted in her seat for the hundredth time in a feeble attempt to put more space between her and Blake. How far from the city were they taking her? She felt her chances of being rescued drop with every farmhouse they passed.

A stoplight flashed in the distance. Zoe glanced over at Blake, twirling the gun on his finger and staring out the window. This was her chance.

She placed her hand on the door handle as the car started to slow, reaching the light. She didn't wait for them to come to a complete stop; summoning all the courage she had, she threw open the door and jumped out. Zoe started running the second her feet hit the ground, stumbling the first few steps but managing to stay upright, much to her own amazement — she wasn't the most graceful person in general.

She scanned her surroundings as she ran. There was a farmhouse about half a mile down the road. The white paint was peeling from the siding but the truck parked in front looked to be fairly new. Someone had to be home. If she could get their attention, she might have a chance. "Help!" Zoe screamed as she ran down the side of the road. A four-foot drainage ditch ran parallel to the road keeping her from cutting into the nearby field.

Tires squealed behind her, but Zoe didn't look back. If they were going to kill her, she didn't want to see it coming. The car pulled in front of her and she skidded to the stop before she ran into it. Her eyes locked on Ian's in the driver seat. He was unbuckling his seatbelt as he opened the door. She spun around, slipping on the loose gravel on the road, and took off running in the opposite direction. She could hear Ian's breath behind her but she didn't ease up. The ditch narrowed up ahead and she was sure she could jump over it and escape into the dried-up corn stalks on the other side.

She readied herself to make the jump when a strong hand closed around her arm and hurled her to the ground. Zoe threw her hands out to break her fall, and her palms scraped against the gravel, taking off the top layer of skin. The right side of her body hit hard, and after a moment she sat up, ignoring the pain emanating from her hip.

Ian loomed over her. "You're beginning to be more trouble than you're worth."

"Then let me go," Zoe pleaded. "I promise I won't tell anyone." She pulled her bleeding hands close to her body. Tears coursed down her cheeks, but she didn't brush them away. What was the point? He was going to kill her.

"It's too late for that. Get up." Ian dragged Zoe to her feet as the car pulled up next to them. "Pop the trunk," he said to Iris, now in the driver's seat.

The woman leaned out the window. "You really want to put her in the trunk? What if she kicks out the taillight and someone notices? It's bad enough you make us kidnappers, let's not be stupid about it."

"For once, would you do what I ask without the lecture?" Ian snapped. Iris threw her hands up and pulled her head back in the window. A second later the trunk popped open. "Blake, do you have anything we can use to secure her?"

"You can't do this to me. I promise I won't try anything else. Please." Zoe clutched at Ian's shirt, but he acted like she wasn't even there.

Blake rummaged through the trunk and emerged with a roll of duct tape. "Will this work?"

"Perfect. We need to do this quickly, before anyone drives by."

Blake ripped off a small piece of tape as he walked over to Zoe. She shook her head violently, tears coating her cheeks. This couldn't be happening. This had to be a nightmare. Any minute she would wake in bed next to Cole. But no matter how hard she shook her head, the scene in front of her did not change.

Blake placed the tape over her mouth, smoothing down the edges. "Can't have you calling out for help."

Ian took the roll of tape and secured her hands behind her back. When he dropped to his knee and wrapped the tape around her ankles, Zoe wavered. She was sure she would fall, but Blake held her steady.

"Help me get her in." Ian rose to his feet.

Zoe struggled as best she could, but Ian and Blake lifted her easily. She was surprised at how gently they placed her in the trunk, removing a metal toolbox and some old sports equipment so that she was the only thing back there.

"I really didn't want to do this, but you didn't leave me any choice." Ian shut the trunk, thrusting Zoe into darkness with nothing but the musty smell of old gym socks to keep her company.

«‹›»

Cole tapped his foot as he waited outside Green Tech's lobby. It was taking his father forever to get there. The only reason Cole wasn't already out looking for Zoe himself was because his dad had told him to wait.

He had already talked to the one police officer who'd showed up, so the second his dad arrived, he could start his search for Zoe. Cole pulled out his keys as the black Cadillac pulled into in the parking lot. Both of his parents were in the car; they must have been on their way out to dinner when he called. His stomach twisted into knots. That was what he should have been doing with Zoe right now.

"There's a cop inside reviewing the security footage," Cole said before Gordon and Alana Wilborn were fully out of the Cadillac. "He can get you up to speed." He started for his own car.

"Where are you going?" Gordon shut the car door.

"I'm going to find Zoe."

"Cole, darling." Alana intercepted him, laying her hands on his shoulders. "Be reasonable. You can't go driving all over the state looking for her. You'll never find her that way."

"Your mother's right. The best thing we can do now is wait and see what the police say." Gordon gently steered him back toward the building.

Once they were inside, Gordon went straight to the police officer in the security office and demanded to hear everything he knew so far. Cole listened intently until he realized that all the police knew was what he had told them. When his father asked to see the security footage, Cole retreated to the quiet of a dark conference room. He didn't think his nerves could handle seeing Zoe with a gun pressed against her back again. He felt so useless. Zoe had been missing for two hours, and all they had managed to do was confirm that she was, in fact, kidnapped.

A shaft of light filled the room, and Cole turned in his chair as his mom walked in. She gently shut the door behind her, not bothering to turn the lights on. The single emergency sign in the corner provided more than enough to see by. He tried to return his mom's soft smile, but he couldn't.

She set a bag a food down in front of him. "You need to eat something."

The smell of fresh bread and Italian dressing drew his eyes to the paper bag stamped with the logo of a nearby deli. A deli where he would often meet Zoe for lunch, at least when he could convince her to take break from the lab. "I'm not hungry." Cole pushed the bag away. He was supposed to be at dinner with Zoe right now. If she wasn't eating, he wouldn't either.

Alana gently rubbed his back, and he let out an involuntary sigh. The last time his mother had held him like was after his last high school baseball game where he had struck out costing them the state title. It had felt like the worst moment of his life, until now. "I know it's hard, darling, but you need to keep your strength up." She sat down next to him. "We're going to find her."

"I don't know what I'll do if anything happens to her, Mom." Cole pressed his palms into his eyes. He couldn't break down now; it wouldn't do anyone any good. He had to be ready in case they needed his help.

"Cole, listen to me." Alana gently turned his face so she was looking him right in the eyes. "Nothing is going to happen to her."

"You don't know that."

"No, but I know Zoe. She's smart and tough. She'll find a way out of this, probably before we have the chance to find her." She took Cole's hand in both of hers and gently squeezed it.

Cole spun around in his chair at the sound of the door opening again. His father stood on the threshold, and Cole looked at him in expectation. But Gordon just shook his head. "I just got off the phone with Jackson—he's putting a team together to handle the media. They're going to schedule a press conference for the morning."

Cole turned back to the wall. Even his brother was more useful to Zoe than he was.

"Alana, why don't you give Victoria a call?" Gordon added. "I don't want her finding out about this from the news."

Cole's mom nodded and stood. "Be strong," she whispered, kissing the top of Cole's head before leaving the room. Gordon took her place in the chair next to him. They sat in silence, the soft hum of the fluorescent light the only noise in the room.

"It's my fault she's gone," Cole finally said after what felt like hours had passed.

"How is any of this your fault?" Gordon turned Cole's chair toward him.

"I made her promise to leave on time so that we could go out to dinner. If I hadn't, she would be safe in her lab. That guy would have come and gone without ever laying eyes on her." Cole could feel his mouth moving, but it felt like someone else was talking for him.

Gordon leaned forward and grabbed the arms of his son's chair. "You are not responsible. We have no idea what this man is after. For all we know, he could have been waiting for her. You can't blame yourself."

A knock came on the door, and Cole whipped around in his chair again. At this rate, he was going to sprain a muscle in his neck. He didn't recognize the middle-aged man standing in the doorway, and he eyed him warily, taking in the freshly pressed shirt and khaki pants, and the gun resting on his hip. The man couldn't be one of his father's private investigators — they tended to dress better.

"I'm Detective Toby Pearson," the man introduced himself. "I'm in charge of Ms. Antos's case."

Cole jumped to his feet. "Have you found her?"

"Not yet. I need to ask you some questions." Pearson motioned toward the table, and Cole slowly sat back down.

"Cole has already told the police everything. Do we need to make him go through it all again?" Gordon rose and rested a protective hand on his son's shoulder.

"Who are you?" Pearson asked.

"I'm Gordon Wilborn, Cole's father and the owner of Green Tech."

"Dad, it's alright." Cole removed his hand. "If it helps bring Zoe home, I'll talk to every person on the force."

Gordon took a step closer to Pearson, placing himself in front of Cole. "I can answer any questions you have. Cole told me everything that happened."

"That's not how this works, Mr. Wilborn. You are welcome to stay, but you won't stop me from talking to your son." Pearson walked to the other side of the table and sat down across from Cole. "What can you tell me about the last time you spoke to Ms. Antos?"

"Her name is Zoe. She hates being called Ms. Antos." Cole planted his elbows on the table and massaged his eyes with his palms again.

"I'm sorry. Tell me about the last time you talked to Zoe." Pearson's tone softened.

"She sounded distracted. She said she wasn't in her car, but I'm sure she was. It always sounds a little different when the call goes through the car. Oh, God, he was probably threatening her—that's why she lied." Cole choked back a small sob. Why hadn't he realized that before?

"Is it really necessary to make him go over all this again?" Gordon interjected.

"I know this is hard, but the more information we can get, the better chance we have of finding her," Pearson soothed.

"It's okay, Dad, I'm fine." Cole sat up a little straighter. He would do this for Zoe. She needed him to be strong. "I knew something was wrong when she asked me to pick up sushi. Zoe hates sushi." A sad smirk crossed his lips as he remembered the first time Zoe had tried to eat it, at some charity event he dragged her to. The face she made as she forced herself to swallow it had nearly made him spit out his drink in a senator's face. Cole didn't think he'd ever laughed that hard in his life.

What if he never did again?

"What did you do after she said that?" Pearson asked.

Cole took a deep breath and forced the memory down. "I came straight here, and the guards told me she had already left. I demanded to see the security footage and realized she'd been taken."

"Did you hear anything on the call that might give us some indication of who was in the car with her or where they were?"

Cole shook his head. He had gone over the call in his head more times than he could count. He wished he had paid better attention, but he'd been too annoyed that Zoe was going to miss another date night.

Guilt threatened to drown him. Cole looked toward the door to avoid making eye contact with Pearson.

"You mentioned that you saw the security footage. Did you recognize the man with Zoe?"

"No." Cole turned back to face the detective. "I've never seen him before."

"Maybe an old boyfriend?"

"Zoe and I have been together for ten years. She didn't date much before that."

"Did she have any enemies? Someone who might hold a grudge against her?"

"Not that I can think of. She doesn't have a huge social circle, just a few close friends."

"Okay." Pearson stood up. "If you think of anything else, call me. Day or night, it doesn't matter. Even if you don't think it's relevant." He held out a card to Cole, but Gordon intercepted it.

"Thank you, Detective." Cole's father got up and opened the door.

"Why don't you folks go home and get some rest? I'll call you as soon as we know anything." Pearson gave the older man a long look before leaving.

"Come on." Gordon returned to Cole. "Let's get your mother and we'll all go back to our house. You need to rest."

His father pulled him to his feet. Cole didn't want leave—this was the last place Zoe had been, and he felt closer to her here—but he didn't have the energy to argue.

«‹«›»»

Zoe lost track of time in the darkness of the trunk. They could have been driving for another ten minutes, or it could have been ten hours for all she knew. Her body ached, and she was acutely aware of how hungry she was. She really shouldn't have skipped lunch to spend time in the lab. To distract herself, she focused on trying to nudge the duct tape off her mouth, working her jaw as best she could, but all she accomplished was filling her mouth with the taste of glue.

Zoe tensed the moment the engine shut off. She was surprised by how soft the light was when the trunk opened. The sun had almost completely set. Cole had to be looking for her by now, even if he hadn't gotten the police involved yet.

Ian towered over her, holding a hunting knife in one hand. Zoe inched back into the trunk as far as she could, though she knew it wouldn't do any good. There was nowhere to go.

"I'm not going to hurt you," he said. "I just want to remove the tape from your ankles so you can walk into the house. Please don't try anything stupid. There isn't another building around here for miles, and I really don't feel like chasing you down again. Okay?"

Zoe wasn't sure what to do. She could easily lie to him and try to run again as soon as her legs were free, but how far would she really get? Her legs had fallen asleep, and with her hands still secured behind her back, she would lose her balance and fall flat on her face.

Finally, she nodded. With one swift movement, Ian cut away the tape, and Zoe awkwardly climbed out of the trunk, stumbling the moment her feet hit the ground. Ian grabbed her under her arms to help steady her, then led her inside.

The house was old, the main living space filled with mismatched furniture that reminded Zoe of her father's hunting cabin. Ian took her over to an overstuffed futon and left her there. She called after him as best she could with the tape still over her mouth, and he slowly made his way back to her. "This is probably going to sting."

Zoe closed her eyes and nodded. The tape pulled at her skin as he ripped it from her mouth; eyes watering, she fought the urge to scream. She wouldn't give him the satisfaction. Slowly, she worked her jaw again. "How about my wrists?"

"Not yet." Smirking, he walked to the kitchen, where Iris and Blake waited for him.

"What are we going to do?" Iris's voice traveled clearly from the kitchen. Zoe wondered if they realized, or even cared, that she could hear them. It wasn't like Iris was trying to keep her voice down. "Kidnapping was never part of the plan."

"Don't you think I know that?" Ian's voice matched Iris's in volume.

"How did it even happen?" Blake asked, much more calmly than the others.

Zoe got up and slowly made her way over to the kitchen, making sure to stay off to the side so they couldn't see her.

"They set up a gate check when I was trying to leave. I had to get out of there before the Arrows realized what I was doing and had me killed. This was the best option I could come up with at the time." Ian paced in front of the doorway, and Zoe pressed herself against the wall to avoid catching his gaze.

"Well, now that we have her, what are we going to do with her? It's not like we can ask her to forget it ever happened and let her go," Blake said. Zoe peeked into the kitchen to see him sitting with his feet propped up on the table.

"We could kill her before anyone figures out we have her," Iris said in a measured way that gave Zoe goosebumps.

"Jesus Christ, Iris, we aren't murderers!" Ian said.

"I didn't think we were kidnappers either, but there's a woman tied up on Blake's couch that tells a different story."

"To be fair, she's not the first woman that's been tied up on that futon," Blake said with a hint of pride.

"You're sick."

"You're jealous."

Zoe eyed the front door. Would Blake and Iris fight long enough that she could make a break for it without them realizing? She'd need a decent head start to even have a shot of getting away. But there wasn't even a hint of light slipping through the curtain on the front window anymore; if she tried to run now, she'd just end up lost in the dark with no way to protect herself. Maybe if she could free her hands?

"We don't have time for you two to bicker. We need to figure out what we're going to do," Ian said. "It's only a matter of time before the Arrows enact their plan, and if we don't come up with a way to stop them before that, then none of this really matters."

Zoe had no idea who the Arrows were or why it was so important to Ian to stop them, but right now, she didn't care. The only thing that mattered was making sure they didn't come back to the topic of killing her.

She would try to run. It wasn't like she had any better options at her disposal.

As she peeked into the kitchen again to make sure they were still distracted, her eyes locked with Blake's. He took his feet off the table and nodded in her direction. "Guys, we have an audience."

There went her chance to run.

Ian shook his head, grabbed Zoe by the arm, and led her back to the futon. "Blake, do you have anything we can use to keep her from wandering off?"

Blake nodded and disappeared. When he returned, he was holding a pair of metal handcuffs with black velvet wrapped around them. "What?" he said in response to Iris's look of disgust, handing the cuffs to Ian.

Ian cut the tape from Zoe's wrists, keeping a firm grip on her arm the whole time, and attached one of the cuffs to the metal armrest of the futon and the other one to her wrist. "Now we won't lose you."

"I think it's time we figure out who you are." Blake walked over and removed her name badge from her hip.

"I'm nobody," Zoe said as Blake sat down in an old armchair and pulled a laptop from his bag.

"Zoe Antos, age thirty-two," Blake said as he stared at the computer. "Undergrad in environmental science from Central Michigan University, master's in chemistry from Michigan State, working on a doctorate at the University of Michigan. Been an employee of Green Tech Laboratories for the last five years."

"Far from a nobody," Ian said.

"Alright," Iris turned to Ian, "maybe she can help us." She didn't even bother to look at Zoe sitting on the futon behind her.

Zoe scoffed. They treated her like a prisoner and then expected her to do what they wanted? These people were out of their minds. "I'm not helping you with anything."

"Then you'll stay cuffed to that futon," Ian said. At least he had the decency to look at her while he spoke. "It's been a long day. Let's get something to eat, then turn in."

The three of them went into the kitchen, once again forgetting about her, Zoe assumed. But Ian returned a few minutes later with a sandwich and a glass of water. "You need to eat something too."

She cautiously took the plate and set it down next to her, then reached for the glass of water. "Thanks." She drank the whole glass at once, her mouth still dry from the duct tape. He took the glass and left, giving her a few minutes of peace to enjoy her sandwich. It was the best PB&J she had ever tasted.

Ian returned with the glass of water in one hand and a small white metal box in the other. He set the water down on the table and took a seat next to her. "Give me your hand."

Zoe pulled her free hand close to her body. "Why?"

Ian rolled his eyes. "I want to clean and bandage your scrapes before they get infected." He opened the metal box and placed it next to him on the futon.

Zoe hesitated before holding her hand out to him. He didn't say anything as he worked, first removing tiny shards of gravel with tweezers, then cleaning the wounds and finally wrapping them in gauze. When he finished, he knelt on her other side so he could work on that hand without removing the cuffs.

"Why are you doing all of this?" Zoe asked as she watched him.

"You're my mess." He continued to work without looking up at her.

She waited a few minutes before asking the question lurking in the back of her mind. "Who are the Arrows, and why do you think they'll kill you?"

Ian paused for a moment, then quickly secured the gauze, making her wince for the first time. "Like I'm supposed to believe you don't know."

"I wouldn't be asking if I knew."

"Then consider yourself lucky." He strode to the closet next to the front door, pulled out an old air mattress, and set it up next to the futon. Then he got down a stack of blankets and pillows, tossed some on the futon for Zoe, and turned out the light.

The darkness enveloped her. Coldness seeped into her bones. She longed to be in Cole's arms, safe and warm. Grabbing the blanket, she arranged it over herself as best she could. Silent tears streamed from her eyes the moment her head hit the pillow.

««« Chapter 3 »»»

Zoe woke to the sound of fingers on a keyboard. She opened her eyes to find the air mattress gone and Blake once again sitting in the armchair with a computer on his lap. She pulled herself up to a seated position; the arm that was attached to the armrest ached.

"Good morning, Sleeping Beauty." Blake set the computer aside. "I've been told to give you five minutes in the bathroom, and then it's straight back to the couch with you." His tone reminded her of a swashbuckling hero from an old pirate movie. Was this whole situation a joke to him?

Zoe didn't say anything as Blake unlocked her wrist and led her to the bathroom. The second she was alone, she locked the door and started searching for a window she could squeeze out of or something she could use as a weapon. Of course, she found neither.

"I don't hear any water going in there. I'd get a move on if I were you — there's only four minutes and forty-five seconds left. Forty-four . . . forty-three . . . forty-two . . ." Blake yelled through the door.

Zoe turned on the faucet to drown him out and splashed some cool water on her face. It smelled earthy; they were getting their water from a well. Where had they taken her that wasn't on a public water system?

Blake banged on the door. "Two and a half minutes gone. You've reached the halfway point."

Zoe rolled her eyes and freshened up as best she could. She would need to be alert and focused if she was going to figure out how to get out of this mess.

More banging. "That's it, time's up. I hope you're decent. I'm coming in."

Zoe stood back and smirked. Did he really think she wouldn't lock the door?

The handle rattled, but the door didn't open. "Very funny, now open up."

Zoe didn't move. There was no reason to be a willing hostage, especially if he was going to be an ass about the whole thing. "No thanks, I'm good!"

"God damn it, Zoe, open the fucking door." The door rattled so much it reminded Zoe of the earthquake that had hit the first day Cole took her to go wine tasting in California. She wondered how far she should push him; somewhere in the house was Ian's gun, though she hadn't seen it since they got here. Blake sounded seconds away from breaking the door down.

Zoe sighed. She might as well open the door.

She turned the knob and stepped aside as Blake came crashing into the bathroom.

"You think you're funny, don't you," he grumbled, picking himself up off the floor.

"Kind of, yeah." Zoe stepped past him and walked back to the futon, trying to find a comfortable position before he re-cuffed her. He retreated to the kitchen, leaving her alone, and she noticed the television remote on the table next to her.

She started flipping through the stations. Maybe she would find something to give her some idea where she was.

Blake returned carrying a plate of food and a mug of coffee. Zoe accepted both and picked at the bacon and scrambled eggs on the plate. They were cold, but she was so hungry she didn't care. Besides, she couldn't be sure they would keep feeding her after she refused to help them.

"Are we the only ones here?" Zoe asked when Blake retook his seat and picked up his computer again.

"Ian and Iris went out to get supplies. We weren't planning on staying here, so we needed to stock up. Especially since there's an extra mouth to feed." His eyes darted across the screen while he talked.

"You know, you could cut back on the grocery bill if you let me go."

Blake smirked and closed the laptop. "Sorry, no can do."

"If this wasn't the plan" — Zoe gestured around the room — "then what was?"

"I'm not going to tell you that, either."

"Alright, then let's start with something simpler. This is an interesting house. Is it yours?" If she could get him talking, maybe he'd let something helpful slip. Besides, she remembered reading an article about a woman who survived a kidnapping by talking to her captor and forcing them to see her as a person.

"Nah, it belonged to Ian and Iris's uncle, I've just been crashing here for a while."

"Ian and Iris are related?" That at least explained why they fought so much. Were they part of some family crime ring? Somehow, Zoe doubted it. They didn't appear to know what they were doing; they'd have to have picked up at least a few basics if this was a family enterprise.

"They're twins." Blake watched her carefully, with that annoying smirk on his face.

"How did you meet them?"

"You sure do ask a lot of questions."

"It's not like I can do anything else." Zoe rattled the handcuffs dramatically.

Blake laughed. "I've been friends with Ian since we were in elementary school. They grew up around the block from me; they lived there with their uncle."

"Where were their parents?"

Blake shrugged. "Dead."

"Oh." Zoe turned her attention to the TV. The morning news was just starting.

"Good morning, Detroit," the anchor said. At least they hadn't taken her out of the state. It was a start. "We'll begin this morning with the kidnapping of Zoe Antos."

"Shit." Blake leaned forward in his chair, tense for the first time since Zoe met him. Maybe this would make him realize this wasn't some silly game.

The front door opened, drowning out the anchor's voice for a moment.

"You guys get over here, we made the news," Blake yelled over his shoulder. Ian and Iris rushed over and sat down on the futon, leaving their grocery bags forgotten by the front door.

"Antos was last seen yesterday afternoon leaving Green Tech Laboratories where she works, with the man pictured here." A blurry picture of Ian standing behind Zoe in the parking lot filled the screen. "Authorities have yet to identify the man in the picture. If anyone has any information about his identity or the whereabouts of Zoe Antos, please call the number below. We will be going to a live press conference with Gordon Wilborn, CEO of Wilborn Holdings, the parent company of Green Tech Laboratories, when we return."

"They don't have a good picture of you — it will be hard for anyone to identify you from that," Iris said. Concern flashed in her eyes as she looked at her brother.

"Yeah, I guess," Ian muttered.

"You could always let me go. I could tell the police you didn't kidnap me, that we were old friends catching up or something like that," Zoe pleaded. She had lost track of the number of times she'd begged them to let her go.

"You're not going anywhere." Ian's harsh tone made it clear she should stop asking.

The commercials ended, and the news anchor returned on the screen. "We will now take you the headquarters of Wilborn Holdings, where Mr. Wilborn will be giving a statement." The picture on the screen shifted to an elegant lobby with an empty podium set up in the middle. Zoe had seen the room countless times, but had never truly appreciated the beauty of it before.

As Gordon approached the podium, several people filled in behind him, including her parents. Her eyes lingered on her father. His normally gruff exterior built up from years working in the automotive plants looked frail and broken. The transformation drove home how much danger she was in. It was as if he had already lost her. Zoe's mom clutched Cole's hand as he led her onto the stage.

Zoe's gaze locked on Cole—her safe place, her home. He was dressed in a suit, his normal work attire, but his eyes were red and tired. His light brown hair was parted differently, like he had run his hands through it a thousand times. She doubted he had gotten any sleep. She knew she would be a mess if their positions were reversed. Her mother's shoulders hung with the weight of worry. Zoe wished she could reach through the screen to let them know that she was alright.

"Thank you all for coming," Gordon started. "What happened at Green Tech Labs yesterday is nothing short of a horrific tragedy. We at Wilborn Holdings care for all our employees, but Zoe Antos isn't just another employee. She's family. She's engaged to my youngest son, Cole."

Zoe gently fiddled with the engagement ring on her finger. They hadn't told anyone outside their families, and now the whole world knew. This wasn't how she had planned to announce her engagement.

"My family will do everything in its power to find Zoe and return her home safely. I'm offering a one-hundred-thousand-dollar reward to anyone with information that leads to her safe recovery," Gordon concluded. "Thank you."

Ian shut off the TV and paced in front of them with his hands on his head. "This can't be happening," he muttered under his breath, over and over.

Blake jumped out of his chair. "Of all the people that work at that lab, you had to go and kidnap the soon-to-be daughter-in-law of the man who's trying to end the world!" He waved an arm in Zoe's direction.

"It's not like I knew who she was at the time," Ian snapped.

"What do you mean, trying to end the world?" Zoe knew she should probably let them continue to act like she wasn't there, but her curiosity got the better of her. "Wilborn Holdings is one of the most charitable organizations in the country. They run charities that bring fresh water and sustainable energy to places that wouldn't have it otherwise. They've replanted millions of acres of forests around the world and remove over a ton of debris from the oceans every year. They're trying to *save* the world."

"You can't be that naïve," Iris scoffed. "Just tell us what you're actually working on so we can figure out how to stop your father-in-law before it's too late."

"The goal of Green Tech is to try to reverse the damage done to the environment."

"You're a liar." Iris leaned closer, and Zoe shrank into the futon to put some distance between them.

"What are you guys, some kind of anti-science zealots? Climate-change deniers who have gone off the deep end? What were you trying to steal from the lab in the first place?" Zoe eyed Ian rather than his sister. She had been so scared of him yesterday, but now he looked nervous, like he had bitten off more than he could chew and couldn't figure out a way to swallow it.

"We're trying to stop the Wilborns from plunging the world into some kind of dystopian horror piece straight out of a teen novel," Blake answered.

Anger built in Zoe's chest. She'd done a pretty good job of keeping her emotions in check up to this point, but now they were attacking Cole's father, one of the most generous people she had ever met. She wouldn't stand for it. "Green Tech is one of the only privately funded environmental research labs in the country, and Gordon Wilborn had to fight the Board to fund it. They didn't think it was smart business since there was no profit to be had, but he convinced them it was their moral obligation. If anything, the Wilborn family are heroes!"

"Gordon Wilborn is one of the most dangerous people in the world. Hell, you're probably just as involved as he is," Blake said. "I was wrong, Iris. We should kill her. It might buy the planet a little more time." He halted in front of her with Iris at his side, and a bead of sweat trickled down Zoe's spine. These people were crazy enough to actually do it.

"Alright, that's enough." Ian came to stand between Zoe and the pair. "Everyone needs to calm down."

"And how do you suggest we do that?" Iris glared at him.

"You took this week off of work and rented that house up north, right?"

"You aren't seriously suggesting I go on vacation, are you?"

"That's exactly what I'm suggesting. And take Blake with you. Go check in and go out to lunch or something. Make sure you're seen."

"This is insane, Ian." Iris threw her hands up. "Do you really think it's safe for us to be out in public right now?"

"The cops are only looking for me, remember? You two need to keep up appearances. This way, you have an alibi."

Iris didn't say anything for a few minutes as she stared at her brother. Ian didn't back down. Finally, she let out a deep sigh. "Fine, let's go, Blake." She grabbed her jacket and stormed out of the house. With a murderous glance at Zoe, Blake followed.

«‹«›»›

The lobby echoed with questions the second Gordon finished talking. The noise engulfed Cole, though he couldn't make out a single word the reporters were yelling at him. Jackson quickly ushered Zoe's parents off the stage, and Cole followed. They went into a small conference room off the lobby, where he collapsed in a chair and watched Jackson close the blinds over the windows.

"Do you think it will work?" Zoe's dad asked. Max Antos had spent his whole life on the assembly line; Cole was certain this was the first time he had ever been in front of the media. It was Cole's fault that the Antos family were now public figures.

"It certainly can't hurt. The sooner they find the guy who took Zoe, the sooner we can bring her home," Jackson said, and Cole shot him a grateful smile. He should have been the one to answer, but he couldn't put the words together right now.

Max nodded and walked over to Cole. "I'm going to take Gail home so she can get some rest. You'll call me as soon as you hear something?"

"Of course." Cole stood up and hugged Max.

"You should get some rest, too. You're no good to my daughter if you're so tired you can't function," Max murmured in his ear.

"I'll try." Cole fought to keep the tears from his eyes. He was the last thing Zoe's dad should be worrying about.

"I'll walk you guys out and keep the press from bothering you," Jackson said. Sometimes Cole forgot how good his older brother was at his job as head of public relations. Cole hated dealing with the press, but that was where Jackson shined. He had a face that was made to be in front of the camera. Their older sister

Victoria loved to suggest that Jackson would make a perfect sales model if he ever tired of the family business.

"Thanks, Jackson," Max said.

Cole didn't think it was possible, but he missed Zoe even more as he watched Max place a hand on the small of Gail's back and escort her from the room. His hand ached as he wondered if he would ever be able to touch Zoe like that again. Something so simple, so innocent — he had probably done it a thousand times, never fully appreciating it.

He sprang from his chair. He couldn't sit and wait any longer; he had to do something or he was going to drive himself insane. Cole didn't consider the press as he left the room, but thankfully they had all gone, a new story somewhere demanding their attention.

He took the elevator up to the floor with his father's office. It would have felt like a normal day at the office if it weren't for the giant hole in his heart.

There were more people in the office than he'd expected for a Saturday. Selfishly, Cole wondered if everyone had come in to help find Zoe, though most averted their eyes as he passed them. His father stood inside his office with the door open, talking to William Conner, one of Wilborn Holding's board members. Thirty-five years of taught manners kicked in, halting Cole off to the side while they finished their conversation.

"You know what was in those files. If anyone were to figure out what we are doing, it would be a disaster," William said urgently.

"They were archived files. The project has evolved tenfold since then," Gordon replied offhandedly.

"But the intent was there, and that's enough." William's eyes bulged slightly behind his horn-rimmed glasses, and a vein on his temple pulsed.

"You're worried over nothing. He's just one person — even if he were to somehow piece together what we are doing, what could he do about it?" Gordon pulled out his phone, and Cole blinked in surprise. He rarely saw his father treat a board member so dismissively.

"You don't know that, Gordon," William argued. "You're clouded by your personal feelings. What we're working on is more important than that."

"Relax, William, before you give yourself another heart attack." Gordon squeezed the bridge of his nose the way he always did when his patience wore thin. "The best we can tell he was only in the building for seven minutes before Zoe first ran into him in the parking lot. He never had a chance to go through any of the files."

Cole's stomach dropped at the sound of Zoe's name. He hadn't realized they were talking about her case.

"Where are the files now?" William asked through clenched teeth.

"They were evidence. The police confiscated them."

"How could you let that happen?" Cole had known William his whole life and never seen him this tense.

"I had more important things on my mind."

William huffed. "I'll make some calls and see if I can get this cleaned up for you. Honestly, Gordon, you need to figure out your priorities before people start to question your loyalty."

"My priorities are the same as they have always been: my family comes first." Gordon's hand went into his right pocket, where he always kept his grandfather's pocket watch.

Cole took it as his cue to cut in. "Dad."

If either man was startled by his approach, they didn't act like it. William held out his hand. "Cole, I'm so sorry for everything you're going through. If there is anything I can do to help find Zoe, please let me know."

"Thank you." Cole shook his outstretched hand and turned to his father. "I'm heading over to the call center. Maybe there's something useful I can do there."

"I'll drive you. We're done here anyway." Gordon placed a hand on Cole's shoulder and led him out of the building.

««« Chapter 4 »»

Cole wasn't sure what he expected from the call center, but it certainly wasn't the string of liars who kept the phones ringing all day. Of course there were dishonest people in the world, but it stunned him that so many would go out of their way to try to get the reward money. Didn't they realize that someone's actual life was on the line — someone he loved more than anything in the world? He would give up all the money he had if it meant she was home safe with him.

When he'd arrived that morning, Cole had felt so determined — finally, he was doing something to help Zoe. His heart would leap in his chest every time the phone rang. He was certain that the next caller would have the clue they needed to find her. But one after another, they let him down. After four hours answering phones, they were no closer to bringing Zoe home.

Cole slammed the phone down in frustration on the latest useless lead. This was pointless. He buried his face in his hands, massaging the heels against his eyes. Was it really possible that it had only been a day since Zoe was taken? Were they any closer to finding her than if the police had waited the customary twenty-four hours before investigating a missing adult?

Cole pulled his hands away at the *plunk* of a canvas bag landing in front of him.

"Your mother sent this over for you." Gordon handed him a bottle of RiverLife water, the only kind his family drank. He guessed it was important to support the brands they owned, but today he didn't much care.

"I'm not hungry."

"If you're not going to get some rest, the least you can do is eat. You need to keep your strength up. Besides, it makes your mom feel like she's doing something useful. I'm surprised she didn't send me down here with bagged lunches for all the volunteers." Gordon let out a small chuckle that Cole didn't return. "She made your favorite," he added, nudging the bag closer to Cole.

Reluctantly, Cole took the bottle of water and downed half of it in one gulp. He wasn't sure of the last time he'd actually had anything to drink. The headache behind his eyes eased ever-so-slightly, and he reached in the bag, pulled out the chicken salad sandwich, and took a bite.

"Feel a little better?"

"Sure, thanks, Dad." Cole tried to smile so that he wouldn't hurt Gordon's feelings. It wasn't his fault Cole had no appetite; his parents were only trying to help. Cole took another small bite out of habit. It did taste good, but part of him felt guilty for comfortably eating when he wasn't sure if Zoe was even being given food.

His dad leaned against the table and surveyed the call center, where he'd only spent an hour himself that morning. "How's it going here?"

"Not good." Cole tossed the sandwich back down. "None of this is actually helping us find Zoe."

"Just give it time."

"She might not have time. I want her home *now*." Cole slammed his fist against the table, and the operators closest to him to shot him uncomfortable, sympathetic looks. He took a deep breath and added quietly, "I just feel so useless."

"We all do. Trust me, she knows you're doing everything you can to find her, and I'd bet good money she's doing everything on her side to find a way home to you," Gordon said. "You two belong together. You're going to get through this."

"I wish I could be as sure as you." Cole turned away from his father and surveyed the room of volunteers answering phones, his heart sinking even further.

"Cole, I was told I could find you here." The voice was familiar. He spotted Detective Pearson weaving between the stations to join them. "Oh, and Mr. Wilborn. You're here, too."

Cole jumped out of his seat. "Did you find her?"

"Not yet, but we found her car."

"Where?" Gordon asked.

"Let's discuss this somewhere more private." Pearson eyed Gordon warily, though Cole wasn't sure why; it was the same question he had been about to ask, his father had just beat him to it.

"There's some offices up here." Cole led them to a small room off the main call center and shut the door, turning to Detective Pearson. "So, what did you find?"

"Her car was abandoned in a Meijer parking lot not far from Green Tech. Her purse was found in the back seat, but her work computer was missing." Pearson gave Gordon a pointed looked. "There was no sign of a struggle or anything to indicate she was injured at that point."

Cole let a small sigh of relief. It was a start. He said a silent prayer that wherever Zoe was, her kidnappers still hadn't hurt her. "Can we trace the location of the computer?"

Gordon pulled out his phone. "I'll have my team start working on it right away."

"While you're at it, tell your team to stop interfering with my investigation, or I'll have them arrested," Pearson growled.

"I wouldn't need to have my private investigators out there looking for Zoe if you were capable of doing your job."

"This isn't helping," Cole interrupted. "Pearson, you found her car in a store parking lot, so there has to be security footage. Does it show what happened?"

"We have people going through all the footage, but it appears they were parked in a blind spot. We assume he had a car waiting there."

Gordon started pacing, his hand on his chin — the same thing he did at work whenever he was trying to piece something together. "It's odd he took her work computer, but left everything else." He stopped pacing and turned to Pearson. "If he wanted money, he would have taken her wallet and tried to drain her bank accounts, wouldn't he?"

"It's impossible to know for sure why he did what he did."

"But you have a theory," Gordon pressed.

Pearson let out a deep breath. "We can't know for sure yet, but we believe that this man was trying to steal information from Green Tech. Ms. Antos was just in the wrong place at the wrong time."

"Is that supposed to make any of this easier? Whether Zoe was the target or not, she's been kidnapped, and she's still in danger." A tear burned down Cole's cheek as he looked from his father to Pearson. "That's the only thing that matters. Once you find her, then you can worry about why."

"If we can figure out why he was there in the first place, we have a much better chance of figuring out who the kidnapper is and where he might be holding Zoe," Pearson said gently. "I know it's frustrating, but this is how the process works. I promise, we're doing everything we can to find her."

Cole nodded and retreated to the corner to try to gather his emotions. Behind him, Pearson added to his father, "I need you to pull together a list of people who might a grudge against Green Tech Labs or Wilborn Holdings. Anyone who was fired, or maybe even interviewed recently and didn't get the job."

"I'll have a list to you within the hour."

That was reassuring, at least—Gordon Wilborn never let anything stand in his way. This wouldn't be any different.

"I'll be at the station for the next few hours. You can send it there." Pearson left the room without another word, and Cole pulled out a chair and sank down into it. His eyes ached, and his limbs felt twice as heavy as normal. He looked out the glass window into the heart of the call center. The phones were still ringing, but he couldn't find any hope there. They wouldn't find Zoe that way, he was sure of it.

"Dad, can you take me home?" Cole looked up at his father, feeling small in his presence, like a child again. He just wanted someone to take care of him.

«‹›»

Ian spent most of the day ignoring Zoe. After sending Blake and Iris away, he went into the kitchen to put away the discarded groceries and never returned. Zoe wondered if there was more to the small house than she realized; she spent at least an hour imagining an elaborate array of well-furnished rooms that Ian could be passing the time in on the other side of the kitchen.

After creating an extravagant indoor lap pool in her mind, she decided to use the time alone more productively. If she could get out of the handcuffs, she might be able to slip out the front door without Ian noticing. Zoe tried to pull her hand through the cuff, but when all she managed to do was bruise her wrist, she decided to see if she could break the chain connecting the two cuffs.

She never would have guessed that handcuffs that were clearly purchased in some seedy adult store would be so strong. After a few fruitless attempt and concluding it would be easier to take the futon apart than to free her wrist, she turned her attention to the television. Flipping through the channels again, she tried to see if there was any new information about her kidnapping. The Wilborns probably had every cop and private investigator in the state looking for her, but the midday news brought her no hope. They simply repeated the same things she had heard that morning.

All she could do was wait. They would find her. She was sure of it.

Until then, she needed to find something to occupy her thoughts. Zoe turned to daytime TV, but tired of it quickly; a person could only watch so many talk shows and sitcom reruns. Besides, another notion kept pulling her attention away.

She couldn't understand why these people thought Gordon Wilborn was dangerous. She had been dating Cole for ten years, and in all that time, she had known his father to be one of the most generous people she'd ever met. Sure, Gordon tended to be a little overinvolved in his children's lives, but that was out of love. He didn't seem capable of anything these people were hinting at.

Zoe's stomach rumbled, and she glanced over at the front windows to find they were dark. It had to be early evening, and they hadn't fed her anything since breakfast. She was about to call out to Ian when he walked in from the kitchen, carrying a plate of food. He set it down on the futon next to her without even giving her a glance. She snatched up the dry ham sandwich, watching him carefully while she took a few bites. Ian took a seat in the armchair and pulled out a computer — *her* computer. Had they figured out how to get past her password? They must have, as Ian seemed to be reading through something on the screen.

Well, if he was going go through her things right in front of her, she certainly wasn't going to sit back and watch silently. "So, Blake said this place belongs to your uncle." Zoe tried to position herself on the futon so that she was facing him. The arm handcuffed to the futon stretched behind her a little, but it wasn't too uncomfortable.

"Blake needs to learn to keep his mouth shut." Ian didn't look up from the computer. She would have to keep pushing until she got his full attention.

"Is that why you sent him away? Was he about to give away your master plan?" She tried to smile, to keep things lighthearted. She wasn't sure she pulled it off.

Ian closed the laptop and looked at her closely. Zoe shrank under his gaze; it was like he could see straight through to her soul. "I sent Blake and Iris away so they wouldn't hurt you. Your connection with the Wilborns scares them. You went from an annoyance to a threat."

"I don't understand how being associated with the Wilborns makes me a threat. What have they ever done to you that makes them so dangerous?"

"To me personally, nothing. It's what they're planning on doing to the rest of the planet that's the problem." Ian shook his head and opened the laptop again.

Zoe was losing him, but she refused to let the conversation die here. Even if he wasn't going to give up any useful information, it was at least better to have someone to talk to. "I'm not sure where you're getting your information, but the Wilborns are trying to save the planet. That's why they founded Green Tech in the first place."

"You're the one with the bad information," Ian responded, barely acknowledging her. She might have gone from an annoyance to a threat, but to her, Ian had gone from a threat to a huge source of aggravation.

"Then change my mind." She tried to cross her arms, but of course she could only move one of them. It felt more awkward than anything. She slowly put it back down at her side. So much for her sense of superiority.

"Why?" Ian closed the laptop again and set it down on the edge of the futon.

"I'm a scientist. I don't like unanswered questions." Zoe cautiously eyed the laptop. If she could get her hands on it, she might be able to send Cole a message to help him find her.

"And what will you do once I tell you what the Wilborns are really involved in?" Ian leaned forward slightly in his chair. Why was everything so intense with him?

Zoe fought the urge to recoil into the futon. "Probably nothing. I won't help you hurt them."

"Then you'll be just as responsible for the end of the world as they are. Maybe more so, since you had the chance to help stop them and you refused."

"I've dedicated my life to helping the planet. I won't let you guilt me about this."

Ian scoffed. "Is that what you're doing in your lab at Green Tech—helping the planet?"

"Yes. I'm working on a way to safely and quickly decompose the plastics clogging the oceans and bioaccumulating in marine life." Zoe really hoped she wasn't giving away anything that would help him. He had been trying to get information about her project, after all. Maybe this was all some elaborate mind game to steal her research? That would make more sense than the Wilborns ending the world.

"Maybe you are, but what about the rest of your colleagues? What are they working on?" He was goading her, she knew it, but she couldn't stop her anger from building. First, he'd attacked Cole's family, and now he was going after her work. She wouldn't stand for either one.

"We're tackling pollution and pollinator preservation. We're researching sustainable farming practices, sources of clean energy, ways to improve drinking water quality." She really should have paid better attention at the last general update meeting they had; at the time, she had only been concerned with giving the update for her department. "We're trying to find the balance between humans and nature."

"That right there, that balance between humans and nature line, that only confirms for me that the Arrows have control of your lab," Ian shot back. "And the fact that you throw it around so carelessly tells me that you are as clueless about them as you claim you to be. Which means you can't help us, even if you wanted to." Ian sat back in his chair and shook his head. Zoe wished she knew what he was thinking.

The front door opened. Blake and Iris were back. The woman came over immediately, standing in front of Zoe with her hands on her hips. "I'm not going to kill you. Not at the moment, anyway."

Zoe tried to raise her chin, but she found Iris so much more intimidating than her brother. "That's comforting," she said with as much strength as she could manage.

"We won't kill you as long as you tell us everything you know about Project Cleansing Rain," Blake added, halting behind Iris.

"She doesn't know anything." Ian got to his feet. "Come on, we need to figure out a new plan." He walked to the kitchen with the pair at his heels.

Zoe's eyes darted to the laptop on the other side of the futon. Her heart raced so fast, she was sure they would be able to hear it from the other room. She held her breath and stretched out as far as she could, gripping the edge of her computer; her whole body relaxed as she brought it to her lap. Unfortunately, that caused the handcuffs to rattle against the futon's metal frame.

She froze, her gaze trained on the doorway to the kitchen.

The seconds ticked by, but nothing happened. She was about to open the laptop when Iris stepped into the room, her gaze landing on Zoe immediately. In a second, she'd snatched the computer from her hands. "What the hell are you doing?"

Before Zoe could answer, Iris slapped her across the face so hard her eyes started to water. Tears burned as they rolled down the side of her face where Iris had made contact.

"What's going on in there?" Ian rushed into the room.

"You need to take better care of your shit!" Iris thrust the laptop at Ian and stormed back through the kitchen. Ian shot Zoe a sympathetic look before chasing after his sister.

Blake returned a few minutes later with a bowl of popcorn and an icepack. "Want to watch a movie?" He sat down on the other side of the futon and handed Zoe the icepack.

"Okay." She gingerly held the icepack up to her cheek, staring at the screen. Blake cued up an old comedy movie she had never heard of.

"How about something to lighten the mood a little?" He flashed her a smile and pushed the bowl of popcorn toward her.

Zoe grabbed a handful and nodded. What could it hurt?

«« Chapter 5 »»

Zoe wasn't sure when she fell asleep. She knew she didn't see the end of the movie, and someone had covered her with a blanket at some point. She pulled at her arm, but it was still cuffed to the futon. Worth a shot.

At the rattle of the cuffs, Blake stirred on the air mattress on the floor next to her. A moment later, he got up, and left without acknowledging her. He returned in a few minutes, holding two cups of coffee.

"Good morning, sunshine, how'd you sleep?" he asked with a smile that was much too big for the early hour.

"Not great." She sat up and accepted the coffee.

"That's a shame. I slept like a rock." Blake sat down in the armchair and picked up the computer leaning against it. At least they weren't using hers in front of her again.

Zoe watched him carefully while she sipped the bitter coffee, wishing for some of that fancy creamer Cole always had for her. She couldn't decide if her captors were a threat or not. They seemed so normal one second, like they could all be friends under different circumstances; then out of nowhere, they would switch and she was certain they would kill her, like in that moment with Iris and the laptop the night before.

The best course of action was to keep trying to engage with them. If they saw her as a real person, not just an annoyance as Ian put it, maybe they would have a harder time hurting her. Besides, she couldn't spend another day with nothing to occupy her mind except daytime television and her own thoughts.

"What are you doing?" she asked.

"At the moment, I'm trying to hack into the police servers to see if they have any leads on where you are," Blake answered brightly. "I want to give Ian a chance to run if they've figured out who he is."

"You really care about him, don't you?"

He looked up from his computer. "I know you might not think so, given that he kidnapped you and all, but Ian really is a nice guy. He only took you out of desperation. Normally he wouldn't hurt anyone."

"Then why does he have a gun?" Zoe raised an eyebrow, but held a smile on her face. She wanted to keep him relaxed now that he was talking.

"We're trying to save the world from dangerous people. He needed to be able to protect himself." Blake shrugged like it was no big deal—only Ian hadn't used the gun to protect himself, he'd used it kidnap her and keep her in line.

Zoe cocked an eyebrow. "Dangerous people like the Wilborns?"

"And others who believe the same things they do."

"And all of this has something to with Project Cleansing Rain?" She was slowly piecing together the bits of information they let slip in front of her. Zoe wanted to be able to pass as much of it along to the police as she could if she was rescued.

No, not *if*, when. She wasn't ready to give up hope. Cole was out there looking for her, and he never let anything stand in his way. He hadn't been deterred when she turned him down the first time he asked her out, when they ran in such different circles in school that Zoe thought it might be some kind of prank. Instead, he joined the same clubs as her, and when they started to get to know each other better, she realized his interest in her was genuine. It got to the point people just assumed they were a couple, and Zoe never corrected them.

"It has everything to do with Project Cleansing Rain," Blake said, breaking into her memory.

"What is that?"

"That's the thing," Ian interrupted, striding toward the futon. "We don't know."

Zoe had no idea how long he had been standing in the doorway to one of the bedrooms listening to them. "If you don't know what it is, then how can you be sure it's dangerous?" She forced herself to keep her cool despite the new, more threatening presence.

"Because we know who's behind it. That's enough," Blake said.

Zoe rolled her eyes. Like most people who tried to discredit the science coming out of her lab, they had no proof, no evidence to support their ridiculous claims.

Ian ran a hand through his hair. "Have you ever heard of the Arrow Equilibrium?"

Zoe shook her head. It sounded like some kind of scientific theory, but she couldn't remember ever studying it in any of her classes or coming across it any of the journals she read.

Ian took a seat next to her. "It's a highly connected, powerful, underground organization that believes it's their responsibility to restore balance to the planet, and they're willing to do whatever it takes to accomplish that goal."

"Which brings us back to Project Cleansing Rain," Blake added. "I was able to get some tracking software onto an Arrow's computer that sends me ghost copies of all their emails. Cleansing Rain seems to be all they're talking about these days."

This whole thing sounded insane. Secret organizations were something from the movies — they didn't exist in real life. Still, Zoe couldn't stop herself from asking, "Whose emails, exactly?"

"That's not important," Ian said. "What *is* important is that they indicated this project would finally bring the planet back into balance."

"What the hell does that even mean?"

"What's the biggest threat to the natural environment?"

Zoe sank back into the futon as she ran through the list of problems plaguing the environment — a list she was working hard to solve. There was one thing that every item had in common.

"Humans." The word slipped from her mouth as nothing more than a whisper.

"Exactly," Ian said with a hint of pride in his eyes, and Zoe's stomach twisted into knots. She didn't want him to be proud of her, she wanted to defy him. To push back, to break free. "So, to restore ultimate balance, you would have to eliminate that threat."

Zoe shook her head. This couldn't be real, it was too far out there. "And you think Gordon Wilborn is somehow involved in all of this?"

"From what we can tell, he's in the inner circle," Blake said.

"There's no way. He would never be involved in something like that. It's not possible." Maybe this whole thing was some kind of elaborate prank. That was the only logical explanation Zoe could come up with. Any moment, people were going to jump out laughing at her for playing along this far—though she didn't know anyone who would go to such lengths just to mess with her.

But the only alternative was that these people really believed what they were telling her, which was so much worse.

Ian got to his feet. "Believe it or not, it doesn't matter. The only thing that matters is stopping him and the rest of the Arrows before they can execute their plan."

"For a secret organization, you seem to know a lot about them," Zoe called after him.

Ian stopped and turned back to her. "My uncle used to be an Arrow before he realized the extremes they were willing to go to in order to accomplish their goal."

"Used to be? This doesn't sound like the kind of group you can just walk away from."

"It's not."

"Oh." Regret heated her cheeks. Whether or not the Arrows are real, or if Gordon was somehow involved, Ian seemed to believe they had killed his uncle. He had lied before—this was personal.

"Yeah, well, now you know. It's up to you to decide what you do with that information. Come on, Blake." Ian disappeared into the kitchen. Blake shot Zoe a sympathetic look and followed him, leaving her with a lot more to think about than when she woke up that morning.

«‹«›»»

Cole paced around the conference room off the lobby at Wilborn Holdings Headquarters while his parents watched him quietly from the table. He wasn't sure how he had let his father and brother convince him to talk to the press. As the youngest, not much was usually expected of him other than to show up and smile. On the rare occasion he had to talk to reporters, he was always given a carefully crafted message to read. But there were no prepared remarks this time. He was on his own.

The door opened, and Jackson walked in. "They're almost ready for you." He patted Cole on the shoulder. "Just remember what we went over. Talk about your relationship with Zoe and what she means to you."

Cole nodded, though he wasn't really listening. "And you're positive this will help us find her?" He wasn't sure how turning Zoe's kidnapping into a Lifetime movie for the press would help bring her home, but Jackson and his father had insisted it would. Cole suspected they had set the whole thing up just to make him feel like he was helping in some way.

"Yes, we need to keep the case front and center in the public's mind. It puts pressure on the police to divert their resources that way," Gordon said.

"And the only we can make sure that happens is if the public cares about Zoe." Jackson directed Cole back toward the table and pulled out the chair next to their mom. Cole didn't sit down.

"Everyone loves a good love story." Alana stood up and wrapped an arm around him. "All you need to do is share yours."

She handed him a bottle of RiverLife. Her go-to fix for any problem—a comforting word and a bottle of water. It was something Zoe and Cole had debated a lot before they started dating. Zoe, ever the environmentalist, argued that Wilborn Holdings couldn't really consider themselves an ecofriendly company while they were putting all that plastic out into the world. She only dropped it after he took her to the facility to prove their bottles were made from 100-percent plant-based material and were completely biodegradable, right down to the cap.

It was one of their more memorable dates. She had been so passionate as she talked to the management team. That might have been the moment Cole fell in love with her.

"I'm not sure Zoe is going to be happy with me sharing our personal life with all of Michigan," Cole said with a weak smile. It felt like a betrayal; there was nothing to smile about until Zoe was home.

"She'll have to come home to yell at you about it." Jackson swatted at Cole's arm, and Gordon shot him a look. He threw his hands up in mocked surrender and went back to the door.

Alana reached up and caressed her son's cheek, turning his head so he was looking at her. "If it helps bring her home, I'm sure she'll forgive you."

"Maybe she'll see it," Gordon added. "Just go out there and talk to her. Zoe needs you to be strong for her right now. Do this for her."

Cole didn't feel strong. He had barely slept more than a few hours since Zoe was taken. It was getting to the point where even simple tasks felt beyond his capabilities. Now they were asking him to be strong, to go out there and string together coherent thoughts for the media. It all felt impossible.

"They're ready for us." Jackson held the door open. Cole nodded once, wiping a tear out of his eye, then headed out to the lobby where the press was waiting.

«‹›»

They left Zoe alone the rest of the day. The TV remote had disappeared. Ian clearly wanted her to spend the day thinking about what they'd told her that morning.

It was a scary prospect. Despite her best efforts to put it all out of her mind, she kept coming back to the Arrows. If she left Gordon out of the equation, she could almost accept it. She had heard about ecoterrorists before, though as far as she could recall they rarely did anything big enough to warrant any kind of concern outside their immediate target. These were people that went after logging companies and construction sites — they targeted equipment, not people. That didn't fit with what Ian and Blake had told her about the Arrows.

The idea of an underground organization out there powerful enough to wipe out the majority of humanity seemed crazy. With the amount of information available, someone would have discovered them by now — someone other than the three people currently holding her hostage. How would the Arrows even go about killing off that many people? She assumed they would want to preserve at least a portion of the human population, themselves included, so they would need to have some control over the extinction event.

It just wasn't possible, especially when she tried to place Gordon Wilborn as the mastermind behind it all. Cole's father was practically a saint. He never passed up a chance to help someone in need. He'd funded countless charities, along with the research lab where she worked. The research lab where Ian believed the means to the end of the world was being developed. Gordon couldn't be involved with a group like that. It went against everything Zoe knew to be true about him.

Unless he was trapped, like Ian's uncle had been? Had Gordon been lured to the Arrows with promises of environmental advocacy, and now he was unable to leave? Was his life in danger, or maybe the lives of his family? Could the Arrow Equilibrium have threatened Cole? She knew Gordon would do anything to protect his family.

A pang of hunger gripped Zoe's stomach. The only thing they had given her was the cup of coffee Blake had brought her when she first woke up, and that had been hours ago. It was so easy to lose track of time with nothing but a conspiracy theory to occupy her mind.

"Um, excuse me." Zoe leaned over on the futon to try to see into the kitchen, where her captors were once again spending their day.

Ian appeared in the doorway. "What?"

"Would it be possible to use the bathroom, and maybe get something to eat?" She gave him a weak smile that she hoped would build on the connection she made with him that morning.

Ian's posture softened. "Sure. Iris is making dinner. It should be done soon." He uncuffed her wrist and walked her to the bathroom. When she came out, there was a bowl of pasta and a large glass of water waiting for her on the end table. Zoe reclaimed her spot on the futon, hesitating a moment before reaching for the glass. She expected Ian to cuff her again, but instead he sat on the floor and leaned against the center of the futon.

Cautiously, Zoe grabbed her pasta and began to eat. It was a nice change, having use of both of her hands again.

Iris emerged from the kitchen carrying two bowls, with Blake trailing behind. She handed one to Ian and took a seat at the other end of the futon without a glance in Zoe's direction. Blake claimed the armchair, producing the TV remote from his pocket. He toasted his glass of water to Zoe but didn't say a word.

The evening news was just starting, and they were all glued to the screen from the first word. "Our top story tonight is the kidnapping of Zoe Antos from Green Tech Laboratories. Antos was last seen Friday afternoon leaving work with the unidentified man seen here."

"At least they haven't figured out who you are yet," Blake said.

"It won't take them long to find this place once they do," Ian said without looking away from his grainy picture on the TV.

"Police have recovered Antos's car from a local Meijer parking lot and are hopeful it will lead them to the missing woman."

Zoe jumped at the clatter of Ian's fork hitting his bowl. Would this new information help or hurt her chances of making it home safely? The closer the police got to finding her, the more desperate her kidnappers became. How desperate would they need to be to act on their threats?

Iris leaned forward and put a hand on her brother's shoulder. "You wiped your prints from the car. You'll be fine." Her voice was kinder than Zoe had ever heard it.

Ian reached up and squeezed Iris's hand. "I tried to, but it's not like I have a lot of practice with this sort of thing. There's a good chance I missed something." He started to eat again, but Zoe could feel the tension radiating from him.

"We will now go live to Antos's fiancé, Cole Wilborn, son of the Wilborn Holding CEO Gordon Wilborn, who will give a statement."

Zoe set her bowl down on the futon and leaned closer to the TV. Hearing Cole's voice would give her the strength she needed to keep going. Her heart skipped a beat when his face appeared on the screen; he looked different, worn down, like it had been years since she last saw him, not three days.

"I have had the privilege of being with Zoe for the last ten years. She is one of the most generous, selfless people I know. She is a better person than I could ever hope to be." Cole had been in front of the press countless times, and despite his dislike for public speaking, he usually came across as a natural. This time, he was having a hard time maintaining eye contact with the cameras. His voice faltered as he spoke, like he was fighting back tears. The bags under his eyes told her he probably hadn't slept since she went missing. "My family is willing to do whatever it takes to bring Zoe home. If it's money you're after, we'll gladly pay whatever you want for her safe return. Please, just send her back to us. And Zoe, if you're listening . . ."

The screen went black. Iris set the remote back down on the end table between her and Blake.

"What the hell?" Zoe yelled, springing to her feet.

"I have no interest in listening to your fiancé profess his undying love for you so he can build sympathy for his family's company. Money that will get filtered to the

Arrows." Iris gestured toward the TV. "They're milking your disappearance for all that its worth. You can't buy press like this."

"My disappearance? You people kidnapped me!"

Iris got to her feet and squared off with Zoe, with Ian still sitting on the floor between them. "You're right, we did, but it wasn't long before they were taking full advantage of it. I bet they're hoping we kill you. Think of all the goodwill a tragedy like that would get them. Their stocks would go through the roof."

Zoe was so angry, she couldn't speak. She clenched her fists and raised her right arm; she had never punched anyone before, but there was a first time for everything.

Ian jumped to his feet and caught her fist halfway through the swing, pushing her back down on the futon. He turned his head toward Iris as he re-cuffed Zoe. "Was that really necessary?"

"Don't forget who's in charge here." Iris grabbed Zoe's half-eaten bowl of pasta and stalked from the room.

Zoe wasn't sure if Iris was talking to her or Ian.

«« Chapter 6 »»

Zoe was beginning to lose track of the days. The air mattress was gone when she woke up from another restless night's sleep, though she was pretty sure Blake had been sleeping on it at some point. The TV was off, and the remote had disappeared again. She was afraid if she spent another day alone with her thoughts, she would crack. For most of the night, her mind had run through theories on how the Arrows had tricked Gordon into joining their cause, entertaining everything from mind control to blackmail, though none of it really seemed believable.

"Have a nice morning?" Ian walked in from the kitchen carrying a plate, and Zoe nearly jumped out of her skin at the sound of his voice. She was so relieved to have a distraction that she ignored the sarcasm in his voice.

"Oh, it was great," she replied with a tone to match his. Ian smirked as he handed her the plate with a single peanut butter and jelly sandwich; Zoe ate it in four bites.

Ian sat down next to her and pulled the remote out of his pocket. The bastard. Would it really have been that terrible to allow her to watch TV? It wasn't like she could use it to contact the police.

The midday news was just starting, and once again her kidnapping was the top story. Unfortunately, they hadn't uncovered any new information. She hoped they might replay Cole's statement from the night before, but they didn't, and her spirits took another nosedive.

Ian turned off the TV as soon as the story ended.

"Wait," Zoe called after him as he got up. He turned to look at her, but didn't say a word. "Can't you let me up for a little while? I've been cuffed to this futon for days. I'm starting to lose my mind."

"How is that my problem?"

Zoe sighed. "Look, I get that I'm your prisoner or whatever, but I'm begging you. There has to be something useful I can do around here. Let me cook dinner or something."

"And how do I know that you won't make a break for it the second I uncuff you?" His voice was calm. If she had upset him with her request, he didn't show it.

"You have my word," Zoe offered with as much sincerity as she could. At least he hadn't walked away. Maybe there was a chance he would let her up after all.

"Not good enough." Ian turned away and Zoe's heart deflated. He had been toying with her, letting her build up a glimmer of hope only to crush it. She collapsed back onto the futon as he walked away—only he didn't go to the kitchen this time, he went to the closet next to the front door. Zoe sat up again, trying to see what he was doing. When he turned back toward her, he was holding his gun. Zoe hadn't seen it since they arrived. "I'm going to need a little extra insurance that you'll behave." Ian placed the gun in the holster on his hip and came over to her. "If you try anything stupid, I'll see to it that you spend the rest of your life cuffed to that futon. Understood?"

Zoe nodded. She couldn't think of a worse threat.

Ian uncuffed her, and Zoe gently massaged her wrist as he helped her to her feet. The man kept a hand on her arm as he led her into the kitchen; to her disappointment, there was no hidden mansion on the other side.

"What's she doing here?" Iris looked up from her phone when they entered the room. She was sitting at the kitchen table with Blake, eating a lunch that looked much more appetizing than the PB&J Ian had brought her.

"She offered to cook and I decided to let her." Ian released her arm. "Do you have a problem with that?" He gave his sister a look Zoe had thought he only reserved for her, though it didn't seem to intimidate Iris nearly as much.

Iris knocked her chair to the floor as she stormed out. "Nope. Like you said last night, she's your problem not mine. You can handle it however you want, but don't expect me to stay and babysit."

"So you can cook?" Blake asked, ignoring Iris's departure. He leaned back in his chair and threw an apple in the air, catching it over and over. Zoe wondered if he was as bored with this whole situation as she was. Ian picked up Iris's vacated chair and sat down at the table. A textbook lay open in front of him; he pulled the gun out and set it on the table before giving the book his full attention. For half a second, Zoe thought about trying to grab it, but she knew she wouldn't be fast enough to beat him.

She stood awkwardly in the middle of the kitchen, unsure if she should start going through the cupboard looking for ingredients or if she should wait to be told what to do.

When no one else spoke, she forced her eyes away from the gun and focused on Blake, answering his question. "A little. My grandmother taught me a few family recipes. Co—" She choked back the rest of her sentence. She was about to tell them that Cole actually did most of the cooking, but they didn't need to know those kinds of intimate details about her life. These people weren't her friends.

"Recipes for what?" Blake asked.

"Perogies were the first thing she taught me to make. They're like a rite of passage in my family."

"I haven't had perogies in years." Blake returned the chair legs to the floor and tossed his apple in the bowl of fruit sitting on the table.

"I could make them now. The ingredients are pretty basic—you probably have everything we need." Perogies would take hours to make. She might even be able to stretch it for the rest of the day if she tried. Anything to keep from having to go back to that futon.

"Make whatever you want," Ian said without looking up from his book.

"Tell me what you need and I'll see if we have it." Blake jumped out of the chair like an overeager assistant. He had to be going stir-crazy, too.

Zoe listed what she needed, and like magic, it appeared on the counter before her. The next thing she knew, the countertop was covered in flour and she was kneading the dough. Her wrist that had been cuffed for the last few days was sore, and she had to be careful not to mess up the bandages on the palms of her hand, but she found the effort needed to turn flour, eggs, and water into dough with her hands extremely satisfying. Blake leaned on the counter next to her, alternating between watching her work and playing on his phone. She would have been enjoying herself if it weren't for the threat that came with the gun still sitting on the table.

"What's he reading?" Zoe whispered to Blake with a nod at Ian. He had barely acknowledged either of them since sitting down.

"Who knows?" Blake shrugged. "He's always studying something. It's hard to keep up. I thought he would have eased up a little when he had to drop out of med school, but I guess some habits are hard to give up."

Zoe glanced over at Ian and tried to imagine him saving lives instead of threatening them.

When his phone vibrated against the table, she jumped for the second time that day, then silently cursed herself. She really wished she could get her nerves in check. Ian glanced at the phone, then stood up and grabbed the gun. Zoe froze, her flour-covered hands hovering over the counter. What had that message said? Were they working with someone else who had just sent Ian the order to kill her?

He walked over to Blake and handed him the gun, and Zoe breathed a small sigh of relief. Blake was a lot less threatening, even with a gun in his hand.

"Iris wants a drink, and she's refusing to come in here." Ian reached into the cabinet next to Blake and pulled out a glass.

"She's always been a little dramatic," Blake said as he examined the gun.

"A little?" Ian rolled his eyes. "I'm going to see if I can calm her down. Keep an eye on that one." He nodded toward Zoe and walked out of the kitchen.

Zoe went back to work on the pierogi filling. Out of the corner of her eye, she saw Blake's phone sitting on the counter; she watched him to see if he would pick it up, but he seemed much more interested in the gun now.

"Can I sneak past you and grab a glass to start cutting the circles in the dough?" Zoe tried to keep her voice calm and natural. What she was planning on doing was extremely risky, but she wasn't sure she would have a better opportunity.

"Sure." Blake stepped away from the counter and Zoe slid past him, grabbing his phone as she went. She opened one of the apps, hoping that would be enough to keep the phone from locking, before slipping it in her pocket.

"Actually, can I use the restroom first?" She forced a smile to distract from the fact that her hands were shaking.

"Sure thing. Right this way." Blake placed his hand with the gun on her back to escort her out of the kitchen. The press of the metal was enough to make her resolve waver.

Zoe held her breath until the bathroom door shut behind her. She wouldn't have long to pull this off.

She took out the phone with a silent prayer. It was still unlocked. Zoe quickly went into the phone's settings and turned on the locator. Then she opened the messenger and put Cole's number in.

Cole, this is Zoe. I'm fine. They are holding me in some kind of cabin in a remote area. I'm not sure where. I turned the locator on for this phone. I hope you can track it. I love you.

Her fingers shook as she typed. The second she was sure her message had sent, she deleted it. Quickly, she flushed the toilet and washed her hands, then opened the door with a smile she hoped looked authentic. "Alright, back to cooking."

Blake walked her back to the kitchen and took a seat at the table. Zoe went back to where she was working, putting the phone back where she'd found it as quickly as she could. She prayed Blake wouldn't noticed it had been moved.

«‹«‹›»›»

There were too many police officers at the station for Cole's liking. As far as he was concerned, they should all be out looking for Zoe. Detective Pearson had called and asked him to come down to the station, and when his father had insisted on driving him there, Cole didn't argue. He was in such a fog, he wasn't entirely sure he was capable of driving anyway.

They had been waiting for Pearson for fifteen minutes already. Cole hoped the delay meant he was busy working on a new lead in Zoe's case.

"Thanks for coming down." Pearson didn't look at them while he walked into his office, his focus instead on the file in his hand. He sat down at his desk and put down the file to give them his attention. Cole was pretty sure he saw Pearson roll his eyes at his father, but he was really too tired to give it any thought.

"Have you found her?" he asked. It was the only thing that mattered.

"No, and we've run out of good leads. That's why I called you down here. I want you to look at the items we removed from Zoe's car and see if there's anything unusual in there." When Cole nodded, Pearson stood. "I'll take you down to evidence."

"Were you able to get any fingerprints from the car?" Gordon asked.

"Just a partial print, but we haven't been able to match it to anything in our system yet."

Cole was having a hard time processing what they were discussing. It wasn't possible they had run out of leads. It had only been four days.

Pearson wasn't giving them all the information. They had to be close to finding Zoe by now.

His phone buzzed in his pocket, startling him out of his thoughts. He doubted anyone from the office would be thoughtless enough to contact him right now, and his family had been running all messages for him through his dad. The only person who had called him directly since this started was Pearson.

There was only one other person it could be.

He yanked out his phone and fumbled to get the screen unlocked, but he didn't recognize the number.

His heart plummeted. It was probably some spam text. His finger hovered over the text icon before he finally opened it and scanned the message.

Could this be real?

"Detective," Cole's voice was barely a whisper as he read the message over and over.

"What is it?" Pearson was at his side in an instant. Cole couldn't find the words to explain, so instead he held up the phone. Pearson snatched it out of his hand, a smirk forming on his lips as he read through the message. "That's a smart woman you have there."

Pearson patted Cole on the shoulder and took off running through the station. Cole and Gordon followed behind.

"Barrett, I need you to trace a phone number for me." Pearson stopped at a desk filled with computers and handed Cole's phone to the woman sitting there.

She typed the number into the computer. "Belongs to an Ian Sutton."

"Does that name mean anything to either of you?" Pearson turned toward Cole and Gordon; Cole shook his head. "Freeman, get me all known residences of Ian Sutton!" Pearson yelled across the room.

The minutes ticked by as they waited, and Cole felt like he would jump out of his skin at any moment. They were close, he could feel it. If only he could speed up time.

"Got it," Freeman called at last. "Sutton rents an apartment downriver and owns a house in Monroe."

"It looks like the cell phone is currently in Monroe," Barrett said.

"Alright, people, this is it." Pearson clapped his hands, quieting the thick excitement in the air. They did it—they found Zoe. "Notify the local police force, have them secure the building, but tell them not to move in until I get there."

Cole picked his phone up off Barrett's desk and opened the text Zoe sent. *We found you. We're on our way. Stay strong.* He hit send.

Pearson snatched the phone out of his hand. "What the hell did you just do?"

"I wanted to let her know that help was coming."

"And what if she doesn't have the phone anymore? You just told the kidnappers we're on our way!"

"I didn't mean to. I didn't think," Cole stammered. His hand covered his mouth as his stomach lurched. He was going to be sick.

"We need to move *now*, people. We just lost the element of surprise." Pearson sprinted from the station, but Cole stood frozen. What had he done? If anything happened to Zoe now, he would never forgive himself. How could he have been so stupid? Tears ran down his face as he struggled to fill his lungs with air.

"It's okay. The police will get there in time. Come on. Let's go get Zoe." Gordon patted him on the back and led him out of the police station. They were on the road before Cole even realized that his father was following the line of police cars down the highway.

They were on their way to get Zoe. He would have her back soon—if his mistake hadn't ruined everything.

«‹›»

Zoe watched the phone out of the corner of her eyes as she filled and sealed the perogies. It had been a half an hour since she'd texted Cole, and nothing had happened. She tried to stay positive, but part of her wondered if Cole even got the message. What if in her panic, she'd typed his number wrong? Or maybe the police weren't able to trace the phone? She had seen it done in movies but had no idea if it was actually possible.

She forced those thoughts from her mind and focused everything she had on rolling out the next batch of dough, letting the pain shooting through her wrist ground her.

Zoe dropped the rolling pin on the counter when the phone buzzed, her gaze shooting to the screen. It could be anything really. A Twitter notification, probably. She didn't have anything to worry about. Still, she couldn't move as Blake got up from the table and grabbed it.

He whipped around to look at her. "What the fuck did you do?"

Zoe didn't answer. Blake grabbed her by the arm and threw her into a chair, then picked up the gun, cocked it, and aimed it directly at her head. Zoe bit the inside of her cheek to keep herself from screaming.

This was it. She wouldn't see Cole again. She would die here.

"Guys, get in here. We have a big problem!" Blake yelled, not taking his eyes off Zoe. She had never seen so much panic in one person.

Ian and Iris ran into the kitchen, freezing in the doorway.

"Blake what are you doing?" Ian's hands were up as if Blake were pointing that gun at him instead of Zoe.

Blake nodded toward the phone on the table. The gun shook slightly in his hand, but he didn't lower it. Iris picked it up. "Shit."

"What is it?" Ian asked.

"We found you. We're on our way. Stay strong." Iris moved to stand behind Blake, the united front as always. Ian still hadn't moved. Zoe wasn't sure if that was a good thing or not. Iris waved the phone in Zoe's face. "Who sent this?"

Zoe didn't answer. She wasn't sure if it was fear or determination that kept words from reaching her mouth, but it didn't matter — she needed to buy herself some time. Help was on the way. She just had to keep them from shooting her.

"Answer her!" Blake waved the gun in her face, and Ian took a few steps forward, but he still didn't intervene.

"Cole." The word came out of her mouth with more strength than she'd thought she had left.

Blake let out a breath, lowering the gun and raking his free hand through his hair. "We trusted you. We let you up, and this is how you repay us?" He shook his head and raised the gun again.

Ian rushed forward this time. "Blake, give me the gun."

Blake didn't move. It was like he couldn't even hear the other man.

Zoe looked from Ian to Blake. "You make it sound like we're just friends hanging out. Did you forget that you kidnapped me? That you're holding me here against my will? I don't owe you anything! Did you really expect me to just wait around for you to decide to kill me?" Every second she talked was a second closer to the police arriving.

"All you've done is made me want to kill you now." Blake's finger moved to the trigger.

"Blake!" Ian lunged in front of Zoe, knocking the table over in the process. "Give me the gun."

"She betrayed us, Ian. Now the cops are on their way here." Zoe could hear the tears in Blake's voice. He'd lost it.

"He's right. We should kill her now while we have the chance, then make a run for it. That way she can't turn us in," Iris said as casually as if they were discussing what to make for dinner.

"No one is going to kill her." Ian reached up slowly and took the gun from Blake's hand, returning it to the holster on his side.

"Why not? If the Arrows go through with their plan, a lot of people are going to die. Why not take out one of their own first?" Iris folded her arms and leaned against the kitchen counter.

"Because we aren't the Arrows. We need to be better than them." Ian turned to look at Zoe. She wished she knew what was going through his head. He had threatened her countless times, but now he decided to show her mercy?

"Then what's your plan? Stay here and wait to get caught?" Iris asked.

"Give me the phone." Iris handed it to Ian, and he immediately threw it on the floor, smashing it to pieces. "Was that still in my name?" Ian turned to look at Blake, who had collapsed into one of the kitchen chairs.

"Yeah, I never got around to changing it to mine."

"Good, then they'll only be looking for me." Ian looked down and nodded as if reading the details of his plan off the floor. "You and Iris need to leave. Now."

"We're not leaving you." Iris took a step toward her bother and put a hand on his forearm. "We're in this together."

"You're leaving. Someone needs to stop the Arrows." Ian squeezed Iris's hand, then pushed it away.

"She'll turn us in the moment she's rescued anyway!" Iris waved her hand at Zoe.

"At least you'll have a head start. Now go."

"If we can't stop the Arrows, the blood of every person they kill is on your hands," Iris said to Zoe. Then she hauled Blake from the chair and out of the house.

Ian watched them leave before turning to Zoe. "Now, what am I going to do with you, Zoe Antos?"

«« Chapter 7 »»

Ian tied Zoe's hands to the chair's arms, then dragged her out to the living room, positioning her so that she was directly in line with the front door. The police would see her the second they entered the house. He forced a piece of cloth between her lips and tied it behind her head—all without saying a word. She might as well have been a piece of furniture.

Now he stood next to the front window, waiting for the police to arrive. It was the closest her kidnapping had come to looking like something out of the movies.

Zoe heard the sirens long before she saw any lights. She guessed they weren't going for the element of surprise.

Ian turned away from the window. "For what it's worth, I'm sorry I dragged you into this. It will be over soon, one way or another." His voice was soft, and for a moment Zoe felt sorry for him—until she tried to brush a loose strand of hair out of her eyes and the ropes securing her to the chair rubbed against her already-tender wrist.

The room filled with endless flashing lights; it was like every cop in the state had been called in. Ian was right—it would all be over soon, and she would be back in Cole's arms.

"Ian Sutton, we know you're in there!" The amplified voice echoed around the room. "Come out with your hands up."

Ian opened the window a few inches, making sure to keep his body out of sight. "No thanks, I'm good!"

"We have the house surrounded. There's nowhere for you to go." Zoe listened for footsteps, trying to gauge how many people were moving around the outside of the building.

Ian looked down at his watch, stalling to give Iris and Blake time to get away.

Guilt flared up in Zoe again; it was her fault that he had to put himself in this position with the cops to save his friends.

She pushed the thought from her mind. This wasn't her fault. She wasn't the one who broke the law. It wasn't her fault Iris and Blake were on the run and Ian was about to get arrested. Or killed.

Still, she prayed he would give up before it came to that. Zoe didn't think she could live with his death hanging over her.

A quick, high-pitched hum preceded the next declaration through the megaphone. "Don't make this harder on yourself than it has to be. Release Zoe Antos and give yourself up."

"I think Zoe's better off in here with me. We've gotten used to each other's company. I'm not ready to give up the only bargaining chip I have." This cocky act wasn't like anything she had seen from him over the last four days. He was putting on a show. Zoe wondered how long the cops would let it continue before they took a more aggressive approach.

"There isn't going to be any bargaining. You either give yourself up or we'll come in there and drag you out. Trust me, the first option will be the best one for you."

"Or I can take option three and kill her."

Zoe whipped her head to the side to look at Ian and was relieved to see the gun was not in his hand. He was bluffing, but the cops didn't know that.

"Zoe!" Cole's voice echoed from outside. He was here.

Zoe tried to yell back, but the gag prevented anything from escaping except a muffled cry. She struggled against her binds; she hadn't bothered to see if she could free herself before, but now that she knew Cole was so close, she desperately wanted to get to him.

"This is going to hurt," Ian warned.

The front window burst into pieces, and a canister landed amid the broken glass. Zoe had just enough time to turn her head and clamp her eyes and mouth shut before the room filled with gas.

Her skin was on fire. Tears rolled down her cheeks from the stinging in her eyes. Her lungs ached. It took all her resolve to keep from breathing in. She felt like she would never escape the cloud of chemicals that filled the room. Just when she was about to take a breath, the front door burst open and someone dragged the chair outside, but she didn't dare open her eyes until she felt the cool air on her face.

People swarmed around her, but none of them wore the only face she wanted to see. They quickly cut her binds and transferred her to a stretcher, and she didn't resist, though it all felt a little excessive. She wasn't hurt. At least the stretcher gave her a better vantage point from which to search the crowd.

"Cole," she tried to yell, but it came out as a choking cough. "Cole!" she tried again.

Out of the corner of her eye, she saw him pushing his way toward her. She reached out to him, and everything faded away the moment his hand touched hers.

"Hey there, beautiful." His free hand cupped the side of her face.

"I missed you." She leaned forward to kiss him, but the pinch of one of the paramedics inserting an IV into her arm reminded her where she was. "What happened to Ian?" Zoe looked to see if he was on a stretcher next to her. She hoped he hadn't resisted when the cops rushed in.

"Don't worry, the cops have him. He can't hurt you." Cole nodded toward one of the police cars, and Zoe turned her head in time to see an officer put him in the back of the car and slam the door. "Are you alright?" Cole watched her carefully, his eyes shimmering with concern.

"I'm fine," she said, though her eyes and lungs still burned. That didn't seem to matter now that Cole was by her side.

"We should get you to the hospital," one of the paramedics said as they unlocked the breaks on the stretcher.

Zoe turned to Cole. "I really don't think I need to go to the hospital. I just want to go home."

"Can we do that?" Cole looked to the paramedic.

"Technically, yes, but we don't recommend it."

"You should go," Cole sighed.

"But I'm fine." Zoe grabbed his hand. "He basically ignored me for four days. He didn't hurt me."

"Then why the bandages on your hands and that bruise on your cheek?" Gordon appeared behind his son, and Zoe choked down a gasp. Why was he here?

"You don't know how happy I am to see you." Gordon leaned down and gently kissed the top of her head. Zoe tensed for a moment, but then forced herself to relax.

"I'm happy to see you, too." She smiled at him and reminded herself she had nothing to fear from Gordon Wilborn. He had always been kind to her. He treated her like one of his own children. She wouldn't let Ian and his conspiracy theories change how she felt about the man.

"The paramedics are right. You really should go get checked out, just to be safe," Gordon said.

"It would make me feel better," Cole said sheepishly.

That did it. Zoe would do anything to ease Cole's stress.

"You'll stay with me?" She arched an eyebrow at him.

"Don't worry, I'm never letting you out of my sight again." He tucked a strand of hair behind her ear and stroked her cheek.

"She's ready," Gordon waved the paramedics over. They loaded Zoe into the back of the ambulance. Cole tried to climb in behind her, but one of the paramedics stopped him.

"I'm going with her," Cole insisted.

"Sorry, that's not how this works," the paramedic said.

"I'm not leaving her." Cole tried again to get in the ambulance, but they blocked him.

"Sir, I'm sorry, but it's for everyone's safety."

"Cole." Panic rose in Zoe's chest. She couldn't be separated from him again. Not yet. She needed him. How could she know that she could trust these people? They could be taking her anywhere. "I changed my mind." Zoe tried to get off the stretcher.

"Zoe, it's going to be fine," Cole said. "Believe me, you're safe. You need to go get checked out."

"We'll be right behind you the whole time," Gordon said.

"Promise?"

"I promise. I won't let the ambulance out of my sight—even if I have to run every red light in the city."

"So are we good here?" The paramedic looked from Cole to Zoe, who reluctantly nodded. "Good."

Zoe's heart stopped for a second as the doors closed, cutting her off from Cole. "You're safe now," she whispered to herself over and over as the ambulance pulled away.

«‹›»

Cole had expected some reporters at the hospital, but there were far more than he could have predicted. Everyone from local news stations to national media outlets was camped out along the hospital driveway. They let the ambulance through, but swarmed the Wilborns' car when they pulled in. Cole strained to see the ambulance, but he quickly lost sight of it as Gordon slowly drove through the sea of reporters.

Cole didn't wait for his father to turn off the engine before he jumped out and raced into the hospital. He needed to get to Zoe. He braced his hands against the counter as he skidded to a halt at the reception desk. "I need to see Zoe Antos."

"She's being brought in now," a woman behind the desk said. "If you'll have a seat in the waiting room, I'll let you know when you can go see her."

"I'm her fiancé," Cole said, smacking the desk.

The nurse raised a brow. "Oh, well in that case, have a seat in the waiting room and I'll let you know when you can go back."

Cole felt hands on his shoulders. He didn't need to turn around know who it was. "Come on, Cole. We'll see her soon."

Zoe's parents descended on them the moment they set foot in the waiting room. "Have you seen her? Is she alright?" Max demanded.

Cole nodded. "I saw her. She looked good. They didn't hurt her."

"Thank God," Gloria said as she hugged him.

"I'm sure they just want to check her out before we can go see her." Gordon led them all over to an empty corner of the waiting room, and Cole collapsed into a chair. Now that Zoe was safe, the last few days were starting to catch up with him.

Alana sat down next to him and rubbed his back. "We got her back. Everything's going to be alright now."

"Did she say anything about who took her?" Gordon asked.

"Gordon, not now."

Cole didn't look at his mom—he didn't want to intercept the dirty looks he knew she was giving his dad. "I only got to talk to her for a few minutes, and that wasn't at the top of my priority list." He let out a small laugh, the stress of the last four days slowly starting to melt away. Somehow, they had made it through relatively unscathed. Zoe was going to be alright. They would be able to put this last week behind them and move on with their lives.

"I don't care what they wanted, I just care we got her back." Gloria sat down on Cole's other side. "I wonder how long they're going to make us wait before we can see her."

"Hopefully not long. I mean, how many tests can they really give her?" Cole said.

"We need to let the doctors do their jobs. I know a few of them here—they'll take good care of her," Gordon said. Cole wasn't surprised; his father knew people everywhere.

Alana squeezed his hand and got up. "I'm going to see if I can find out what's going on. Jackson," she said to her oldest son, who was still standing near the waiting room entrance, "go see if you can convince the press to leave."

"What would you like me to tell them?"

"Just give them a generic statement that she is fine and we are glad to have her home," Gordon offered.

"And throw in a thank you to the police force," Alana added, making her way over to the nurses' station. Jackson nodded and left the hospital, and Gordon claimed the now-vacant seat next to Cole.

"Are you sure she didn't give you any idea what her kidnapper was after?" he asked, softly enough that only Cole could hear. "I mean, it couldn't have been money, or they would have demanded a ransom when all of this started. It all seems a little strange, doesn't it?"

"Ask the police. It's their job to figure that out."

Cole wasn't sure what to make of his dad's questions. It wasn't like Gordon to push for information. Then again, nothing about this situation was normal. Cole assumed they would find out what the kidnapper had wanted at some point, but as long as Zoe was safe, he didn't care what that lunatic had been after.

Cole got up and went up to the desk to help his mom. He knew he really should be the one handling this.

«« ‹› »»

They wheeled Zoe directly to a private room. She had no idea if that was standard protocol or a perk of being engaged to a Wilborn. She was only alone for a few minutes before an older woman with a warm smile walked in.

"Hi Zoe, I'm Dr. Northrop. The Wilborns asked me to take care of you while you're here."

"You know the Wilborns?" Zoe wasn't sure why that surprised her. People seemed to know the Wilborns everywhere she went.

"I've been friends with them for years. You and I actually met last year at their Christmas party."

"Oh, I'm sorry, I didn't remember." Zoe had met so many people at the Wilborn parties that it was rare for her to remember any of them. It usually didn't matter, since Cole was always by her side and he had a gift for remembering people and details about their lives.

"I would have been shocked if you did," Dr. Northrop chuckled. "Now, let's get started. Are you hurt anywhere?"

Zoe was only half-listening, still trying to process the fact that the Wilborns had requested which doctor would examine her. Was that something normal people did? Was there a reason they didn't want another doctor to look her over? It wasn't like she was a complicated case that would require a specialist.

"I'm sorry, what did you say?" she asked when she noticed Dr. Northrop looking at her expectantly.

"How about something more direct?" Dr. Northrop gently grabbed her hand and held it up. "Can you tell me what happened here?"

"I scraped them pretty badly the first day when I was trying to get away. They don't hurt much anymore."

"The paramedics did a nice job with the bandaging."

"Actually, he did that." Zoe remembered the care Ian took while cleaning and wrapping her hands. Now he was in jail, and no matter how much she tried not to, she felt responsible for that.

"He? As in the kidnapper?" Zoe nodded. "Well, then I'll leave them alone until the police come to take pictures, but I want to take a look at them before you leave." Dr. Northrop turned to the computer to enter her notes.

"The police?"

Dr. Northrop turned back to her. "They need to take pictures of your injuries for evidence. It shouldn't take long. In the meantime, I'm going to send someone in for some bloodwork, and then we can send your family back." She gave Zoe one last smile before leaving.

Zoe leaned back on the bed and tried to relax. She didn't have long, though, as a nurse and uniformed officer with a camera walked in moments later. Zoe tried to be friendly as they poked and prodded her, but it didn't seem to matter to either of them. So she let herself zone out, knowing that once this was over, she would be able to see Cole again.

"That'll do it," the cop said, bringing Zoe out of her trance. She hadn't even realized the nurse was gone. "Detective Pearson should be along once to ask you some questions once he's done processing Sutton."

"Okay, thanks."

Familiar faces appeared at the door the moment the officer was out of sight. Zoe's mom rushed to her and enveloped her in a hug. "We were so worried about you." She buried her face in Zoe's shoulder and started to cry. At least ninety percent of her mom was on the bed with her, and part of Zoe wanted to get up and offer her the whole thing; she seemed like she needed it more.

"It's alright, Mom, they didn't hurt me." Zoe gently patted her back, unsure how to handle the situation. Shouldn't her mom be the one trying to comfort her? Zoe caught Cole's eye. He had the biggest stupid grin on his face she had ever seen. She mouthed "help" as her mom continued to cry on her, and he came over and gently pulled her mom off of her, hugging Gloria until she finally stopped crying.

Zoe's dad leaned down and kissed the top of her head. "You really had us scared."

"Sorry, Dad." She knew it wasn't her fault, but she hated that they'd been so worried.

"We're just glad we got you back safe and sound. I thought Cole was going to start going door to door until he searched every house in the state if we didn't find you soon." Alana wrapped her arm through Cole's and leaned her head on his shoulder for a second.

Zoe let a laugh escape her lips as she imagined Cole banging on random doors, trying to find her. It felt good to laugh. Normal.

"We haven't talked to the doctor yet, but she seems fine." Gordon stood on the other side of the room with a phone to his ear.

"Who's he talking to?" Zoe nodded toward Gordon.

"Victoria." Cole took a seat on the edge of her bed and grabbed her hand. He fiddled with her engagement ring, filling her stomach with butterflies. She would have given anything to be alone with him right now.

"Isn't it, like, the middle of the night in London?"

"Let me check." Gordon turned to Zoe, forcing her to acknowledge the others in the room. "Do you feel up to talking to Victoria?"

Cole's older sister was a force to be reckoned with. If she put Victoria off, the woman would check in constantly until she got what she wanted. It was best just to get it out of the way. "Sure." Gordon handed Zoe the phone. "Hi, V."

"Are you really alright? Dad told me you were going to be fine, but you know how he is, always the optimist." Victoria sounded extremely cheery for the time of day.

Zoe had thought she knew Gordon, but after everything Ian, Blake, and Iris had told her, she wasn't sure she really did. She hadn't seen anything that might suggest he was hiding an alter ego, out to eliminate human life on the planet. Zoe decided the only reason she had started to question Gordon's character was due to the stress she was under. Now that it was gone, she couldn't fathom a reality where Gordon Wilborn was anything less than the generous, loving father he seemed to be. "Your dad wasn't lying."

"You do what the doctors tell you, do you hear me?" Victoria said in that mom voice that always made Zoe feel like a child despite Victoria only being five years older than her. "And make sure that brother of mine takes good care of you."

"He always does." Zoe squeezed Cole's hand and smiled at him.

"Good. Well, we'll see you in a couple of days."

"You're coming home? Is it for work?" Zoe asked. Victoria was so busy running the London branch of the family's company that she usually only came home for major events.

"No, we were flying home to help look for you, but since you're home now, we'll celebrate instead."

"You really don't have to do that." Zoe was exhausted just thinking about one of Victoria's parties. All she wanted was a few days alone with Cole and then for things to go back to normal.

"Of course we do, you're family. Besides, the kids are starting to pick up English accents. They could use a good dose of the States. Shoot, I hear the baby. I have to run. See you soon. Bye!"

"Bye, V." Zoe handed the phone back to Gordon. "Are we going to video chat with Jackson next?" she asked with a playful smile.

"Jackson's here, actually," Alana said. Zoe looked around the room, half expecting him to jump out of the closet.

"He's out front handling the press." Cole answered her unasked question.

"I noticed a cop leaving your room when we were coming back," Gordon said.

"Yeah, he was taking pictures for evidence or something."

"Pictures of what?" Max asked.

Zoe held up the hand that wasn't holding Cole's. "My injuries."

"I wish they would have told us they were going to do that," Gordon muttered. "I could have had the family lawyer come down."

A lawyer? Why would she need to have a lawyer present? Zoe eyed him sidelong but didn't have a chance to question him before Dr. Northrop returned.

"How is she?" Gordon asked before the doctor had made it halfway across the room.

"If you give me a few minutes to do my job, I'll tell you." She proceeded to check Zoe's chart and the computer that was monitoring her vitals, then carefully unwrapped the bandages on her hands and took time with her examination, while every eye in the room remained fixed on them. Zoe admired Northrop's strength. Had she been in the doctor's place, she would have cracked by now.

"Zoe is going to be fine," the doctor finally said.

"I told you," Zoe said with a sense of satisfaction. No one in the room met her gaze; they were all looking intensely at the doctor.

"The biggest issue is dehydration," Dr. Northrop added. Alana pulled a bottle of RiverLife water from her purse and handed it to Zoe. She looked to the doctor, who gave her a reassuring nod, before opening it and taking a sip. It was the best sip of water she had ever had. Zoe had been drinking RiverLife ever since she'd started dating Cole, but had forgotten how much fresher it tasted compared to the lukewarm tap water she'd been given the last few days. "We have her on an IV that should eliminate any risk. The scrapes on her hands are healing nicely, though I want you to keep them clean so they don't get infected," the doctor said to Zoe. "There's some minor bruising on your right hip and around your left wrist, but nothing serious. You'll probably be sore for the next few days. What you really need is rest and plenty of fluids."

"So I can go home?" Zoe asked hopefully.

"I want to get the rest of that bag into your system, then I don't see why not," the doctor said with a warm smile.

"Thank you, Dr. Northrop," Cole said.

"I'll go start your discharge paperwork." The doctor and Alana exchanged a looked before she left.

"Excuse me," a new voice called from the doorway. The badge-wearing detective didn't wait to be given permission to enter. He walked over the edge of the bed. "Hi, Zoe, I'm Detective Pearson. I've been heading up your case."

"Thank you for finding me." She would have given him a hug if she could, but Gordon had come to stand at the head of the bed next to her. Was he trying to protect her from this man? Did he not trust Pearson, or was it something else?

"You did that yourself." Pearson beamed. "If you're feeling up to it, I'd like to ask you some questions."

"Of course, I—" Zoe started.

"Do we have to do this right now, Pearson?" Gordon cut her off. "Zoe is under doctor's orders to rest." He shifted to block Zoe from Pearson's view.

"I just need to talk to her; I'm not asking her to run a marathon. We believe Ian Sutton had accomplices who are still at large, and the sooner we can find them, the better." There was a hint of anger in Pearson's voice that Zoe felt sure was reflected on his face, but the only thing she could see was Gordon's back.

"Mr. Wilborn, I really don't mind. I don't think the doctor would have any issues with me talking to the detective." Zoe reached out to try to gently guide Gordon away from her line of sight.

"Great." Pearson sat down on the foot of her bed so that the only way Gordon could get between them would be to dive across it. "So, Zoe, do you know if Sutton was working with anyone?"

Zoe's smile faltered. This should have been an easy question for her to answer. "Umm," she started, then stopped again. Why couldn't she tell Pearson about Blake and Iris? They were probably a bigger threat to her than Ian was. She should want them all behind bars where they couldn't get to her, but she couldn't bring herself to speak their names. Her eyes traveled to Gordon. The veins in his neck pulsed as he held back his anger.

What if they had been right about the Arrows and Gordon? What if that was why he didn't want Zoe talking to the cops? Iris and Blake could be the only thing that stood between the Arrows and the end of the world. If Zoe turned them in, and the Arrows pulled off their plan, it would be Zoe's fault, just like Iris said.

She shook her head no, tears dripping down her face.

"Hey," Cole whispered, brushing a tear away. "Are you alright?" He leaned over and searched her eyes for the answer when she didn't speak.

Zoe quickly choked back her tears. "Yeah, sorry."

"See, Pearson, I told you this was too soon." Gordon turned to Zoe. His smile was kind and gentle, but there was something hard in his eyes. "You don't have to do this now. You need time to process everything you've been through." Was he trying to keep her from talking to the cops, or was he trying to protect her? Zoe wasn't sure.

"I am pretty tired. I haven't slept more than a few hours since I was taken. I'm sorry, Detective Pearson, could we do this another time?" Maybe it would be best to talk to the cops without Gordon standing over her.

"There you have it." Gordon grabbed Pearson by the arm and guided him off Zoe's bed and toward the door. "Let me show you out."

Pearson yanked his arm from Gordon's grasp and looked back at Zoe. "How about you come to the station tomorrow and we can talk through what happened? No pressure, just a conversation." She gave him a weak smile and nodded. "Good, then get some rest and I'll call you tomorrow." He patted the bed gently and left.

Cole grabbed her hand. "Is there anything I can get you?" He seemed completely unaffected by what had just happened.

"I just want to go home, take a shower, get something to eat, and go to bed." Zoe tried to focus on Cole, but she kept looking over at Gordon, who smiled at her from his post by the door.

His intent was clear — he wouldn't let anyone else in to see her that he didn't approve of.

«« Chapter 8 »»

Two hours later, Zoe was finally released from the hospital. Somehow, Cole had convinced their parents to go home, promising he wouldn't leave her alone. The media was still camped out in front of the hospital when they left; apparently, Jackson hadn't been successful in persuading them to leave. They were able to catch the press off guard as Cole sped out of the parking lot while Zoe ducked down in her seat. Gordon had left them his car, and she was grateful for the custom tinted windows. She wasn't sure she would ever be ready to face the media.

Zoe stared out the window as Cole drove down the highway, humming along to the radio. She hadn't seen him this relaxed in a long time. He had been so stressed with work and with the amount of time she was spending in the lab recently, and the kidnapping must've escalated it even more. To see him so at ease was a welcome change—this was the Cole she'd fallen in love with back in college.

The blurring mile markers along the highway put her in a trance as she looked out the window. Ian had taken her farther south than she realized; they were practically at the Ohio border. As much as she wanted to, she couldn't stop thinking about Ian, Iris, and Blake—not after the way Gordon had acted with the detective tonight. She wasn't concerned they would come after her again; her fear was that they might have been right about the Arrows after all, and now there was no one out there to stop them.

"Cole, you just passed the exit to my apartment," Zoe said as the off-ramp zoomed by her window. He hadn't even slowed down.

"We aren't going to your apartment. We're going to my house."

"My place is closer."

"And mine's in a gated community with a security guard posted at the entrance twenty-four hours a day." Cole glanced over at her, checking to see if she was upset.

She rolled her eyes and smirked at him. "No one's coming after me."

"We can't know that for sure. We have no idea what that bastard wanted." He clenched the steering wheel with both hands. "And what if Pearson is right and he was working with other people? They could try to take you again."

Zoe reached over and put her hand on Cole's leg. He freed one of his hands from the steering wheel and covered hers with it. "It's not like Ian was targeting me or anything," Zoe reminded him gently. "I was just in the wrong place at the wrong time."

"I don't like you saying his name." Cole put his hand back on the steering wheel and looked straight out the windshield.

"Why not?" There was no way he could be jealous of the man who kidnapped her.

"It makes it harder to forget what you've been through." He reached down and squeezed her hand again. "I want to put the last few days behind us and move forward. Which is why I think we need to talk about your apartment."

Zoe cocked an eyebrow. "What about it?"

"I think it's time you got rid of it and moved in with me. The engagement is public knowledge now, and I don't want to wait any longer to start our lives together."

"You could always move into my apartment," she said with a wicked grin, and Cole turned to look at her in shock. Her cheap one-bedroom apartment was a shoebox compared to his professionally decorated five-bedroom house. She had teased him mercilessly when he purchased it last year; it was more room any thirty-five-year-old needed. She knew he thought it was a modest house, and compared to his parents', it was. It wasn't even on the water, he tried to argue—like that was standard and not a luxury for the rich.

That house was one of the reasons she'd kept her tiny apartment for so long. She didn't want to forget where she came from. She would join the wealthiest family in Michigan when she married Cole, and she had started to come to terms with everything that meant, but she wanted to hold on to her piece of the real world for as long as she could.

"If that's what you really want," Cole forced the words out after a long pause.

It was too much; Zoe burst out laughing. "I'm only kidding, Cole. Of course I'll move into your house. I'm pretty much living there now anyway. I still have six months left on my lease, though."

"That's not a problem. I could pay off the rest of your lease with the cash in my wallet. Or we can use the space for storage." The happiness was back on Cole's face.

Zoe smacked his arm. "I should make you live there so you can experience what it's like to be normal."

"Normal is all relative. To me, this is normal. And it will be to you soon, too." Cole smirked at her and pulled his car up to his neighborhood gate. The security guard waved them through, and Zoe noticed there were actually two in the booth instead of one. Had Cole requested extra security?

He pulled into the driveway and rushed around the car to open Zoe's door for her, ushering her into the house. "Alright, I believe you said shower, food, and then bed."

"That's right."

"So you head upstairs and take a shower, and I'll bring you up something to eat."

"You're a prince." Zoe kissed him longer than she normally would have, trying to make up for all the kisses she had missed while she was captive. They were both a little breathless when she pulled away, and Zoe felt herself relaxing more and more with every passing minute.

Cole was right. It was time to start living their lives together.

«‹›»

Cole had three pans going on the stove. He didn't have any idea what Zoe wanted to eat, so he was making all her favorites. It was the least he could do after everything she had been through.

He smiled to himself when he heard the shower turn on upstairs. She was really back; he hadn't imagined it. Somehow, they had made it through this whole ordeal and come out the other side unharmed.

Cole was dicing up chicken for a quesadilla when his phone rang. He quickly answered it and put it on speaker so he didn't have to stop cooking. He wanted to have the food ready when Zoe got out of the shower—he had no idea if she'd been given anything to eat while she was being held, and the thought made him sick.

"Hey, Dad," he said as he dumped the chicken into the pan, stepping back as the hot oil sizzled and splattered.

"Cole, did you guys make it home alright?" The speaker made his dad's voice sound more intense than normal.

"Yeah. Zoe's up in the shower now. We're good." Cole dropped a handful of pasta into a pot of boiling water and stirred the homemade marinara sauce warming next to it. Good thing he'd frozen some the last time he made it.

"Good. Was the extra security I hired there when you got home?" Gordon asked in an all-business tone.

Cole froze. "What extra security?" He hadn't noticed anything at the house. Did that mean there was something wrong? Was Zoe in danger? The shower was still running upstairs, and Cole was certain that he would have heard something if she was in trouble. He fought down the surge of panic that started to build in his chest.

"For the front gate. Nothing intrusive, I promise. You won't even realize they're there," Gordon said more gently. "I just want to make sure everyone is safe. If Pearson is right and this Sutton guy wasn't working alone . . ." He trailed off. They were both quiet. Cole knew what his dad was going to say—he had been thinking the same thing since they got Zoe back. Cole didn't think he could survive going through this again. He would do everything he could to keep Zoe safe, and it seemed his dad would, too.

"I did notice some new faces at the guard shack," Cole said. "Thanks for thinking of that. Zoe keeps saying they won't come after her again, but we can't know that for sure. I'll sleep better knowing there's an extra set out of eyes out there." He went back to cooking.

"I would do anything to keep you guys safe, you know that." The intensity of his father's voice sent a shiver down Cole's spine.

"I know, and we both appreciate it. I wish I would have thought of it myself. I'm supposed to be the one taking care of Zoe." Cole sighed, wondering if he would ever be as good of a husband and protector as his father was.

"You have more than enough to worry about. Let me handle this. I can hire some private security for Zoe if you want me to."

"She'll never go for that." Cole tried to suppress a laugh as he imagined Zoe sandwiched between two bodyguards walking into work.

"Well, the offer's there if you need it. Maybe bring it up in a few days before she heads back to work."

"I'll ask her, but I can already tell you what the answer will be."

"Fair enough. By the way, did she mention anything about the guy who took her or what he wanted after we all left?"

"We didn't really talk about it." Cole turned off the burners and started to plate the food. Zoe had to be almost done in the shower by now. He needed to wrap this up so he could get back to her.

"I wish I knew what he was after. Then I could be sure that you were safe. Especially with Victoria and the kids coming home. What if these people go after one of her kids next?" His father seemed determined to keep the conversation going, much to Cole's annoyance.

"Well, if you had let Zoe talk to Pearson, we might have more answers." Cole carefully arranged the food on a plate.

"I didn't want to push her too soon. I had her best interest in mind."

"If she says anything about it, I'll let you know, but I'm not going to ask her to about it. Look, Dad, I have to go." The shower had turned off upstairs. Cole grabbed two bottles of RiverLife water from the fridge and put them on the tray.

"Alright. I'll check in with you guys in the morning. I love you, Cole. Goodnight."

"'Night, Dad, love you too." Cole put down the phone and headed up the stairs to the bedroom with enough food to feed them for days.

《《》》》

Zoe turned on the shower in the master bathroom to let the water get hot. She loved the massive rainfall showerhead. Taking off the bland blue sweats the hospital had given her — they were two sizes too big, but at least they were clean — she dropped them in the trash can next to the sink. Zoe didn't want any reminders of the last few days.

When she stepped into the shower, the hot water scalded her, but she didn't turn it down. She closed her eyes and focused on the drops hitting her skin, washing away everything that had happened over the last four days, cleansing her soul.

Was this what it would be like when the Arrows released their toxins? Would people think it was just a normal rain when really it would kill them?

Zoe's eyes flew open, and she stepped out of the water instinctively as her breathing quickened. She sat down in the corner of the shower and tucked her knees into her chest so the water couldn't hit her.

She would never be able to move past what had happened to her until she could prove, once and for all, that Ian was wrong. Or worse, that he was right. Either way, she needed to know what Project Cleansing Rain was and how it was connected to the Wilborns; she wouldn't be able to put her mind at ease until she did.

Zoe took a few deep breaths and slowly rose to her feet. Tentatively, she stuck her arm back in the stream coming from the showerhead. She wasn't sure what she thought would happen as the hot water rolled down her skin, but she watched it carefully for any signs of damage.

Of course, there were none. She was being ridiculous. Whatever Project Cleansing Rain was, it didn't have anything to do with Cole's shower. She took a deep breath before stepping back under the showerhead. She tried to wash at a normal speed, but her hand was shaking so much she dropped the shampoo bottle twice. Relief washed over her when she finally turned the water off and stepped out.

She needed to pull it together; she didn't want Cole to see her like this, and she didn't want to explain why she was now suddenly terrified of the shower, or about Cleansing Rain, the Arrows, and how it all might be connected to his family.

Zoe waited until she felt her heartrate return to normal before leaving the bathroom for the large walk-in closet. She had a complete wardrobe at Cole's, but she didn't want that. Instead, she grabbed a pair of his pajama pants and one of his old college T-shirts and put them on. She felt safe dressed in his clothes, his scent surrounding her at all times, reassuring her that she was where she belonged. It gave her the strength she needed to push the Arrows, Ian, and Cleansing Rain to the back of her mind.

For now, anyway.

Cole was waiting for her on the bed with a tray of food. "I wasn't sure what you wanted, so I made a few things." There was the kind of shy awkwardness in his voice she hadn't heard since they first started dating. She went over and wrapped her arms around his neck, hugging him tight. Zoe would have stayed there all night, but when her stomach started to growl, she gave him a quick kiss on the cheek and sat down on the bed. After surveying the tray and trying to decide what she wanted to eat first, she finally picked up the chicken quesadilla and took a bite. It was easily the best thing she had tasted in her entire life.

"I know people like to spread rumors that I'm only with you because of your family's money, but I want you to know that it's entirely because you can cook," she said between bites.

"And here I was thinking it was my charming personality and dashing good looks." Cole lay down on the bed next to her, using his elbow to prop himself up.

Zoe leaned down and kissed him. It felt so good to be able to do that whenever she wanted again. "Nope, it was always about the food," she whispered in his ear as she pulled away.

"As long as I know where I stand." Cole reached around her to grab a piece of garlic bread off the tray, and Zoe playfully swatted his hand away.

"Go get your own!"

"Half of that was supposed to be mine."

Zoe moved the tray out of his reach. "I've lived off peanut butter and jelly sandwiches and half a bowl of spaghetti the last four days. This is all for me." She waved her hand over the tray.

"I'll have you know I barely ate anything while you were gone." Cole's voice was playful, though his words sent a pang of guilt shooting through her. She pushed it aside; she wouldn't let anything ruin this moment with Cole.

"Well, whose fault is that? I'm sure you had people shoving food in front of you the whole time. I can't help it if you didn't eat it. It's the same reason you always leave those fancy benefit parties hungry when I don't. While you're busy schmoozing all those rich and important people, I'm making friends with the waitstaff. You need to have your priorities in order." Zoe picked up the piece of garlic bread he had been reaching for, dipped it in the pasta, and took a large bite to drive her point home.

"I can't argue with that." Cole made a grab for the food again, which Zoe blocked, then got off the bed and headed for the door.

"I'd kill for a glass of wine," Zoe called after him.

Cole stopped in the doorway. "You're dehydrated. I'm not sure wine is what you need."

"The doctor said to drink plenty of fluids—she didn't specify which ones. The last time I checked, wine is in fact a fluid."

"What am I going to do with you, Zoe Antos?" Cole shook his head, a huge smile on his face, and headed downstairs.

«« Chapter 9 »»

Sunlight streamed through the curtains when Zoe woke up the next morning. She rolled over to see Cole sitting on the bed, working on his computer, already dressed. "Good morning, sleepyhead." He set the computer on the bed and leaned down to kiss her.

Zoe stretched, enjoying having the full range of motion back in her arm. "What time is it?"

"Almost ten."

She hadn't slept that late since she was an undergrad. "And how long have you been up?"

"I got up around seven." Cole brushed her hair out of her face.

"Why didn't you wake me?" She sat up, pulling the covers with her, not quite ready to give up the comfort of the bed.

"Because you need your rest. I was afraid I would wake you up during my conference call this morning, but you snored right through it."

Zoe smacked him in the stomach. "I don't snore."

"Whatever you say," he chuckled.

"I would have been fine if you went into the office. You didn't have to stay here all morning watching me sleep."

"There is nowhere else I want to be right now." Cole opened his arms, and Zoe scooted over into his embrace, laying her head on his chest.

"I could stay here all day with you."

"As great as that would be, Detective Pearson has been calling all morning to see if you're up to giving a statement." Cole stroked her hair.

Zoe took a deep breath. She would have to talk to the police eventually; might as well get it over with. "Yeah, I think I am."

She could do this. Maybe she would even get some of the answers she was searching for.

"I'll give him a call while you go get dressed," Cole said.

Zoe got ready in a haze, with so many thoughts running through her head that they all blended together. She barely remembered getting into Cole's car or the drive to the police station. She thought she would be nervous as she walked inside, but a sense of calm fell over her—a calm that shattered the moment she saw Gordon standing in the lobby with a man she didn't recognize.

"What's your dad doing here?" she whispered to Cole.

"I called him while you were getting ready. He wanted to come down and support you." Cole didn't seem to think it was odd that his dad was here—and maybe it wasn't. Though Zoe wondered if he was going to try to stop her from talking to the police again.

Gordon hugged Cole in greeting, then Zoe. It had been their normal way of greeting one another for years, but this time she tensed as she gingerly hugged him back. "How are you feeling?" Gordon asked as he held her at arm's length and looked her over. If he noticed she was on edge, he didn't say anything.

"I'm a little nervous." There was no reason to lie, though she left out that he was the one making her nervous, not the police.

"You have nothing to worry about. There's someone I want you to meet." Gordon gestured to the man with him. "Zoe, this is Frank Hangerman. He's been the family's lawyer for years."

Zoe looked from Cole to Gordon. "I don't need a lawyer. I didn't do anything wrong. I was the one that was kidnapped, remember?"

"It's just a precaution. We don't want the police twisting your words around or thinking you were somehow involved," Frank said with a smile the curled like a cartoon villain's. "After all, you did walk away with barely a scratch on you." Was he really suggesting that her kidnapping wasn't traumatic enough to be believable?

"Ms. Antos." Detective Pearson entered the lobby and joined them, watching Gordon and Frank out the corner of his eye. "Thanks for coming down."

"I'm sorry I wasn't able to answer your questions last night," Zoe said, trying to ignore the three men standing behind her, watching her every move.

"I'm glad you're feeling up to it now. Let's head back and go over what happened." Pearson held the door open, and Zoe walked through without hesitation. The others started to follow, but Pearson blocked the doorway. "I only need to speak Ms. Antos right now.

The rest of you can wait out here. I'll bring her back out when we're finished."

Frank held out his hand. "I'm her lawyer."

Zoe fidgeted. She really didn't want Frank back there, but would Gordon get suspicious if she said that? She wasn't sure if she could trust him or not. If he was an Arrow, the last thing she wanted to do was alert him that she knew the truth.

The best thing she could do was go along with it. For now, anyway.

Pearson turned to look at her, and she mouthed, "I'm sorry." Hopefully he at least understood this wasn't her idea.

"Fine," Pearson grumbled, leading them back to an interrogation rom. Zoe took a seat, and Frank sat down right next to her. She inched her chair a little to the right to increase the space between them.

Pearson smirked as he sat down on the other side of the table, making a display of moving his chair directly across from Zoe. "I know it's probably the last thing you want to do, but I need you to walk me through everything that happened to you the day you were kidnapped."

Zoe took a deep and nodded. Then she recounted the events that led up to her being taken, including how she first ran into Ian while he was trying to steal some documents from the lab, how she had gotten them past the gate check, how they'd transferred cars, and how she'd eventually ended up bound in the trunk. She was careful not to mention Blake or Iris.

Pearson listened intently, jotting things down on his notepad every once in a while. "And once he got you to the house, what happened?"

Zoe shrugged. "He ignored me for the most part. He kept me handcuffed to the futon in the living room and just let me up a couple times a day to use the bathroom, until the last day when I begged him to let me cook to break up the boredom. That's when I was able to steal his phone."

"Did you see anyone else while you were being held there?" Pearson looked her directly in the eye. Did he suspect she was lying?

"I would hear voices in the kitchen sometimes, but Ian was the only one who came into the room I was being held in."

Pearson pulled two pictures out of a folder and placed them on the table in front of her. "Have you ever seen either of these people?"

Zoe looked down at the pictures of Blake and Iris, her heart sinking.

She didn't owe them anything. It should have been easy to tell Pearson that they were there too, but she couldn't. If the Arrows really did exist and were planning some world-ending event, then by keeping Iris and Blake out of jail, she was doing her part to save the world. "They don't look familiar, sorry."

"Did Sutton ever give you any indication of what his plan was?"

"No." Zoe shook her head. "I wish he had. It would make this whole thing a little easier to understand." She shot Frank a cautious smile. He did not return it. Was it possible that he was an Arrow? If Gordon was, it would make sense that the people around him would be, too.

Pearson looked over his notes. "You said you first saw Sutton when you were leaving work on Friday, when you helped him pick up the files he dropped. Is that correct?"

"That's right." Finally, something she could be truthful about.

"Do you remember what was in any of those files?"

Again Zoe shook her head. What she did remember was the way the hairs on her arm stood up when she noticed details of her project in those files. "Were they ever found?"

Pearson got up and retrieved a box from the cabinet in the room, setting it in front of Zoe. "Do you recognize this?"

Zoe's eyes widened, and her hands itched for the files. "That's the box Ian had."

"We're going to need that research back. It's all classified," Frank said, and Zoe turned to look at him. That was why he was really here, to protect the company's interests — or the Arrows'. If there was any difference between the two.

She stopped herself mid-thought. When had she decided the Arrows were real? She was a scientist, she needed proof, and right now she didn't have any. The best course of action was to pretend that Frank wasn't there. "Do you mind if I take a look?"

Pearson pushed the box toward her. "Go ahead. These were found in a stolen car in Green Tech's parking lot shortly after you were reported missing."

Zoe stood up so she could easily see what was in the box — what was so important that Ian had risked everything to get it.

"Miss Antos," Frank started, "now is not the time to satisfy your curiosity. I think it would be the best use of everyone's time to continue with any other questions Detective Pearson has so he can get back to the case."

"If you have somewhere else you need to be, don't let me keep you," Zoe said as sweetly as she could. "I'll be fine here on my own."

"That's not appropriate."

Zoe rolled her eyes and turned back to the smirking detective. "May I?" She motioned to the box.

"By all means," Pearson said.

Zoe pulled out the first file and started to read it. There was nothing unusual in it, nothing that proved the Arrows were real, but something else did catch her focus.

She'd been certain she saw her project's description on the documents when she first ran into Ian, but this was more than a simple project overview; these were detailed research notes on their theory to safely break down plastics in the ocean. It was a theory her boss, Brett, claimed to have developed, but it wasn't his name at the end of the report. Instead, it read Dr. Sami.

"Have you ever heard of Hamid Sami?" Pearson asked. He seemed to be on board with the whole "ignore Frank" thing.

"No." She didn't look up from the research notes in her hands.

"He was killed in a car accident fifteen years ago. That's his research." Pearson gestured to the file in her hand. "He also happens to be Sutton's uncle."

Zoe's eyes shot back to him. Blake had told her Ian's uncle was dead, but he'd failed to mention that the man used to work for the Wilborns. "You think this was personal for Ian?"

"It appears that way. From what I've pieced together, it seems Sutton was trying to steal that research to force Green Tech to give his late uncle credit for his work."

Zoe closed the file. "Where do I come into play in all of this?"

"We aren't entirely sure. It's possible he was going to use you as leverage to get his uncle's work and hadn't come up with a way to do it yet."

Zoe sat back down, lost in thought. Pearson's theory was certainly more believable than the story about the Arrows. There was just one thing that didn't add up. "What would he gain from having his uncle's contributions to the project acknowledged? It's not like there's any money involved in environmental research."

"Miss Antos, please remember that your work at Green Tech is confidential," Frank said through gritted teeth. Zoe wondered if any of his clients had ever outright ignored him before.

Pearson leaned forward in his chair and locked eyes with Frank. "You can keep her from talking, but there are other ways to get the information I need. It won't take much to get a warrant and seize everything at Green Tech."

"You could try, but you won't be successful. No judge in the state would allow that to happen. The work Green Tech is doing isn't relevant to this case."

"Not relevant," Pearson echoed in disgust. "The information in that box is the entire reason there's a case in the first place. Zoe was kidnapped because she stopped someone from stealing that information."

"Exactly, she stopped him. Meaning the information was never stolen. It was simply misplaced."

"We don't misplace files, especially not in stolen cars in the parking lot," Zoe said before she could stop herself.

"Miss Antos, I think you've said enough." Frank shot her a warning look, then stood and turned to Pearson.

"I'll be filing the paperwork to have Green Tech's research returned today."

Frank stared at Zoe until she got to her feet as well. She was about to follow him out of the door when something in the box caught her eye.

She quickly shifted the folders aside to reveal a small black drone; it looked like the deployment system for her project, but she hadn't realized they had already built a prototype. Zoe's team had made some progress breaking down microplastics in the controlled setting of the lab, but they were years away from real-world trials. So much could change before then. Why waste time and resources to build a delivery system now?

Unless they were planning on using it for something else.

"Let's go, Miss Antos," Frank said from the doorway. With a last fleeting look at the drone, Zoe followed him from the interrogation room.

«‹›»

Cole paced in the lobby of the police station while his father sat and watched. He understood that the police needed to talk to Zoe, but why had they insisted on doing it alone? She'd frozen when Pearson tried to ask her questions at the hospital; what if it happened again and he wasn't there to support her? All he wanted to do was sit quietly next to her and hold her hand while she relived everything she went through.

"Cole, why don't you sit down?" Gordon said for what had to be the tenth time.

Cole looked at his watch, then back to the door leading into the station. "It's been almost an hour. What could be taking them so long?"

"I'm sure everything is fine. I would have heard from Frank if it wasn't. These things just take time." Gordon patted the empty chair next him, the same gesture he had used on Cole as a child.

Reluctantly, Cole sat, telling himself it was because he wanted to and not because his father had told him to. "Why is Frank here?" Cole had known the man his whole life, so when he saw him there that morning, he didn't question it—Frank's job was to help protect the family. The only reason he was starting to question it was because Zoe had found it odd. She was his barometer for what was normal. Growing up the way he did, he'd never realized how skewed his sense of normalcy was until they had started dating. She brought him down to earth.

"Some highly classified research was taken from Green Tech as part of the investigation, and we need to get it back," Gordon explained. "But since he was going to be here anyway, I didn't see the harm in having him go back with Zoe in case the cops try to pressure her."

"What kind of research?" This was the first time Cole had heard anything about it. He was sure it had been mentioned while they were trying to find Zoe, but at the time, the only information he could take in was the fact that they still hadn't found her.

"It's nothing, really," his father said offhandedly. "Just some papers from a failed experiment. I'm not even sure if it has anything to do with her case, but the Board wants to make sure it doesn't fall into the wrong hands. Some of the chemical formulations that the lab first came up with to tackle oil pollution were actually quite dangerous to humans."

"Why did we keep information like that?" Cole thought the company's do-no-harm policy would require all those documents to be destroyed after the risk to human life was discovered.

Gordon took off his glasses and squeezed the bridge of his nose. "They should have been destroyed a long time ago. I'm not sure why they never were. If the proper procedures had been followed, all of this could have been prevented. We should set up an audit of Green Tech's data archive to make sure nothing else slipped through the cracks."

Cole nodded and was about to agree when the door to the station opened. He jumped to his feet as Zoe appeared with Pearson and Frank. She looked different—he could almost see the gears turning in her brain. What had Pearson put her through? He should have insisted on going back there with her.

"Are you alright?" Cole grabbed Zoe's hands and brought them to his chest as he searched her eyes.

Zoe shook her head as if she there were an Etch A Sketch in her mind that contained all her thoughts. "Yeah, I'm fine." She gently pulled her hands free and smiled, but it was fake.

"If you think of anything else, please don't hesitate to call me." Pearson held out his card; Gordon reached for it, but Pearson jerked it way, looking Zoe straight in the eye. "Even if it doesn't feel relevant to the case, I want to know about it." Pearson stretched his arm out to Zoe, who finally took the card.

"What was all that about?" Cole asked once Pearson was gone.

"No idea." Zoe slid the card into her back pocket.

"Did he give you any idea what Sutton was after?" Gordon asked.

It was the same question he had been asking ever since Zoe was rescued, and Cole was getting tired of it.

He knew his dad meant well, but when Zoe was ready to talk, she would. Until then, he wished people would let it go. He leaned over and whispered in Zoe's ear, "You don't have to answer that. We can just walk away and go back to bed if you want."

Zoe took a deep breath and squeezed Cole's hand. He turned toward the front door, but felt some resistance from Zoe. She wasn't following him. "The police think he was trying to get credit for the work his uncle did while at Green Tech before he died."

Cole turned back to Zoe. "His uncle worked at Green Tech? Did you know him?"

"No. I've never heard of him." Zoe looked from Gordon to Frank and then back to Cole. "I'm pretty tired—could you take me home?"

"Of course." Cole wrapped his arm around her and started to lead her from the station.

"Zoe," Gordon called after them, "what was the uncle's name?"

Cole didn't stop walking. His father could get his information from someone else. Zoe had done enough.

«« Chapter 10 »»

Cole woke up later than normal on Saturday. He had cooked Zoe a fancy dinner the night before, and they were finally able to make up for all those date nights they missed. The past few days had been pure bliss as they spent every second together, slowly putting the kidnapping behind them.

Cole stretched out across the king size bed and found Zoe's spot was empty. Panic shot through his gut; had she been taken again? He sat up, searching the room frantically for signs of a break-in. When he heard the TV downstairs, he let out a deep breath, pulled on some sweats, and headed down.

Zoe was sprawled out on the couch watching some home improvement show with a large cup of coffee cradled in her hands, wearing his old Central Michigan University hoodie. She had been stealing his clothes more than normal this week, but he didn't say anything about it. He would have gladly given her his entire wardrobe if it made her feel safe.

Cole shuffled over and plopped down next to her.

"Good morning," she said with a small chuckle.

"How long have you been up?" He reached for her coffee, and she reluctantly handed it over. He took a few sips, then handed it back to her.

"Not long. You look terrible, by the way," she grinned, reaching over and ruffling his hair.

Cole nuzzled her neck, then lay down with his head in her lap. "Well, someone kept me up late last night."

"Oh, I'm sorry," she said in mock offense, "you didn't seem to mind."

"You can keep me up like that any time you want, but this is what you have to deal with when I don't get my beauty sleep."

"Then why don't you go back to bed? It's not like we have anything going on today. Go sleep 'til you're pretty again." She bopped him on the nose.

Cole hesitated. He had been putting off telling her about their weekend plans. He knew she would try to get out of it if she had the chance, and it would have ruined the surprise. "That's not entirely true."

Zoe pushed him off her lap. "What do you mean?"

She really looked annoyed, but there was no turning back now. Cole sat up on the other side of the couch. "We have to go to my parents' house for dinner tonight. I told you about that, right?" He knew full well he hadn't told her—in fact, he was under strict orders not to. Cole had tried to warn his family it wasn't a good idea—Zoe wasn't a fan of surprises—but they had insisted.

"No, you didn't." Zoe folded her arms and glared at him.

"Sorry," he said sheepishly. "Victoria planned some kind of fancy dinner for the family."

Any soft romantic feelings lingering from the previous night vanished at that, leaving her scowling. "Does *fancy* mean I have to get dressed up?"

"You can go in sweats for all I care, but you'd have to deal with the wrath of V." He smiled, trying to break the tension. It did not work.

"Isn't there any way we can get out of it?" The hint of desperation in Zoe's voice nearly broke Cole's heart, but it was too late to call the whole thing off. Besides, his family would kill him if they were a no-show tonight.

"I doubt it, but you can ask V when she gets here in an hour." It was only fair to deflect the blame to his sister; the whole thing was her idea, after all.

Zoe threw her hands up. "Why is she coming here?"

"She has a whole spa day planned for the two of you. Mani-Pedis, hair, the whole thing. Didn't she tell you?" This time, Cole wasn't lying. The last time he'd talked to Victoria, she promised she would check with Zoe before making any appointments.

"No. Apparently it's a family trait. I guess I have to go take a shower and get ready." Zoe threw the blanket to the floor and stormed from the room.

Cole sighed and lay back down on the couch. This was not how he'd wanted to start today.

After a few minutes, he made his way to the kitchen, poured himself a bowl of cereal, and sat at the large marble island to eat while scrolling through this phone. He kept looking up at the ceiling for some indication that Zoe was on her way back down.

The front door opened instead, and Victoria appeared. "Where's Zoe?" She looked around the kitchen as if Cole were keeping her locked away in a cupboard.

"Getting ready," Cole said through a mouthful of cereal. "And fair warning, she's kind of pissed, like I warned you and Dad she would be."

Victoria grabbed the box of cereal and took a handful. "Well, it's too late to call it off now." She popped a few pieces of the sugary cereal into her mouth. "I can't believe you eat this stuff. How old are you?" She dumped the rest in her mouth.

"Old enough to use a spoon like a civilized person."

"Shut up." Victoria took another handful of cereal from the box. "And don't worry about Zoe. I promise, by the time I bring her back, she'll be so relaxed and pampered there's no way she'll be angry at us."

"Good morning." Zoe appeared behind Victoria with a false smile, and Cole loved her for trying. He knew his sister was a lot.

Victoria spun around, quickly dumping the cereal in her hand into the trash. "I'm really sorry I'm springing this on you."

"It's fine." Zoe made her way over to the fridge and grabbed a bottle of water.

"I swear I texted you about it earlier in the week, and since you didn't say anything, I figured you were fine with it."

Zoe leaned on the kitchen island. "I don't have my phone anymore."

"What happened to it?"

"It was thrown out of the window of a moving car while I was being kidnapped." Zoe causally took a sip of her water.

Cole glanced awkwardly at Victoria. He should have thought of that and gotten Zoe a new one days ago. They had spent nearly every moment together since she was rescued, and he didn't realize she didn't have a phone anymore. No wonder there had been so few interruptions.

"Right." Victoria's smile faltered for a second before coming back full-force. "Anyway, we should be going if we don't want to be late for our appointments."

Cole stood up and gave Zoe a soft kiss. He lingered by her ear and whispered, "Try to have fun and relax a little."

"You owe me big time," she whispered back before allowing his sister to whisk her out of the house.

«‹«›»

Zoe was exhausted by the time Victoria dropped her back off at Cole's house. After their salon appointments, Victoria had insisted on taking her shopping. It was a good thing she lived in London, because it would take Zoe six months to recover from their outing. She plopped down on the bed, arms still laden down with shopping bags, without a second thought to her carefully styled hair. The woman had put so much hairspray on it, Zoe wasn't sure it would ever move again.

Cole emerged from the bathroom dressed in a perfectly tailored three-piece suit, and Zoe's heart fluttered. He looked like he belonged on the cover of a men's fashion magazine.

"How was your day with Victoria?" Cole stood in front of the full-length mirror and straightened his tie. Zoe wondered how much effort it would take to convince him to blow off the party and have a repeat of their previous night.

"I don't know how your sister manages to run a company, raise three kids, and still have that much energy left over. She's not human." Zoe didn't move as she talked. The slow spinning of the ceiling fan was hypnotizing her. If she closed her eyes, she was pretty sure she would be asleep in five minutes.

Cole sat on the edge of the bed. "I got you something while you were out."

"I think I've gotten enough for one day." She lifted her arms to emphasize the shopping bags still hanging there.

"This is something you'll actually want." He reached over to the bedside table and pulled out a new phone. "It's the same number, and I think we were able to recover everything." He handed it to her, looking extremely proud of himself.

"Thank you." She puckered her lips, waiting for him to come kiss her. She didn't have the energy to move. Cole did exactly that, then got off the bed. "I guess I should get ready for the party," Zoe said, looking at the new phone.

Cole sat in the armchair in the corner and started to put on his shoes. "You're not moving."

"I'm thinking about moving. It's a start."

"Well, don't think for too long. We have to leave in twenty minutes." Cole left the room with a chuckle.

Reluctantly, Zoe sat up and sorted through the shopping bags, then slipped off her tennis shoes and started to undress. She struggled to get into the new dress Victoria had insisted on buying for her—a simple strapless black thing with a flared skirt that cost as much as a month's rent on her apartment. Zoe's favorite part was that it had pockets.

She put on a simple pearl necklace and a matching pair of earrings that she kept at Cole's in case of an impromptu dinner or social function, which happened with alarming regularity. Cole was terrible about telling her of their social engagements until the last minute. Her hair and makeup were already done, so the only thing left was shoes; she sorted through the bags until she found a pair of ankle boots she had bought at a discount shoe store she'd forced Victoria into—payback for the day of high-end shopping with clerks who wouldn't leave her alone.

Zoe picked up her new phone and silently cursed herself. It had only taken her five minutes to get ready; she could have lain on the bed for another ten minutes and still had plenty of time. Accepting defeat, she started to make her way out of the room—then noticed Cole's laptop on the table next to the armchair.

He had been going out of his way to keep her from looking at it all week, and for the first time she really wondered why. Was it possible it was something to do with the Arrows? She had been trying to forget about The Arrow Equilibrium, but it kept forcing itself to the forefront of her mind.

Picking up the laptop, Zoe took a deep breath and opened it. The screen was locked. With shaking hands, she typed in a password; he usually used the date and location of their first official date. Part of her hoped that it wouldn't work, but a moment later, his desktop appeared with a picture of the two of them as the background. She brought the cursor to the documents folder, then hesitated.

Could she really do this? Cole had never given her a reason not to trust him. Yet here she was, ready to violate his privacy based solely on information given to her by a group of people who had kidnapped her.

She quickly shut the laptop and set it back on the table. Zoe wouldn't let Ian and his conspiracy theory destroy her relationship. Leaning back in the chair, she took a few deep breaths to calm her nerves before heading downstairs.

Cole was on the phone in his office; she stayed back so that she wouldn't overhear what he was talking about. She didn't want a repeat of what she went through upstairs. He ended the call abruptly the moment he saw her, and a wave a paranoia washed over her. Maybe she should have looked at the files on his computer. It was clear he was keeping something from her.

"Who was that?" she asked, eyeing the phone in his hand.

"Nobody. Work. It's not important. You look beautiful." The words fell out of his mouth as he quickly stashed the phone in his pocket.

Zoe walked over to him and wrapped her arms around his neck. "What are you hiding?" she asked as seductively as she could to mask the very real concern bubbling in her gut. This had to be a side-effect of the kidnapping, and she would do everything in her power to beat it.

"You'll find out soon, I promise." He kissed the tip of her nose. "Come on, we should get going." He took her hand and led her out to the car, and the ball of panic in Zoe's gut grew with every step they took.

Was this it? Was he taking her to meet the Arrows and begin the end of the world?

«« Chapter 11 »»

The drive to the Wilborns' house was uneventful. Zoe even started to relax as she sang along with the radio, though she noticed that as her nerves were melting away, Cole's were building. His knuckles were white from gripping the steering wheel, and his left leg hadn't stopped bouncing since they left their house. She was about to ask him what was wrong when his parents' house came into view, complete with a large white party tent set up in the backyard and a line of cars around the block.

Zoe turned to look at Cole; his eyes were glued to windshield. "Cole, what's going on?"

He pulled into the driveway ahead of those still waiting to get to the front of the line. He didn't answer until he had put the car in park. "It's a surprise?"

"You know I'm not big on surprises."

"It's an engagement party." The moment the words were out of his mouth, he breathed a sigh of relief like a huge weight had lifted off him.

This was what he had been keeping from her all week. She couldn't believe she had begun to question if he was part of an elaborate terrorist group when this was his real motivation. "Whose engagement party is it?"

"Ours. It was my dad and Victoria's idea. You know how the two of them get. Don't be mad."

Zoe closed her eyes and took a deep breath. She wasn't mentally prepared for this. That tent could easily hold three hundred people, and she would probably only know a handful of them. "I'm not mad, it's just a little overwhelming."

"I know this isn't your thing. If you want, we can leave now."

It was a tempting offer, but they couldn't just leave after everything his family had done for her — not just with the party, but making sure she was rescued. She could put on a smile and enjoy the party they'd put together for her. "Don't be silly."

Cole flashed her a huge grin and jumped from the car, running to open her door before the valet had a chance. He helped her out and pulled her in for a kiss. "I don't deserve you."

"Make sure you remember that when I steal all the blankets tonight," she smirked. Cole wove his arm through hers and led her around the house to the tent.

"Surprise!" Victoria was standing outside waiting to hug them. "You both look incredible. Wait right here for one minute." She turned on her heels and disappeared behind a white flap.

Zoe laughed. "This is our party, and we aren't even allowed to go in."

Cole shrugged. "I take no responsibility for my sister's dramatics."

"Ladies and gentlemen," Jackson's amplified voice echoed through the entire backyard. "It is my honor to introduce you to the couple of the night: my little brother and the woman who is way too good for him, Cole and Zoe!"

"I think that's our cue." Cole took her hand, and together they walked into the tent, which erupted into applause at the sight of them. Zoe fought the urge to look behind her to see if someone more important had come in. The tent looked incredible, with strings of lights above making the whole place twinkle. Elaborate centerpieces adorned the countless tables set up around the perimeter. This wasn't the first backyard party like this she had been to at the Wilborns, but it was the most elaborate. Especially since they had pulled it all together in less than a week.

Their parents were waiting for them in the middle of the empty dance floor, Gordon clapping more enthusiastically than anyone in the tent. That was when it hit Zoe, how much he must have been affected by her kidnapping. How much they *all* had been. There were moments when she was handcuffed to that futon that she was sure she would never see any of them again, and they must've felt the same. Now they were all here, safe and together.

Zoe quickly hugged her parents before turning to Gordon. They both had tears in their eyes as she allowed him to pull her into a hug, warm with love.

Jackson ran over, swooped her up, and spun her around. "Welcome to the family. If my brother ever gives you any trouble, you let me know and I'll set him straight."

"I'll keep that in mind," Zoe laughed as Jackson put her back down. She retreated to the safety of Cole's arms. "This is all wonderful. Thank you."

"After everything you've been through, the two of you deserve the very best," Alana said.

The band started up, and Victoria appeared and shooed everyone else off the dance floor until Zoe and Cole were alone with three hundred pairs of eyes on them. Zoe quickly scanned the crowd; she didn't recognize a single face outside of their families.

"I'm guessing she wants us to have the first dance of the night." Cole held his hand out.

"She does know that this isn't the actual wedding, right?" Zoe shook her head slightly as Cole led her around the dance floor. If this was what a last-minute engagement party looked like, she couldn't imagine what the Wilborns would put together for the wedding when they had months to plan it. She also had no idea what song the band was playing, but it didn't matter. The only thing that did was that the two of them were here, together, taking the first step toward their new life together.

Zoe rested her head on Cole's shoulder and breathed in. She didn't want this moment to end, but slowly the dance floor began to fill around them, first with their parents, then with Victoria and her husband, along with Jackson and whatever woman he'd brought as his date for the evening.

The moment the song ended, Cole led Zoe off the dance floor and over to the bar.

"You read my mind," she said as Cole handed her a glass of red wine.

"Congratulations!" An older man made his way over to them. Zoe was sure that she had met him before, but she had no idea who he was.

"Zoe, you remember William Conner—he's one of Wilborn Holdings's board members," Cole said as he shook the man's hand. Zoe was always grateful when he did things like that; he was much more at ease in this setting than her.

"Yes, of course. How are you, Mr. Conner?" Zoe's smile faltered slightly. Could she be shaking an Arrow's hand?

"I'm wonderful. You're home safe, and we're celebrating young love. That must have been quite the experience you went through." His words had a casual pleasantness to them, but they sent a shiver down Zoe's spine.

"I'm just glad that we can put it all behind us and move on." She prayed that would be enough to end the subject. She did not want to spend the evening fueling everyone's curiosity about the kidnapping.

"Gordon mentioned that they were after some research from your lab. Do you know if they got their hands on it?"

Of all the things to ask, why was he focused on the research? Unless it really did contain some details on the Arrows' plans, and he was part of them?

Cole squeezed her hand—their signal that he would handle it from here. "Zoe, I think I see your friend Sasha over there. We should go say hi. If you'll excuse us." Cole nodded to William and steered Zoe across the tent.

"Thanks for the save," she said once they were out of earshot.

"Do you want to go? I don't want you to have to spend the evening dodging questions like that."

"No, it's fine. I don't want to upset your family after all the work they put into this."

"You really are an incredible woman." Cole kissed her deeply. "Let's go dance — that way, no one can interrogate you."

«‹›»

Cole grabbed a bottle of RiverLife water from one of the roaming waiters as he made his way across the party. He always found it amusing that regardless of how fancy the occasion was, his parents always insisted on serving bottled water to their guests. Maybe they saw it as a way for some free advertisement.

He scanned the tent for Zoe. No matter how hard he tried to stay by her side, it was impossible. They both kept being pulled in separate directions. Zoe's parents kept taking her to greet various distant relatives that had flown in for the party, while he kept being pulled away to discuss work. Apparently, several of his operations managers had been told not to bother him while he spent the last week home with Zoe, and several minor issues had escalated to huge problems he would have to solve on Monday.

The only thing he cared about right now was finding Zoe and making sure no one else had bothered her for details about the kidnapping.

Instead of his fiancée, Cole saw his parents sitting together at a table off to the side of the tent. It was rare for the two of them to be alone together when they were hosting a party. They were pros at moving about the room and making sure everything was perfect. Cole changed direction and headed toward them, sitting down next to his mom, who was feeding Victoria's six-month-old son a bottle while she gently rocked him.

"Have either of you seen Zoe?" Cole leaned over and tickled the infant's belly. His heavy eyelids shot open, and he giggled as Cole made faces at him.

"Not recently." Alana swatted Cole's hand away and shifted the baby so he could no longer see his uncle.

"I'll keep looking, then." Cole started to rise.

"I'm sure she's fine," Gordon said. "Sit down for a minute. You haven't stopped moving since that party started." He flagged down a waiter, who brought a round of drinks over to them.

"If you insist." Cole sat back down and took the drink his father offered him. "Thanks again for all of this."

"How did Zoe handle the surprise?" Alana asked.

"Better than expected," Cole smiled. "I mean, she was really annoyed this morning when V showed up, but by the time we got here, she was alright. I hope she's enjoying herself."

"I'm sure she is. I saw her at a table laughing with a group of your friends from college a little bit ago," Gordon said. "I hadn't seen her that at ease in a long time. I knew this is what you both needed after the stress of last week."

"And you were right, as usual." Cole raised his glass to his father.

"Was I also right that no one would ask Zoe about the kidnapping?"

Cole shifted in his seat. "Almost."

"What does that mean? Did someone bring it up?" Alana asked as she shifted the baby to her shoulder and gently tapped his back.

"Conner ask her about it when we first arrived."

"He did what?" There was a hardness in his mom's face he hadn't seen since he dared Jackson to dive into the pool from the roof of the pool house when they were teens.

"It's not a big deal, Mom. You know how he is."

"What did he ask her?"

"He wanted to know about the research the kidnapper was after. Probably afraid it would affect our stock prices somehow." Cole took a sip of his drink, cursing himself for even bringing it up.

His parents shared a look. Cole had given up trying to figure out what those silent exchanges meant years ago. More than once, he had seen them hold an entire conversation without ever actually saying a word. "Take the baby." His mom stood up and gently handed Cole his nephew. "I'm going to have a word with William."

Cole watched helplessly as Alana stormed off across the tent. He looked down at the sleeping baby in his arms and back up at his father. He couldn't read the expression on his face. "What was all that about?"

"It's nothing." Gordon glanced across the tent, then back to Cole. "You can give him to me and go enjoy your party." He held his arms out for the baby and shooed Cole away.

<<<>>>

Zoe worked her way through the tent, thanking all the guests for coming. Unfortunately, she had lost Cole, and she kept introducing herself to people she had clearly met several times in the past. They forgave her, hinting at the extra stress she was under recently and clearly hoping she would give up some details about her kidnapping. No one had been bold enough to ask outright since William Conner, though, and Zoe couldn't keep the idea that he might be an Arrow from popping into her mind every time she saw him.

In fact, she found herself questioning if everyone she talked to could be some kind of undercover terrorist.

Her stomach growled in the middle of a conversation with yet another board member and his wife, finally pushing the idea of an apocalypse from her mind, and she scanned the room for one of the waiters walking around with trays of food. This was a dinner party, after all, and dinner parties typically included food. She spotted one of the waiters entering the tent with a fresh tray of food, and was about to excuse herself so she could go corner him when something stopped her. The waiter looked familiar, almost like . . .

Zoe shook her head. It wasn't possible. He wouldn't risk coming here.

By the time she came to her senses, she had lost sight of the waiter in the crowd.

She needed to get some air. Zoe excused herself from a conversation that she wasn't really a part of anymore and left the tent. The cool fall air raised goosebumps on her arms, but she didn't care. She stared over the black glass of the lake and tried to center herself.

"Not enjoying your party?" The voice was eerily familiar.

Zoe whipped around to see Blake making his way toward her, dressed in a waiter's uniform. Fear started to build inside her, but she stood her ground. He was on her turf now; she wouldn't let him scare her.

"What are you doing here?" She knew she should have walked away, or called the security team that Gordon had hired for the night, but her curiosity got the better of her.

He held up his empty food tray. "This is my actual job, you know, when I'm not trying to stop an underground organization from ending life as we know it."

"That's how you were able to get tracking software on the computers at Wilborn Holdings." The Wilborns always used the same catering company for all their private and corporate events. She wondered how many times Blake had been in the same room as her without either of them realizing it.

"When opportunity strikes." He flashed her a smile, but it did nothing to calm the anxiety that was growing with every stop he took toward her.

"Don't come any closer, or I'll call security," Zoe warned.

Blake held up his hands. "I'm not here to hurt you."

"Why should I believe that?"

"If I was going to hurt you, I wouldn't do it at a party full of witnesses." He gestured toward the tent, but there wasn't another person in sight. Would they even hear her over the party noise if she screamed?

"That's not very reassuring."

"I just want to talk to you." Blake closed the distance between them. "With Ian locked up, we don't have a lot of options left to get the information we need to stop the Arrows."

"What does that have to do with me?" Zoe crossed her arms, slowly rubbing them. She wasn't sure if she was trying to warm herself up or expel some of the nervous energy mounting inside her.

"You have an inside connection. And since you didn't turn Iris or me in to the cops, I thought there was a chance you might be willing to help."

Zoe didn't say anything. Yes, she wanted answers, and some things Gordon had been doing since her rescues were suspicious, but that was just the scientist in her making her question things. It didn't mean she believed their theory.

"Here." Blake held out a flash drive. "This is everything we know about the Arrows. Go through it and come up with your own conclusions."

Zoe took the flash drive, putting it in her dress pocket without saying anything.

"There you are!" She jumped at the sound of Cole's voice. He walked over to her, took off his jacket, and draped it over her shoulders. "What are you doing out here?"

"Um, I wanted to remind the caterer that Victoria's kids are allergic to shellfish." Zoe hated how easy it was becoming to lie to Cole. It rolled off her tongue without a second thought.

"Always thinking of others, even at her own party," Cole said to Blake as he wrapped his arms around her. "How did I get so lucky?"

"She does seem like the type of person who always does the right thing." Blake's eyes bored into her so hard she had to look away. "Well, if there's anything else, you know how to find me." He nodded toward the pocket Zoe had put the flash drive in, then walked away.

«« Chapter 12 »»

Zoe had built up her return to work so much in her mind that she was sweating with nerves by the time she pulled into the parking lot at Green Tech, eyeing the row of chargers in the back of the lot where she normally parked. She hadn't realized how far away from the building they were.

She made a sharp turn and pulled into the spot right by the lobby that was reserved for Gordon and his staff when they visited. No one would say anything about her taking it.

Her stomach was in knots as she walked into the building. Zoe wasn't sure if she was more nervous about something happening to her again or how her coworkers would act now that she was back. She really didn't want another celebration; she just wanted things to go back to normal.

To her relief, the biggest thing her team had come up with was printing off a sign that read, *Welcome back Zoe!*, and taping it to the outside of her cube. There wasn't even anyone there to greet her. Granted, she was normally one of the first people to arrive, and she had left even earlier than usual this morning. A new laptop was waiting for her on her desk with a sticky note containing her new password and access code. She wondered if the police had recovered her old computer from Blake's house; it hadn't been in the box of files Pearson had shown her. Maybe Blake had grabbed it when he left with Iris.

She booted up the computer, trying to decide what to work on first. Her team had been in the middle of running a test on a new decomposition formula agent when she was kidnapped, and she was anxious to dive into the results. On the other hand, now would be the perfect time to start digging through Green Tech's servers to see if she could find any references to Cleansing Rain or The Arrow Equilibrium. She didn't expect anyone else from her department to be in for at least another half hour.

Zoe's hand went to her pocket and the flash drive Blake gave her. She hadn't looked at it yet, and it was driving her crazy not knowing if the answers were on it, but what if it contained a virus? For a second, she thought about plugging it into the computer, but quickly dashed the thought from her head. Work first, conspiracy theories second.

She opened her email to find almost a thousand messages waiting for her. She shouldn't have let Cole convince her not to check them while she was home last week. It would take her days just to dig herself out of email jail. Opening the most recent email, Zoe began reading through it. A second later her cell phone rang, flashing Cole's picture on the screen. Her stress instantly evaporated.

"Good morning," she said, turning away from the computer.

"I know I promised I wouldn't bother you all day, but you left so early this morning I didn't even get to wish you luck on you first day back." It was clear that Cole was in the car on his way to work.

"And you wanted to make sure that I made it into the office alright," Zoe finished for him.

"Can you blame me for being worried?"

"Not at all. I think it's sweet that you called. In fact, I need you to do me a little favor."

"Anything."

"Can you let your dad know I took his parking spot? I don't want them to tow my car in case any bigwigs show up at the lab today and see an unauthorized vehicle in their spot." Zoe spun her chair in slow circles as she talked.

Cole laughed. "I'm sure he'll be thrilled to hear you're using it. If you're not careful, he'll have the spot assigned to you permanently."

"Let's not get crazy. I just . . ." Zoe trailed off. She didn't want to admit she was nervous about crossing the parking lot, about the way the gun barrel had felt pressed against her back as Ian forced her to take him to her car. They weren't coming after her again, she was safe, but she couldn't completely shake the fear. "I was just feeling a little lazy and didn't want to walk all that way to the building. I'm sure I'll be back to parking at the chargers tomorrow."

"You sure you're alright?" Cole asked.

"Yeah, of course. I'll see you at home tonight after I'm done at the library. I love you."

"I love you, too. Call me if you need anything."

"I will. Bye." Zoe hung up the phone and turned back to her computer and her full inbox. Not wanting to deal with it, she got up and headed down to the lab.

She wasn't surprised to find it dark. She switched on the light and went into the vestibule, donning her lab coat before heading inside, where she pulled down the slides containing samples from the last two weeks of testing and made herself comfortable in front of one of the microscopes. She went through them in chronological order, finding some minor decomposition in the first week that she thought looked promising. In last Tuesday's sample, the breakdown rates had skyrocketed.

Zoe pulled the slide out to make sure it wasn't misfiled, then put it back in the microscope to make sure she saw it correctly. She did.

She pulled out the binders of notes and flipped through them to see if anyone had made any changes to the parameters of the experiment, but everything looked normal. The sample had been taken in the early afternoon, which was odd—samples were normally pulled first thing at the beginning of each shift. She looked at the time and realized it would have been taken right after she left the police station. Was there was some kind of connection, or another coincidence?

According to the notes, Brett had been the only one to pull samples since Tuesday. What was the rest of the team doing? Zoe racked her brain for the last time Brett had pulled a sample; he had been pretty hands-off since she was promoted to lab supervisor a year ago.

"Pretty amazing, isn't it?"

Zoe whipped around to see Brett leaning on the doorframe. She had been so engrossed in her work that she hadn't heard him come in. Her smile faltered as she met his gaze; was she scared of Brett? She had been working with him since she started at Green Tech five years ago, and they had a great working relationship. Zoe tried to push her uneasy feelings aside. "Any theories on what caused it?" she asked.

"A few, but we can get to that in a minute." He walked over to her and held open his arms. "First, welcome back."

Zoe hesitated a moment before she got up and hugged him. She had been comfortable hugging him before she was kidnapped, and was determined not to let the ordeal change that.

Brett released her and sat down on the stool next to her. "We were all so worried about you."

"Worried you might have to start training a new lab supervisor to replace me," she joked.

"That was a big part of it," Brett chuckled. "Do you have any idea what he wanted with you?"

"I don't think he wanted me at all." Zoe studied him carefully. Brett had been at Green Tech since it first opened, and ever since the police station, she'd been racking her brain to come up with a logical reason why he was passing off Dr. Sami's work as his own all these years. The only thing she had concluded with absolute certainty was that Brett was hiding something, and she wanted to know what it was.

"What do you think he was after?" Brett watched her just as closely—the same way he looked at her when posing a new idea about their project. Like he could read Zoe's thoughts on her forehead.

"I don't know for sure. He didn't really tell me anything. The police seem to think it had something to do with his uncle, Dr. Hamid Sami. Have you heard of him? Apparently, he used to work here."

"I knew him," Brett said, and Zoe blinked rapidly. She had expected him to deny it. "Hamid and I actually established this department together. He was one of the smartest people I've ever met. His death was a real tragedy, but at least his work gets to live on through us."

"It's funny, I don't remember seeing his name on any of the old research files."

"You'd have to go pretty far back into the archives to find it. Anyway, I have a meeting I have to get to. Take some time to go through all the data, and later we can meet up to exchange theories." Brett smiled and left the lab.

Everything about their exchange was completely normal, but it left Zoe feeling even more paranoid than before.

«‹›»

The energy at the office was different when Cole arrived. Everyone he passed in the hall brought with them an air of tension he didn't expect, even for a Monday morning. Conversations stopped the moment he came into sight, and whispers followed him as he left. He should have expected that, he supposed; while he had been checking in with the office all last week, it was his first time actually coming in since Zoe's kidnapping and rescue. There were bound to be rumors and speculation on what had happened.

He went into his office and fired up his computer. Cole had tried his best to keep up with it while he was off, but as the head of manufacturing operations in North America, he received hundreds of emails a day.

Most were just courtesy updates or people adding him because they thought it would make the recipient respond faster. Scanning the most recent items in his inbox for anything that he would actually have to respond to, he saw nothing pressing, though Green Tech had been mentioned in several emails over the last few days, more than he had seen it mentioned in the last year. Green Tech was his father's passion project, and he maintained oversight of the lab. It had worked out well when Zoe started working there. She had almost refused to even interview for the job because she was dating Cole. The only reason she had agreed to it was on the condition that Cole had nothing to do with the operation of the lab.

After skimming through the rest of his email, Cole headed toward Jackson's office, swinging by the break room for two cups of coffee. They had an informal meeting every Monday morning to make sure they were both up to speed on what was happening across the company. As head of communications, Jackson needed to be made aware of any potential issues in their manufacturing operations that could result in a media frenzy.

Jackson was on the phone when Cole arrived, and waved him in without breaking stride. Cole set Jackson's coffee on the desk before taking a seat.

"It's like I told you the last time you called, Ms. Antos is not available for comment. If the situation changes, I'll let you know." Jackson shook his head and hung up. "Sorry about that." He grabbed the coffee and took a sip.

"How many interview requests does that make now?" Cole asked. They'd started about an hour after she was rescued and hadn't let up much since. Jackson was handling it all personally even though it wasn't technically business-related.

"Too many to count. Are you sure she isn't willing to go on camera and make a statement about the kidnapping? It would certainly make my job easier."

"Sorry, she's made it very clear she doesn't want to talk to the press." Cole hadn't actually told Zoe about the interview requests, but they had discussed her giving press releases before, and she always shut them down right away. He was certain her answer would be the same now, so why add to her stress by mentioning it?

"So, what's new in your world?" Jackson leaned back in his chair. "Have you even gotten caught up yet?" He smirked at Cole the way only an older brother could.

Cole shot him a dirty look. "As a matter of fact, I have." Though the others didn't always take him seriously since he was the baby of the family, he was actually quite good at his job, and even found that he enjoyed it most of the time. Cole lived for the high-stakes decision-making and problem-solving that came with manufacturing. "RiverLife has increased sales by thirty percent over the last two weeks."

"That's great. The marketing department put together a series of ads for the holidays that I think are going to play really well."

Cole laughed. "Please tell me they aren't putting bottles of water in children's Christmas stockings."

"Hey, you do your job and let me do mine. How about the rest of your plants? Any delays I should be aware of?"

"Nope, everyone is making their numbers. We should be able to stay out of the press for a while."

"I wouldn't be so sure of that. Haven't you heard what's coming from Green Tech?" Jackson set his coffee down and leaned forward in his chair.

"I heard a few people mention it on my way in, but I assumed it had to do with Zoe's kidnapping." Cole leaned forward. There hadn't been any notable news from Green Tech in a while, certainly not anything that would warrant bringing Jackson's team in. The only things that came from the lab were published in journals no one outside of the scientific community would ever bother with.

"They've had some kind of breakthrough. I actually think it came from Zoe's department." Jackson searched through the stack of papers on his desk. "Something about discovering a way to safely break down the plastics in the ocean." He handed Cole the report.

"Really? How?" Cole quickly read through the document, but couldn't understand most of what it was saying. Jackson would need an interrupter from the lab to write a press release the general public could keep up with.

"Don't ask me — you're the one engaged to the scientist. All I know is they're trying to determine a date to do a field test, and from the sound of it they would like it to happen sooner rather than later."

"That's incredible." Cole handed the paper back. The timing seemed fast, but he didn't know anything about scientific procedure. He was sure they had done countless tests in the lab before they got to this point. Zoe had been working on the project for the last five years, after all.

"Yeah, but it means a lot of extra work for me and my team."

"Somehow, I think you'll live." Cole got up and tapped Jackson's desk. "I have a call with the California plant. Let me know if you want me to get Zoe to explain any of the big words in that report to you."

«‹«›»»

Zoe spent most of the morning in the lab, poring over the slides and data collected while she was gone. As much as she tried, she couldn't find a reason for the sudden increase in the decomposition rate.

She went to Brett's office in the afternoon to hear his theory, a logical explanation she hadn't put together yet. But Brett's admin told her that he'd left early, another development that made her skin crawl. In the five years Zoe had worked at Green Tech, she could recall exactly three times that Brett had left right after lunch—once when his mother had passed away, and twice when his sons were violently ill at school. She tried not to read into his unexpected departure now.

Since she couldn't get any answers in the lab, she wrapped up her day by whittling away at her inbox. The whole time, her hand kept drifting to the pocket where Blake's flash drive was stashed. When it became too much to bear, she left the office and headed to campus.

The campus library was fairly empty when she arrived, but Zoe still walked around until she found a secluded computer station. Checking over her shoulder a few times, she finally inserted the flash drive.

She waited for something to happen, for the screen to fill with skulls and crossbones or a threatening message to appear, but the only thing that opened was the file explorer window. They were all .pdf files expect for one: a Word document with her name on it. She felt like it was going to jump through the screen and bite her. Slowly, she opened it.

Zoe

I know it's risky trusting you and that you have no reason to believe anything we told you. Like you said, we kidnapped you, you have no reason to be loyal to us. But I also know you're a good person. I could tell after spending a few minutes with you. This is every shred of evidence we've been able to find about The Arrow Equilibrium. Ian has written hundreds of pages of theories on what they're planning, but I've left that out. I want you to go through everything and draw your own conclusions.

Blake

A phone number was listed at the bottom of the letter. Zoe closed it and turned her attention to the hundreds of other files on the drive, scanning the list to see if there was a logical starting place, but she couldn't tell from the file names. They were going to make her work to get the answers she wanted, so she scrolled to the top of the list and started to go through them one at a time.

There were news articles going back to the late sixties, everything from protests and vandalism to corporate sabotage and an alarming number of accidents and disappearances. She remembered a few of the stories, like the death of Senator Guzman a few years ago. His family had insisted he was murdered, but it was quickly ruled a suicide and disappeared from the press. Zoe did a quick internet search to see if she could find any more details about it, but it was almost like the event had been completely erased from history.

Then there was the 737 that had crashed into an airport fifteen years ago, ruled engine failure. Zoe wondered which of the 215 people who'd died had been the Arrows' target.

Next were the invoices and manifests for chemicals coming into and leaving Green Tech. She recognized some of the ones used in her lab, but there were others she didn't. It wasn't surprising, given the size of Green Tech and the number of projects being worked on, and Zoe couldn't see anything incriminating in them, but clearly Ian thought they meant something.

After a while, her scientifically trained eye couldn't help but pick up on the similarities and patterns in the stories. She started making subfolders on the drive to organize the files. After reading through about twenty articles, she pulled a notebook from her bag to put together a timeline of events. This was just another experiment for her to solve; she collected data and developed theories based on that.

And she wasn't sure she liked where the data was leading her.

Zoe glanced down at the computer clock. She had been at the library for three hours and only made it through a third of the documents. Cole would start to worry about her soon. Just one more — then she would head home.

The next file was a .pdf of an email chain, with the first message addressed to Gordon Wilborn. Zoe let out an audible gasp that drew the attention of those working near her; she hadn't realized the tables around her were now occupied. Up to that point, she hadn't seen any evidence to implicate the Wilborn family, but now she couldn't deny their involvement.

Her eyes danced over the screen as she quickly read through the chain. It all seemed innocent, and she chastised herself for jumping to conclusions. Just because they had an email with Gordon's name on it didn't mean he was actually involved in anything.

Then she saw the last message.

It came from William Conner, the man she'd met at her engagement party who was so concerned with her kidnapper's motives. The message was short and to the point:

The other founders are anxious to hear how Project Cleansing Rain is progressing. Will you be at the meeting tonight?

Zoe stared at the screen as she struggled to comprehend everything that short message implied. Not only was Gordon a member of The Arrow Equilibrium, but if Zoe was reading this right, he was one of their founding members. There went her theory that he had been tricked into joining.

She jumped when her phone vibrated against the table, and she scrambled to answer it, nearly dropping it in the process. "Hello?" she said in a loud whisper.

"Zoe, are you still at the library?" Cole asked.

"Yeah, sorry, I lost track of time."

"How much longer do you think you're going to be? I want to hear how your first day back went." He sounded like an eager schoolboy waiting to be told he had won a prize.

"I'm packing up now. I'll be home soon. I love you."

Zoe closed out all the files and removed the flash drive. She needed more time to figure out what it all meant. The one thing she knew for sure was that she couldn't let that drive out of her sight.

«« Chapter 13 »»

It amazed Cole how quickly they fell back into their normal routine. Though Zoe was nervous about returning to work, by Wednesday all of that seemed to have vanished. She was working long hours again, and he had to fight to get her attention at dinner. She always got like this when there was something big happening at the lab. Cole didn't bring up what he heard about the breakthrough in her department, and neither did Zoe; she would tell him when the time was right, and until then he promised himself he wouldn't push her.

At work, things returned to normal as well. Whatever had kept his plant managers from bothering him while he was home with Zoe was over. His inbox was full of updates on the latest issues and production schedules for their manufacturing plants across the world. Wilborn Holdings had their hand in so many different industries that it was sometimes hard for him to remember every product they made.

He was reading through a sales report for their outdoor sports line when his phone rang, and he checked the number. It was Tyrone Roberts, the plant manager at the RiverLife bottling plant. Cole had always like Tyrone; the man didn't care at all about a person's title or position, he just wanted the job done. He'd taught Cole more about manufacturing operations than every collage class he had taken combined.

Cole picked up the call. "Hey, Tyrone, how's things at RiverLife?"

"You tell me. I'm looking at next week's production schedule and it's double what we are doing right now."

"That doesn't make any sense." Cole wedged the phone between his shoulder and ear so he could pull up the production schedule. Sure enough, their production target was double this week's.

"That's why I figured I'd call you before I start scheduling overtime only to find out that some pencil-pusher up there fat-fingered the report and I've blown my operating budget for the year."

Cole suppressed a laugh. "Could you guys even make these numbers?"

"I'd have to bring on a full third shift, and we couldn't have a single breakdown, which of course never happens. So realistically, no. I could push all the equipment to the max, but you and I both know that will lead to bigger issues down the line."

"Yeah, I don't want you to do that. Let me check on this before you do anything, alright?" Cole printed off a copy of the production schedule.

"You're the boss. It's good to have you back. I'm glad everything worked out," Tyrone said, the normal confidence in his voice faltering slightly.

"Thanks," Cole said, and meant it. "I'll get an answer to you on this by the end of the day." He hung up, grabbed the report off his printer, and headed toward his father's office.

The door was slightly ajar when he got there. Normally he would walk right in, but there was someone else in the office speaking with his father. He was about to turn around and head back to his own office, figuring he'd come back later, when his father's voice stopped him in his tracks.

"You can't really be accusing me of having anything to do with Zoe's kidnapping." Gordon wasn't yelling, but it was close. Cole moved closer to see if he could figure out who he was talking to.

"I'm not accusing you of anything, Mr. Wilborn. I'm simply asking a question. You're the one who's jumping to some pretty interesting conclusions." The second voice was much calmer—and it was familiar.

Cole peeked through the crack in the door and spotted Detective Pearson sitting at his father's desk. Gordon stood with his knuckles pressed into the wood. "Then why are you here, Pearson? Zoe is home, her kidnapper is behind bars—there's nothing left for you to do."

"See, that's where you're wrong. Now I need to figure out why Ian Sutton broke into Green Tech in the first place, and I think you know more about that than you're letting on. So, why don't you tell me about your history with Hamid Sami?"

"What's there to tell? We met in college, became friends, grew apart, then he died in a car crash fifteen years ago."

"You left out the part where the two of you started Green Tech Laboratories together, which he was in charge of for ten years. That his name is on the research papers Sutton tried to steal."

"If you already know all that, why are you bothering me?" The tension radiating from Gordon was palpable all the way out in the hall.

"I know you're hiding something, Mr. Wilborn. I don't know what it is yet, but I'll figure it out." Pearson stood and headed from the office. Cole stepped behind the door so the man wouldn't see him as he left.

Once the detective was gone, Cole cautiously knocked on the office door. Gordon barked, "What is it now?"

Cole stuck his head in. "Do you have a minute?"

"Cole, of course," his father's voice calmed. "Come in." He waved his son in as he sat down at his desk and rubbed his temples.

"Was that Pearson I just saw leaving? What did he want?" Cole walked over and took a seat across from his father.

"That was nothing. I think the detective is looking to turn Zoe's kidnapping into something bigger than it is. Maybe he's hoping to get a promotion out of it or something. Has he been in contact with you or Zoe?"

"No," Cole shook his head. He was sure Zoe would have told him if the police had called her again.

"Good." Gordon nodded, looking off into the corner of the office, most likely replaying the conversation with Pearson in his head. He had the uncanny ability to recall even long-forgotten dialogues in detail. "I'm going to make a few calls and make sure he doesn't try to harass either of you. I'm not sure what he's hoping to find. There's already more than enough evidence to put Sutton away for what he did to Zoe."

"I'm glad. I don't want to think about that man being free."

"You didn't just come here because of Pearson, did you?" Gordon eyed the paper in Cole's hand.

"No. I wanted to talk to you about the adjusted production schedule for RiverLife." Cole handed the printout to him. "Those numbers can't be right, can they?"

Gordon studied the paper for a minute. "They look right to me." He set the paper down on the desk and adjusted in his chair.

"Are you sure? I know our sales are up, but they don't support an increase in production that large." Cole nodded to the paper. "Did we secure a new contract I'm not aware of?" As much as he hated to admit it, RiverLife was a luxury brand. It was priced slightly higher than most bottled water on the market, and while they did well, he didn't think there was a lot of room to expand their distribution in the US.

"We're looking into expanding our overseas sales. There's a short timeline to get it in people's hands if we're going to have the impact we need." Gordon shifted in his seat again, signaling the conversation was over.

"Alright." Cole stood. "I'll let the facility know to start ramping up production." He gave his father one last look, then left the office, already dialing the phone. He would talk to the sales director before he had the plant start producing bottled water they would never be able to sell, then talk to his dad again when he wasn't so distracted.

«‹›»

There was an unfamiliar car parked in front of the house when Zoe got home.

She said a silent prayer that it belonged to one of the neighbors, but that was unlikely. She had been hoping to spend the evening going through the rest of the files on the flash drive. Now that she was confident it didn't contain a virus, she had been spending every free moment with its contents. She only needed a few more hours to make it through the last of the files. What she would do when she finished was still up in the air, but if Blake's goal was to convince her that the Arrow Equilibrium was real and that Gordon Wilborn was involved, he had succeeded.

Was it too late to turn around and head to the library?

Sighing in defeat, she got out of the car and opened the front door to find Cole on the other side, putting on his jacket. "Where are you going?"

Cole held his hands up. "None of this was my idea." He grabbed his keys and wallet off of the table next to the door.

She kissed him on the cheek. "That doesn't answer my question."

"I've been banished, so I'm heading to the bar to have a drink with some friends."

"Who banished you?" Zoe tried to look around him to see if she could see anyone else in the house.

"You'll see." He pointed toward the family room. "I ordered dinner for everyone. It should be here soon." He stepped around her so he was closer to the door. "I'll be back in a few hours. I love you." Cole kissed her and ran from the house like he'd robbed the place.

Zoe set her stuff down at the front door and slowly made her way to the living room. It was packed with catalogs, material samples, racks of table covers, a bin full of flowers, and several place settings and centerpieces on two long tables that hadn't been there when she left for work that morning. Alana, Victoria, and a woman Zoe didn't know sat on the couches, flipping through catalogues.

"What is all this?" she asked.

Alana jumped to her feet and led Zoe back to the couch, where the other women waited. "Zoe, I'd like to introduce you to Rachel Beck. She is the best event planner in the state."

"It's nice to meet you." Zoe shook the woman's hand and scanned the room again. No wonder Cole had hightailed it out of there.

"I know you probably haven't even started to think about what you want your wedding to look like." Alana retook her seat on the couch. "But with Victoria still in town, I thought this was the perfect time to get started. We all need to focus on something happy."

Zoe nodded. The flash drive in her pocket could wait a few hours. What harm was there in looking at some wedding things? It would be a good distraction from the constant thoughts of the end of world that played on repeat in the back of her mind now. "You're right." She took a seat next to Victoria. "Where do we start?"

"Did you have any ideas for a theme?" Rachel asked, pulling out a tablet.

"Simple." Zoe eyed the three-tiered candelabra in the corner of the room with a string of diamonds draped over it. "Elegant."

Alana turned to see what Zoe was looking at and laughed. "We can work with that. Nothing has been set in stone."

"Of course, I just brought samples of some of our more popular pieces, but we don't have to use any of it," Rachel agreed.

"I thought of you when I saw these." Alana grabbed some white calla lilies from the bin and handed them to Zoe.

"I do like these. I also really like orchids, maybe we can include them somehow," Zoe offered. Both Alana's and Rachel's eyes lit up, much to her relief. Zoe had always gotten along with Alana, even if she found her intimidating at times; the woman never seemed to mind that Zoe wasn't from the same world as the Wilborns and always made her feel welcome.

She wondered if Alana had any idea what her husband was planning with the Arrows. Alana had nothing to do with Wilborn Holdings, spending her time heading up a few charities she'd founded. It wouldn't be that hard for Gordon to have kept it from her all these years.

The doorbell rang, and Alana went to pay for the food. Victoria scooted closer to Zoe with a stack of catalogues in her lap. "Let's talk about what's really important: your dress."

Zoe laughed. "You don't have models hiding somewhere to put on a fashion show, do you?"

"I would have if I'd had a little more time to plan," Victoria smiled, handing Zoe one of the catalogues. "For now, these will have to do. I've marked a few of my favorites that I think you should try on."

"Of course you have." Zoe opened the catalogue to the first page Victoria had marked. Surprisingly, she really liked the dress. She let herself get lost in the pages of the bridal catalogue with Victoria, pointing out parts of dresses she liked and what she didn't. Out of the corner of her eye, she saw Rachel taking notes. They were probably going to reach out to a designer and have them design a custom dress, a perk only available to the extremely wealthy.

Zoe found that she was enjoying herself as they talked wedding details, though the threat of the Arrows was always in the back on her mind. She hadn't been able to find anything about timing in any of the files Blake gave her. Would Gordon wait until she married his son to end the world? Would Alana and Victoria be spending all this time planning a wedding they knew would never happen? Somehow, she doubted it. If either of them knew anything about the plan to end the world, they would be focused on preparing their families for that, not on which chair coverings looked the best with which silverware.

No, Zoe was certain that Gordon was the only member of the family who knew about The Arrow Equilibrium. Now, she had to decide if she should tell the rest of them, or keep it to herself. If she could get the rest of the Wilborns on her side, maybe they could band together to convince Gordon to stop his plan.

But that would risk him finding out that she knew before she was ready to confront him. Zoe knew what the Arrows were capable of; what she didn't know was if Gordon would go to the same extremes to keep her quiet.

«« Chapter 14 »»

Zoe went to Brett's office late Thursday morning. She had only seen him in passing since their conversation in the lab her first morning back, but they usually had lunch together on Thursdays, and she was hoping to finally hear his theory on the rapid decomposition with their experiment. She should have spent more time digging into the data, but she had been distracted by Blake's flash drive, going through the last of the files that morning. Her mind was drowning in information, and she needed to step away from it if she was going to have any chance of making sense of anything.

"Hey Tammie, is Brett around?" Zoe said to Brett's administrative assistant. The light was on in his office, so Zoe figured he would be close by.

"You just missed him, actually," Tammie said.

"Oh. Do you know when he'll be back? I was really hoping to catch him sometime today." It was starting to feel like Brett was avoiding her. Before her kidnapping, not a day had gone when he didn't check in with her.

"He got called into a last-minute meeting downtown at Wilborn Holdings Headquarters, so I doubt he'll be back today. I can call him if you want?" Tammie reached for the phone.

"No, that's okay. I'll try to catch him tomorrow." Zoe turned to leave, and out of the corner of her eye she saw a box sitting on Brett's desk; it looked exactly like the one she had seen at the police station. Apparently, Frank had been successful in getting the documents returned.

In that moment, she wanted nothing more than to go through the files in that box again.

"Tammie." Zoe turned back to her. "Have you had your lunch yet?"

"No, and at this point I'm not sure I'm going to get one. Brett took off so fast I didn't get a chance to grab anything. He doesn't like both of us to be gone at the same time, so I'm stuck here until the end of the day."

This was exactly what Zoe was hoping for. If she could get Tammie to leave for a few minutes, she would be able to see what was in the box. "I wouldn't mind covering for you if you want to run out and get something."

"You have better things to do than babysit the phones. I have a granola bar, I'll be fine." Tammie waved her away.

Zoe's gaze went back to the box. "It's really not a big deal. I need to take a break to help me refocus anyway. Honestly, you'd be doing me a favor."

"Well, if you're sure . . ." Tammie said, already reaching for her purse.

"I am." Zoe nodded and gave the other woman the biggest smile she could. This was all perfectly normal.

Nothing suspicious going on, even though she had never once offered to cover for Tammie while she ran out for lunch.

"Thanks, Zoe." Tammie grabbed her phone off the desk and got up. "I shouldn't be gone more than twenty minutes."

"Take your time." Zoe sat down in the now-vacant chair behind the desk and forced herself to relax, even though every muscle pulsed with energy. She had to make sure Tammie really left; the last thing she needed was to get caught going through files in her boss's office while he was gone. She wasn't sure being engaged to the owner's son would be enough to keep her out of trouble if that happened.

Once she was sure it was safe, Zoe snuck into Brett's office, shut off the light, and brought the box to the floor. The protype drone was still in the box, and she pulled it out and took a few pictures before setting it aside. Next, she pulled the files out one-by-one and took pictures of every page. She didn't have time to go through them now to find the relevant information; Tammie might be back at any minute. Zoe finished taking photos of the last file, grateful that Cole had gotten her a phone with decent memory, then carefully returned everything to the box. She made sure to place it back exactly where she found it. Brett had such an eye for detail that he might suspect something if the box was moved even a little.

Zoe slipped out of the office and reclaimed the admin's chair, grateful no one had called while she was in Brett's office. She didn't want to get Tammie in trouble. It wasn't long before she saw the woman walking back to the desk with bags from the local sandwich shop in her hand.

"Hey, Zoe, anything come up while I was gone?" Tammie set the bags down on the desk.

"Nope, everything was quiet. No one even knew you were away." Zoe plastered a huge smile on her face. It didn't feel natural, but she hoped Tammie wouldn't notice. "Well, I should get back to work." She stood and hurried away.

"Wait," Tammie called after her, and Zoe froze. "I picked up your usual order as a thank-you." The woman held out one of the bags.

"That's so nice of you. Thank you." Zoe took the bag and tried to walk away at a more natural speed, the crinkling of the paper bag announcing her presence as she moved through the halls. She needed to figure out how to stop her hands from shaking.

She made it back to her desk without anyone stopping her, then fished Blake's flash drive out of her pocket, checking that no one was around before putting it into the computer. She opened the letter from Blake and scrolled down to where his phone number was listed.

Was she really going to do this? Could she betray her company, Cole's family, by giving away confidential information? What if this was all some kind of set-up to get her to steal for them? Could they have fabricated the files to lead her down the path they wanted her to go on?

No, she needed to trust her instincts, and they were telling her that Blake wasn't trying to manipulate her.

She picked up her phone and texted him.

Can you meet me somewhere tonight? I have something for you. As she set her phone back down, she wasn't sure how long it would take him to respond, or if he even would.

It started buzzing instantly, and she scrambled to pick it back up.

Blake: How do I know I can trust you? This could be a trap.

Zoe: If I was going to turn you in, I would have done it by now.

Blake: Fair point. Where do you want to meet?

Zoe: My apartment around five? There's a spare key attached to the back of the wreath on the door. You can wait inside.

Blake: It's a date ;)

Zoe rolled her eyes. There was one thing she did want to know. *How did you know this was me?*

He responded, *You're the only person that has this number beside Iris, and she isn't this nice to me.*

Zoe shook her head and smirked. She deleted the messages, then plugged her phone into the computer and began transferring the photos she had taken in Brett's office to the flash drive, her work forgotten.

«‹›»

Zoe's nerves grew exponentially the closer she got to her apartment. She had felt so sure she was doing the right thing when she sent those messages to Blake, but the high of successfully stealing the documents had worn off. Now that she was about to willingly walk into a room to meet with one of her kidnappers, she wasn't so sure. Blake had been the one concerned about a trap, when maybe she should have been. He could have been at her apartment for hours. Why had she told him where the extra key was?

She approached the door cautiously and found it was still locked. Maybe Blake had backed out. A small part of her was relieved; he had threatened to kill her, and she wasn't exactly thrilled to be alone with him again. It took her three tries to get her key in the lock and open the door.

"Welcome home, darling, how was work?" Blake was sprawled out on her couch, watching TV. At least he wasn't holding a gun this time.

"Make yourself at home." Zoe shut the door, but made sure to keep it unlocked so she could make a quick getaway if necessary.

"Don't worry, I have." Blake waved a bottle of RiverLife water he must have gotten out of her fridge. "This is a nice little place you got. I was expecting something fancier, what with your fiancé's money. Should we be expecting him anytime soon?"

"I pay for this place myself." The familiar defensiveness rose in Zoe's chest like it always did when people suggested she was using Cole for his money. "And no, I'm meeting Cole for dinner at his house later tonight."

"Separate places? Is there trouble in paradise?" Blake put on a face of mock concern.

"No, I just haven't had a chance to move my stuff over there yet." Why was she answering his questions? She hadn't called him here so they could catch up. "Look, we're getting off topic." Zoe set her stuff down on the counter and walked over to Blake.

"Right, you said you have something for me." He got up and met her halfway.

"Here." She held his flash drive out to him.

"I didn't really need that back. I have copies of everything that's on there."

"I went through everything, organized it, and added my notes," Zoe said, still holding the flash drive out to him.

Blake ran his hand through this hair. "So you believe us?"

Sweat gathered under her arms. Maybe Blake had turned up the heat. She thought about taking her jacket off, but that would only slow her down if she needed to make a quick escape. It was best to leave it on and deal with it.

"I do, and I want to help if I can." She shook the flash drive in front of him, her arm growing heavy as she held it out. Blake didn't seem to notice. She could almost see the gears in his head turning. "I was able to get pictures of all the files Ian was trying to steal, and I added those to the drive. They aren't the best quality, but I figured it was better than nothing."

Blake finally took the flash drive from her. "That was pretty risky."

"It was a lot less risky for me than it was for him. At least I work there."

"How did you know what files Ian was after?"

"They were all in an evidence box. It wasn't too hard to figure out."

"Thanks." Blake pocketed the flash drive.

"Now you guys can figure out what the Arrows are up to and how to stop them, right?" Zoe assumed they had a plan. Why else would they have gone to all the trouble of stealing the research if they weren't going to act on it?

"That's what we hoped those files would tell us," Blake said sheepishly.

"You hoped." Zoe crossed her arms. She had been kidnapped and held at gunpoint because they *hoped* to find the information they needed.

"I mean, we know the Arrows want to kill off most of the human race, but we don't actually know how they're going to do it. I don't know what Ian planned to do once he got the information. He was the mastermind behind all of this. He said he was keeping us safe by not telling us anything."

Zoe couldn't believe what she was hearing. These guys had to be the worst criminals on the planet. Though, were they really criminals? If they were right, they were trying to save the world from the real criminals—the ones like Cole's father. "So you need Ian?"

"Yeah. Too bad someone called the cops and got him thrown in jail."

"Too bad he kidnapped someone." Zoe raised an eyebrow.

"Touché." There was no malice in Blake's smile. Maybe they could be on the same side.

"Take the information and see if you can make any sense out of it. Then meet me back here tomorrow night. I'll see what I can do." Zoe turned and left, feeling pretty good about how she'd handled the situation.

«‹›»

Cole had gone all out, setting the table with the nicest dishes he had, lighting candles, and even pulling out the cloth napkins his mother had bought him when he moved into the house last year. They were impractical, but made from recycled material, and Zoe loved them. He wanted this dinner to be special for her.

She had only been back to work for a few days, and she was already more distracted than before. She barely said anything to him about work, which surprised him; normally, Zoe would tell him in excruciating detail — most of which he didn't understand — what she was working on in the lab. Now, he barely got more than a "fine" out of her when she got home, before she disappeared with her laptop. With everything he had been hearing at the office, she had been key in that major breakthrough at Green Tech. He would have thought she would be talking about it nonstop.

Maybe the kidnapping was affecting her more than she was letting on. Zoe tended to keep things to herself rather than burden him with her feelings, and she didn't want him to feel guilty about what happened. But he didn't want her to keep her feelings inside in order to protect him, either; he wanted to be there for her, to be strong for her.

Tonight, he was determined to prove he could do just that.

The front door opened right as Cole was taking dinner out of the oven. "Hey, sorry I'm a little late. There was traffic."

Cole set the tray of lasagna down on the stove and went to meet Zoe. "That's okay." He gave her a second to get her jacket off before wrapping her in his arms and kissing her more passionately than their normal "welcome home" peck.

"What was that for?" Zoe purred.

"Aren't I allowed to kiss my fiancée?" Cole cocked an eyebrow at her, pulling her in tighter.

"Of course you are." She took a deep breath. "Dinner smells amazing."

Cole finally released her. "I just took it out of the oven. Go have a seat and let me take care of everything." He went back to the kitchen while Zoe headed to the dining room. He could feel her watching him as he plated the lasagna. "How was work? Anything exciting happen today?" Cole set the plates down on the table and took his seat across from her.

Zoe looked away. "It was fine." She picked up her fork and started to eat. "Nothing out of the ordinary. I spent the day in the lab trying to make sense of the latest test results."

She was keeping something from him. Was it just the project, or was there something else going on? He hated to pressure her, but he needed to get her talking. How was he supposed to help her if she didn't tell him what was going on? "Anything seem unusual?"

Zoe set down her fork and looked at Cole. "All of it is unusual, if I'm being honest." Worry gleamed in her eyes, though he had no idea what it was about. Maybe he should suggest she talk to a therapist? He had been reluctant to bring it up, but she might want to talk to a professional after everything she had been through.

Before he could find the right words, Zoe sighed and added, "I can't make sense of any of the data. It doesn't line up with anything I've seen before."

So this was about the project. Zoe always did take her work to heart. "Should it? I mean, this is a completely new formulation, right? Shouldn't the results be different?" He really should know more about Green Tech, even if it didn't fall under his control. It would be good to have some basic knowledge about what was going on there so he would be able to hold up his end of the conversation.

Zoe looked at him strangely, as if she had been talking about something else. "Yes, it's a new formulation, but the results shouldn't be that drastically different from what we've seen in the past. I was hoping to get Brett's thoughts on the data, but he's been unusually busy since I came back."

"I actually ran into him today. I keep hearing that exciting things are coming out of Green Tech." This felt more normal than anything since he'd gotten Zoe back.

Her eyes darted up from her plate. "What have you heard?"

"Just that's there's been progress on some of the projects." Cole took a sip of water. "That's why Brett was at HQ—he was giving an update to the Board."

Zoe adjusted in her seat. "Really? Does he do that often?"

"Occasionally. At least a few times a year." Cole was dying to tell her what was going on with Green Tech, but he couldn't; it had to come from Brett. When Zoe first took the job at Green Tech, they both agreed that they wouldn't be involved in each other's work. It was more a promise Cole had made Zoe that he wouldn't interfere and give her an unfair advantage. Not that she needed — she was brilliant. It was why his dad had wanted to her become the lab manager down the line, something neither of them had discussed with Zoe yet.

Zoe played with her food for a few minutes, looking like she was a million miles away. Cole watched her closely, not sure what to say to get the conversation going again.

"I'm pretty tired." Zoe finally set down her fork, having only eaten a few bites. "I think I'm going to go take a shower and go to bed. Thank you for a wonderful dinner."

She got up and left the table without looking at him, and Cole slumped. He had the old Zoe back one second, and she was gone again just as quickly. He wished he knew how he could help her.

«« Chapter 15 »»

Now that Zoe had passed the information back to Blake, she could finally concentrate on her work. She still hadn't accounted for the spike in the decomposition rate, so she decided to run the test again and see if they got the same results. The only variable was that she was the only one gathering the results this time. She didn't want to accuse Brett of tampering with the experiment, but at this point she would believe almost anything.

"Hey, Zoe," Brett said as he entered the lab. "I heard you were looking for me yesterday."

"It wasn't a big deal. I was just going to ask you to lunch." Zoe had a hard time meeting his eyes. She wasn't sure if Brett was involved with the Arrows or not. He certainly didn't have the money or power Ian had suggested the rest of the Arrows did, but after what Cole told her last night about Brett giving the Board updates, she couldn't deny it was a very real possibility. She had no idea who she could trust anymore. "How was your meeting?" Zoe tried to keep her tone friendly. She couldn't let him know that she was now afraid of him when the last time she'd seen him, they were friends.

"It went really well. The Board was really excited about the progress we've made. They want to do a real-world test in two weeks."

Though Brett sounded genuinely excited, Zoe was pretty sure he had lost his mind. "You mean two years, right? After we've had a chance to replicate the results, have it peer reviewed and vetted in front of the ethics board?"

"No, two weeks."

"As in fourteen days?" Zoe was going to be sick.

"Yes," Brett laughed.

"You told them that was crazy, right? We can't possibly be ready to field test that soon." There was no way this could be happening. This had to be about Project Cleansing Rain. There was no other explanation for Brett having abandoned all reason. She was in the same room as a member of The Arrow Equilibrium. Dizzy, she clutched the lab table to steady herself.

"Of course not. This is the biggest opportunity of our careers. I wasn't going to jeopardize that. We've been working on this project since Green Tech started. We deserve this." Brett pulled out the chair next to her and sat down, staring at her with such manic intensity she had to fight the urge to run from the room.

"But we don't even know for sure that the formulation was successful! It could have been a fluke. We need to run *several* more rounds of testing before we can draw any real conclusions. This isn't how things are done." She needed to appeal to the scientist in him. Even if he was corrupted by the Arrows, he was still a scientist at his core. Deep down, he had to know this was insane. She just needed to reach that part of him.

"Zoe, I would have thought you'd be happy, given this was your formulation. The Board has complete confidence in you. They even decided to name the project after you. They're calling it 'The Antos Solution,'" Brett said. "I know it's not the most scientific-sounding, but the marketing team thinks the public will love it."

Since when did a legitimate research facility need a marketing team? This was too much to wrap her head around. Why did they want to tie her name to it? When this failed, she would be held personally responsible. Her name would go down as one of the biggest scientific jokes in history. Or worse, if this ended up being connected to Project Cleansing Rain as she suspected, her name would be tied to the end of the world. She choked down the bile that found its way into her mouth. "What body of water are we going to test it on?" Maybe they had chosen an isolated pond to run the test.

Brett laughed. "We're trying to break down plastics in the ocean. We'll run the test there."

"What ocean?"

"All of them."

"We can't launch untested chemicals into every ocean! It could have catastrophic consequences we haven't even thought of yet," Zoe pleaded.

"None of the chemicals we use have any known hazardous effect to the environment. That's why you chose them in the first place, isn't it?" He had her there; they were always cautious of what they chose to work with so they wouldn't cause an adverse reaction in another part of the environment.

"What about permits and stuff? We can't get those in two weeks." She was grasping at straws, but she didn't know how else to stop this.

"Don't worry about that. Wilborn Holdings has people taking care of all the details. You've done your part," Brett smiled.

Was it possible that Wilborn Holdings could really cut through all the red tape and safety checks to make this happen? Wouldn't other people get suspicious and raise the alarm? And was the whole company really involved? Was Cole?

She pushed the thought from her mind. The only thing that mattered right now was buying more time, and currently she was losing that fight. "What about the delivery system? I know they have a prototype, but we're going to need hundreds of them. Our engineering team won't be able to get that done in two weeks."

"We've been manufacturing the drones for months now. We have more than enough to run the test. You're always so focused on your work, you miss the bigger picture." Brett chuckled, though Zoe wasn't sure what part was supposed to be funny. "Enjoy your success, Zoe. This is all happening because of you." He stood and left the lab, and Zoe sat there in shock, watching his empty seat slowly rotate in front of her.

This had to be a dream. Any minute now, she would wake up in bed with Cole.

When that didn't happen, she turned back to the lab table, where she'd been in the middle of setting up another test run. Maybe if she could show that the previous trial was tampered with, she could get the field test called off. She had to do *something*.

«‹›»

"We got a big problem," Zoe announced as she walked into her apartment, where she knew Blake would be waiting. He had probably been there most of the day.

Sure enough, he was sitting at her small kitchen table with a computer in front of him. Zoe hadn't given him the Wi-Fi password, but after watching him hack into the police system, she was sure he didn't need it. What really surprised her was that there were two other people with him. She should have expected Iris to come at some point, but Zoe had no idea who the older man sitting next to her was.

"What's the problem?" Blake asked, looking up from his computer.

Zoe glanced at the unknown man sitting at her table. Could she speak openly in front of him? Blake and Iris had to trust him if they brought him here, but was that enough? She was starting to believe that she couldn't trust anyone anymore.

"Blake, I thought you said she was going to help us. Now she can't even speak," Iris smirked.

"Iris, be nice," the older man scolded, and Iris slumped back in her chair. He turned to Zoe. "Go on."

Swallowing, she said, "Whatever Project Cleansing Rain is, it's happening in two weeks."

Iris shot to her feet, leaning her palms on the table. "How can you be sure?"

Zoe wanted to back away—of all her kidnappers, Iris was the most threatening—but she made a concentrated effort to hold her ground. This was her apartment, after all. "I was told this morning that the Wilborn Holdings' Board wants to run a field test of my plastic decomposition chemical in two weeks, even though the project is years away from actually being ready. All the files Ian was trying to steal point to the fact that my department has really been a cover for the Arrows' plans since its conception." She'd suspected this since she first started going through the data, but saying it out loud made it real. Her life's work was a scam, just a cover story to end human life on the planet.

Iris sank back down in her chair. "I thought we'd have more time."

"Go get Ian so we can figure this out." Zoe took a thick envelope from her purse and held it out. She had been nervous carrying it around all day and was glad to finally get rid of it.

Blake took the envelope and eyed it suspiciously. "What's this? Plans on how to break Ian out of jail?"

Zoe rolled her eyes. "It's money for his bail. I thought it would look suspicious if I went down there and paid it."

"We don't need your charity," Iris said.

"Then don't think of it as charity, think of it as an investment in the continuation of the human race. Unless you think you can stop the Arrows without Ian—then by all means I'll take it back." Zoe held her hand out for the envelope.

Blake held it close to his chest and turned to Iris. "You know we can't do this without him."

"Where did you get that kind of money, anyway?" Iris demanded

"Gifts from my engagement party. I assume most of the guests there were Arrows. It seemed like a good use for their money."

Iris's lip twitched up into a smile for a second before the scowl reappeared.

"I'll be back soon." Blake grabbed his jacket off the back of his chair and left.

"So," Zoe said awkwardly. Should she leave? There really wasn't anything more she could do at this point. She walked over to the refrigerator and pulled out three bottles of RiverLife water, then set them on the table and took a seat across from the stranger. "I'm Zoe."

"I've heard all about you, Ms. Antos." He extended his hand to her. "I'm Doctor Hamid Sami, Iris and Ian's uncle."

It was a good thing Zoe hadn't taken a drink yet, because she would've choked at the name. This was the man who started her department and yet received no credit—the one who'd been killed in a car accident fifteen years ago.

"But I thought . . ." Zoe looked to Iris, who shrugged.

"That I was dead," Hamid finished with a knowing smile.

"Well, yeah." Zoe took a sip of water, not sure what else to say.

"Don't feel bad. The rest of the world believes I'm dead, too."

"And we'd like to keep it that way," Iris chimed in.

"The Arrows didn't kill you?" The idea that the Arrows had killed Ian's uncle was one of the first pieces of evidence to make her think they could be real—but that was a lie. Was everything else a lie, too? Was this all some elaborate plan to get her back? She wondered if she should try to leave and call the cops. How far would she make it before Iris caught up with her?

"They certainly tried." Hamid's smile vanished. The faraway look in his eyes, like he was being forced to remember a time in his life he would rather forget, was enough keep Zoe from running to the door.

"What happened?" It was rude to ask, but she didn't care. Zoe needed to know the truth from the one person in the apartment that hadn't done anything to hurt her. She needed answers, from one scientist to another.

"I joined the Arrows when I was in college. At the time, it was just a small group of people who wanted to protect the environment. I never thought it would be anything more than a college activist club trying to make some small changes in the world, but I was wrong. Our numbers grew quickly outside the university, and the bigger we got, the more powerful and secretive things became. I didn't bother myself with the details; I was too busy with my work. By the time I realized what they were planning and the lengths they were willing to go to in order to get it, I was in too deep."

"You tried to get out?"

Hamid nodded. "Shortly after Ian and Iris came to live with me, I went to Gordon and told him I didn't want any part of it anymore. We had been friends for years, so I figured he would understand. Then things started to happen. There was a chemical leak in the lab when I was the only one there. That's when I quit my job. Next was the failed robbery. That was the worst, because Ian and Iris were sleeping in the next room. I think that was what stopped them from killing me that time. The kids came running into my room, and the robbers fled. They didn't want any witnesses."

Zoe covered her mouth. "That's terrible." How could Gordon have been so cruel to a man who was his friend?

"Things quieted down for a while after that, but I knew they would be coming after me eventually. It was eleven years after I left Green Tech that the hit-and-run happened. I knew it was the Arrows. They had me. Even if the crash didn't kill me, several of the doctors at the local hospital were part of the Equilibrium, and they would see to it that I didn't make it out of there alive. So

I didn't give them the chance. I was able to get out of the car and blow it up before emergency personnel arrived on the scene. I stayed hidden until they cleared the crash. Ian and Iris were able to nurse me back to health, and I've been in hiding ever since. Up until this morning, only three people knew I was alive. Now it's four." The weight of his trust hung over her as he looked at her across the table.

Several minutes passed, and no one said anything. Finally, Zoe rose to her feet, unable to take it any longer. "I haven't had dinner yet—would you like something to eat?"

"That's very gracious of you, thank you." Hamid nodded and smiled.

With a sigh of relief, Zoe left the table and went to search the kitchen for something to make, something that would fill the time until Ian and Blake returned. How long did it take to bail someone out of jail? She pulled out some beef and a few vegetables that had almost turned and set to work. She had no idea what she was making. With her back to Iris and Hamid whispering at the table, she started to relax, but it was short-lived.

Zoe whipped around as the front door opened and Blake walked in with Ian trailing behind. She had told herself that she was ready to face her kidnapper, but now that it was actually happening, she was having second thoughts. She moved to the other side of the small kitchen island, hoping he wouldn't notice her right away.

Iris jumped to her feet and ran over to Ian the second the door had closed behind him. She put her hands on his shoulders and looked him up and down. "What happened to you?"

Ian's arm was in a sling and his right eye was swollen shut. "I was attacked the first night in jail. I'm pretty sure they would have killed me if one of the guards hadn't stepped in. The two others that were there just stood by and watched it happen."

"Why would the other prisoners attack you? It's not like you have any enemies in there," Blake scoffed.

"It had to be the Arrows. I'm sure they know by now what I was after when I broke into Green Tech."

"At least you're safe now." Iris hugged her brother tightly.

Ian's eyes locked on Zoe as he hugged Iris back. "What's she doing here?" He gently pushed his sister away.

"This is her place," Iris said.

Ian walked over with a slight limp that hadn't been there the last time she saw him. He leaned across the island toward her. "Why?"

Zoe clutched the back of a chair, hoping it would make her shaking less noticeable. "Blake showed me all the information you had on the Arrows." Her voice was steady and calm. She could do this—she could face him.

Forcing her fingers to release the chair, Zoe moved around the island so they were on a more even playing field. This wasn't like when she was handcuffed to the futon and he was towering over her; she was not the victim here. She wouldn't allow herself to slip back in the role of hostage.

"Are you saying you believe us?" Ian raised an eyebrow. Zoe wondered if it hurt, given the bruises on his face.

"Yes. I managed to get copies of the files you were trying to steal, but Blake needs you to make any sense out of it. I want to help."

Ian ran his good hand through his hair and started to pace. "Are we all just supposed to sit here and pretend to be friends? Are you forgetting she's the reason I've spent the last two and a half weeks in jail?"

"Did you forget that you kidnapped me, tied me up, held me at gunpoint, and threatened my life on more than one occasion?" Zoe put her hands on her hips. None of this was her fault, and she wouldn't feel guilty about it.

"That's enough, both of you." Hamid stepped between them. "All of that is in the past now. We have to work together if there's any hope of stopping The Arrow Equilibrium."

Ian sat at the table next to Iris without saying a word. Zoe was about to join them when her phone rang, flashing Cole's number. "I have to take this."

She half expected them to stop her, but no one did.

"Hi, Cole." Zoe was acutely aware that everyone in the room was listening to her.

"Zoe, where are you?" Cole sounded worried. Had something happened?

"I'm at my apartment. I wanted to grab some things to bring to your place." She didn't even have to think about the lie, and it made her sick.

"I'm coming over." There was an urgency in his voice that made her nervous.

She glanced over at the table, where the others were watching her like the evening's entertainment. "Cole, you don't need to come here. Tell me what's going on."

"My dad just called. Ian Sutton made bail. He's sending a security team over to our house tonight."

"Isn't that a little excessive? I'm sure he isn't going to come after me again. I mean, isn't that a violation of his bail or something? Why would he risk it?" Zoe's gaze went to Ian, who smirked at her.

"I'm not willing to risk it," Cole said.

"Look, I was just about to leave anyway. Why don't you meet me at home and we can talk about this more?"

"I'd feel better if you weren't alone right now."

"I'll be alone longer if I wait for you to get here. I'll meet you at home. I'm leaving now, okay?" She had to keep Cole from coming to the apartment at all costs. What would he do if he found her here with Ian?

"Fine, but if you aren't there in an hour, I'm sending out a search party."

"I love you, too." Zoe hung up the phone and walked straight into the bedroom, where she grabbed a duffel bag from under her bed and started stuffing clothes into it. Cole would be suspicious if she showed up emptyhanded.

Once she gathered enough stuff to make her lie believable, she walked back out to the kitchen. Everyone was still sitting at the table. "Blake has all the information I found. We can regroup tomorrow if you have a chance to get through it all. Blake knows how to get in touch with me. Right now, I have to go convince Gordon Wilborn that I don't need a private security detail to protect me from you." Zoe waited a second for anyone to object, but they all remained silent. "Lock up when you leave."

«« Chapter 16 »»

"Zoe isn't going to be okay with this," Cole said as he paced around his living room. His father sat in an armchair, watching him, with two men dressed in black suits standing off to the side, whom Cole was trying to ignore.

"She doesn't have to like it. She just has to agree to it," Gordon said, as if Zoe was a company he was trying to acquire under the Wilborn Holdings name.

Cole eyed the men in suits. They were from a private security firm Wilborn Holdings hired for all their major events, but it was the first time his father had hired them for personal security. He wasn't even sure how this would work. Were they just going to stand there and watch everything he and his father did?

He hadn't given it much thought when his father first brought up the idea of private security. Sutton was in jail, and even though the police believed he wasn't working alone, there was no evidence to support that.

Zoe felt safe without it, and Cole wasn't going to force it on her.

But things were different now. Sutton had made bail, something Cole would have thought impossible given how high it was. That meant Sutton had someone powerful helping him, and that made him dangerous.

"Cole, sit down. Zoe won't be home for an hour. We have time to come up with a strategy to make her see reason."

"She's my fiancée, not a difficult client." Cole plopped down on the couch.

Gordon sighed. "That's exactly my point. We're putting her in a difficult position, but we're doing it for her safety."

It would be hard to make her understand that they were trying to protect her when Zoe was convinced she wasn't in any danger. "If Sutton was really only after credit for his uncle's work, do we really think that he would come after Zoe again? I mean, what does he have to gain from that?"

"Who knows how these people think? He could come after her for any number of reasons. Maybe he thinks she can get him back in the lab, or that she has access to his uncle's work and can get it for him. Maybe he'll come after her because she put him in jail. People like him don't think logically. I'm not willing to risk her safety, are you?"

"Of course not." Cole's blood turned to ice. It would destroy him if anything happened to Zoe again, especially if he could have done something to stop it.

He got up and started to pace again, hoping the movement would dispel the chill in his bones. Gordon leaned forward in his chair. "Good. Then you need to make her see this is for her own good."

"And if she doesn't see it that way?"

"If anyone can convince her, it's you." Gordon stood and joined the two men in the corner. "Cole, this is Matt Tucker. He'll be guarding Zoe."

The younger of the two men stepped forward, and Cole looked over his strong, muscular frame and expressionless face. He guessed those were good features for a bodyguard. "Mr. Wilborn," Tucker said, "I have ten years of experience with private security, and before that, I was a Marine. I assure you that nothing will happen to Ms. Antos while under my protection."

"And what exactly will that entail?"

"I will drive her to and from work and anywhere else she needs to go. At work, I'll escort her to the building and coordinate with the security team there to make sure all entrances are monitored around the clock. We know Sutton gained access to the lab through one of the emergency exits that was propped open, so we'll be patrolling the perimeter to ensure there are no other breaches. When she is here, I'll be stationed outside the house and alert you to anyone approaching. We have been provided with an approved list of visitors. Anyone else will have to be approved by you or Ms. Antos."

Cole turned to Gordon. "I want to see that list." He might forgive his father's intrusion in their life more than he should, but he wasn't about to let his dad say who they could and couldn't see. "What about other places, like the store or at the campus? Zoe likes to study at the library there."

"In any area we can't secure, I'll be by her side. I can't say that she won't notice I'm there, but I will try to be as unobtrusive as possible."

"That, right there." Cole pointed at Tucker. "That's where we'll lose her."

"Which is where you come in," Gordon urged. "You know what to say to make her agree to this."

Gordon put his hand on Cole's shoulder, but he shrugged it off and went to the other side of the room. He needed space to think clearly. A picture of him and Zoe on the table caught his eye—a selfie he had snapped last year while they were out hiking. Just the two of them, alone in the woods. He longed for the simplicity of that moment. "I can't lie to her."

"No one's asking you to lie. You simply need to make her understand that this is in her best interest and we wouldn't be asking otherwise."

Cole turned around and slowly nodded. His father was right; it was a small sacrifice to make until Sutton was behind bars for good and they were sure Zoe was safe.

«‹›»

Zoe's stomach twisted into knots as soon as Cole's house came into view. She recognized Gordon's Cadillac in the driveway instantly. She had mentally prepared to argue with Cole during her drive home, but she hadn't factored his father into the equation. Even though she had known him for years, she wasn't comfortable fighting with him, especially now that she knew he was part of The Arrow Equilibrium. What if the rest of the family was there, too? She wouldn't put it past them to gang up on her to pressure her into agreeing to their security detail.

She wished she could turn around and head back to the apartment. Right now, she would feel more at ease with her kidnappers than walking into Cole's house.

There were two nondescript black cars parked in front as well; Zoe assumed they belonged to the security detail Gordon had hired. It wasn't a good sign that they were already here. How was she going to convince them that she wasn't in danger without giving away what she was actually doing? Should she pretend to be afraid of Ian? No, Cole would see through that, and it would give Gordon all the leverage he'd need to force the security detail on her. She needed to stand firm and stick the facts—at least the facts as far as they knew. Ian wasn't after her, and he never had been.

Zoe rehearsed the story in her head a few times before getting out of the car, then hesitated on the doorstep before turning the knob. Cole rushed to the door to greet her. She was in his arms before she fully crossed the threshold.

"Thank God you made it home safely," he said into her shoulder.

"Of course I did. I told you, no one is coming after me. I'm sure I'll never lay eyes on Ian Sutton again." Zoe hugged him back, though not with the same intensity. The guilt of her lie was already taking hold. Over Cole's shoulder, she spotted Gordon and two men in suits standing in the living room.

She released Cole and made her way over to them. It was time to fight back.

"This really isn't necessary," she said with what she hoped was a reassuring smile.

"It's just a precaution," Gordon said. "We don't know who put up the money for Sutton's bail or where he went after he was released."

It was me, I paid his bail, Zoe thought, but she could never tell them. "I'm thankful for that, but I really don't believe I'm in any kind of danger. I was never his intended target. I was just in the wrong place at the wrong time. Why would he go to all the trouble of tracking me down now?"

"Revenge," Cole offered without really looking at her.

His father must have told him what to say. Zoe tried to suppress a laugh, but a small chuckle escaped. "Revenge for what?"

"For stopping him from stealing the research he was after. For alerting the cops and getting him thrown in jail," Gordon answered promptly. "I'm ashamed to say that we didn't have any leads on where to find you until you sent Cole that text. You alone are responsible for stopping him, which you should be proud of, but it puts a target on you."

Zoe didn't know what to say. In one sentence, Gordon had taken her from victim to hero to target. It was no wonder people followed him—he could almost get Zoe herself to believe she was in danger. But she had been within arm's reach of Ian only an hour ago, and he hadn't hurt her.

"I still don't think he would come after me. He's not some kind of criminal mastermind. Most of the time, he didn't seem like he knew what he was doing." It was the most honest thing she'd told them so far. "The fact that he left his phone where I could get it in the first place should tell you that. I think he's just a guy who made a bad decision in a moment of panic."

"That only makes him more dangerous." Gordon took both of her hands in his. His touch was tender, like he was dealing with an irrational child, and Zoe fought the urge to pull away. She had never been uncomfortable with his gestures of fatherly affection before, and if she was now, he might suspect she knew who he really was.

"Sutton's proved that he doesn't act rationally. He thinks with his emotions. There's no way to predict how someone like that will behave. It's better to take precautions, at least until we can track him down and make sure he doesn't come anywhere near you."

Zoe felt her face fall. She hoped they would see it as a realization that her safety was at risk and not concern over Ian. How long would it take them to figure out she was the one who gave Blake the money for his bail? To figure out that she was helping him? They had to know he was going after the Arrows—look what had happened to him in jail. Did they suspect she was involved somehow? Was the security detail there to keep her safe, or to keep her from digging further into Project Cleansing Rain?

All these questions spun through Zoe's head until she wasn't sure what she thought anymore. All she wanted to do was go back to a time before she ever knew about The Arrow Equilibrium.

"Cole, can I talk to you alone for a minute?" Zoe walked into his office and prayed he would follow her without protest. If she could get him on her side, there was a small chance Gordon would back down—her last chance.

She held her breath until the door closed behind Cole. Then he turned to face him. "I'm really not comfortable with this."

"I know, and I wouldn't be asking if it wasn't important." Cole at least had the decency to look embarrassed.

Zoe crossed her arms. "I really don't think my safety is at risk."

"It's only for a little while." Cole ran his hand through her hair, and Zoe softened slightly. This wasn't his idea; she knew she shouldn't take her frustration out on him.

"I don't like the idea of someone following me around all day." Zoe let her arms fall at her sides. She had lost, but she wasn't willing to admit it yet.

"He can wait outside for you once they've secured the area." Cole wrapped his arms around her, a small smile on his lips. He knew she was almost ready to give in. "Do this for me. I was so worried when he took you. I couldn't live with myself if something happened to you."

"Fine," Zoe said with an overexaggerated sigh. She would have to find a way to help bring down the Arrows without her new babysitter finding out. It just added another layer of complications to an already-complicated situation.

Gordon looked at them expectantly once they returned to the living room. "One security guard, and they wait outside for me," Zoe answered his unasked question.

"Agreed. Though he will be driving you to and from work and anywhere else you need to go," Gordon added.

Zoe turned to look at Cole for backup, but he didn't look shocked by the news. "I guess that will be fine," she finally said, feeling like she had accomplished nothing and Gordon was getting exactly what he wanted.

The Arrows would know where she was at all times.

«« Chapter 17 »»

Zoe had been at the lab for an hour and she was itching to reach out to Blake. Her new bodyguard, going only by Tucker like some kind of celebrity, had picked her up in the morning, driven her to work, and walked her to the lobby. The whole ordeal was highly embarrassing, but she put up with it for Cole. He had been through enough, and she didn't want to add to his stress. If the bodyguard helped put his mind at ease, she would find a way to deal with it — for now.

Still, she couldn't be sure that Tucker wasn't a spy for the Arrows, or that he would actually stay in the lobby until she was done for the day. When an hour had passed without her spotting him, she figured she was in the clear. Zoe ducked into an empty conference room, pulling out her phone as she went, and pulled up Blake's number — stored under her graduate advisor's name in case Cole ever looked at her phone. Not that she thought he would invade her privacy like that, but like Gordon had said last night, better safe than sorry.

The phone only rang once before a male voice answered, "Yeah?"

"Blake?" He was usually much more verbose when he answered.

"No."

Zoe pulled the phone away from her ear to double check that she had dialed the right number. "Ian?"

"Depends on who's asking."

"It's Zoe." He chuckled, and she frowned. "What is it?"

"Blake has you in his phone as *handcuff chick* and that didn't really narrow down for me."

"Oh, that's just lovely." Zoe rolled her eyes even though no one could see her.

"He's always the charmer. Look, Blake's out right now. He has to keep up appearances, you know? Do you need me to pass along a message?"

"I actually wanted to talk to you, I just didn't know how to get in touch with you."

"Really? Why would you want to talk to the guy who kidnapped you?"

Zoe chose to ignore the sarcasm in his voice. "I wanted to warn you." She tried to sound sincere; Ian had no reason to trust her, so she would have to be the one to take the risk and trust him, like he had when he first told her about The Arrows. "I wasn't able to convince the Wilborns that I don't need a private security detail. Gordon also mentioned he has a team working to track you down on the pretense of making sure you don't come near me."

"Won't they be surprised when they find out you're the one that keeps reaching out to me," he scoffed. "You might want to talk to a therapist about that."

"I was trying to give you a heads up," Zoe snapped. "But if you want a repeat of what happened to you in jail, feel free to ignore it. I'm not sure why I bothered."

"I'm sorry," Ian said, all humor gone from his voice. "I appreciate what you're trying to do, even if I don't fully understand why you're helping us. I know the Arrows are after me, and I know what they're capable of. I'd be a fool if I wasn't afraid of them." He paused and took a deep breath. "You should probably stay away from us. I don't want you to get hurt. It's too late for Iris, Blake, and me. We're already in too deep, but you can still walk away from this before anyone finds out that you're involved."

"I've read all the evidence you have. How do you expect me to walk away when I know what they're trying to do?"

"Your notes were pretty insightful. You made a couple connections I missed. I wanted to talk to you about that, but it's probably not a good idea for us to meet back at your apartment tonight."

"Probably not." Zoe searched her mind for a safe place they could get together. She didn't want to wait; the Arrows were moving fast, which meant they needed to move faster. "Could you get to the U of M library, say around six?"

"What about your security detail?"

"I go there a few days a week after work to study, so it wouldn't raise any suspicions, and the bodyguard is supposed to wait outside of the building for me. As long as you're there before me, it shouldn't be a problem."

"And if he decides to do a sweep of the building first?"

"He's only one person, it's not like he can survey every person in the building. I'll do what I can to keep him from coming in, but if he does, you'll have to make sure he doesn't see you. You managed to break into Green Tech without being detected, I'm sure you can handle this."

"You are full of surprises, Zoe Antos."

"So you'll be there?"

"Yeah, I'll be there." Ian hung up the phone.

《《〈〉》》

The library was crowded when Zoe arrived, with midterms around the corner. Zoe didn't wait for Tucker to open her door once the car was parked. She headed toward the entrance, determined to ignore him. She wanted to make it clear to everyone that while she had agreed to the private security, she'd only done so under protest.

"I need to do a sweep of the library before you go in," Tucker said once he caught up with her. She had managed to make it into the lobby, at least.

"Do you really think someone is going to try to hurt me in the middle of a crowded library? How would Sutton even know I'm here?" Zoe said, knowing that Ian was waiting for her somewhere in the building.

"It's my job." His face remained expressionless. Zoe was sure he wasn't thrilled about his current assignment. Surely there had to be more exciting things he could be doing instead of babysitting her, especially since she was in no danger—and she suspected Tucker knew it too.

"Fine," she relented.

"Wait here. It will only take a few minutes," Tucker said.

"And how can you be sure that someone isn't going to come in off the street and get me while you're doing your sweep?" She knew she was pushing his buttons, but she couldn't help herself. This whole thing was ridiculous.

Tucker scowled at her before going to talk to the nearby campus security guard, who couldn't have been more than twenty years old. They returned together. "He is going to keep an eye on you while I complete my sweep of the building. Stay here or I'll let Mr. Wilborn know that I think you need a second security guard." Tucker took off without another word, leaving the threat hanging in the air.

Zoe quickly pulled out her phone and texted Blake. *Incoming.*

"So are you, like, famous or something?" the security guard asked. Zoe very much doubted that he would be able to do anything to actually protect her if a situation arose.

"No. I'm nobody." Zoe opened an app on her phone and pretended to read an article.

"Then what's with the bodyguard?"

"My fiancé's family has more money than they know what to do with." She continued to look at her phone, though her focus was elsewhere. Every sound made the hairs on her arms stand on end. Had she given him enough warning to hide? What would happen if Tucker spotted Ian? Would there be a fight?

She breathed a small sigh of relief when Tucker finally returned. "Is it safe for me to go study now?" she asked, failing to keep the sarcasm out of her voice.

"Yes, ma'am."

Zoe rolled her eyes and started off toward the heart of the library with Tucker following. "Where are you going?"

"With you," he said matter-of-factly.

"I'm not going to have you hovering over me while I try to study. Besides, the agreement was that you would wait at the entrance."

"With all due respect, that was the agreement when you were at work, inside a secured facility, not in a public place." Tucker towered over her, but she wouldn't let him intimidate her into compliance. She was going to be a Wilborn; it was time she started acting like it. Technically, he was an employee, and she didn't have to listen to him.

"No, that was the agreement for everywhere, so go have a seat by the door." Zoe pointed to the small table and chairs next to the library entrance.

Tucker stared her down, and for a moment she felt herself wanting to cave under the scrutiny, but she held firm. Finally, he said, "I'll come check on you every forty-five minutes."

"That's not necessary."

"It's not negotiable." He turned away and took up a post by the library's entrance.

With renewed confidence, Zoe made her way into the heart of the library, found a table in the corner, and set up her computer. She needed to have a cover for when Tucker came to check on her. She set an alarm on her watch to make sure she was back in time, then set off to find Ian.

Zoe had no idea how she would find him. It was entirely possible he hadn't shown up. Would she tell her if he wasn't able to make it, or just leave her wondering?

She wandered around aimlessly for a while, peeking in every study room that she passed. Just when she was pull out her phone to text Blake again, she heard someone whisper, "In here."

Zoe turned to see Iris standing in the crack of door leading to a housekeeping closet. Zoe glanced around to make sure Tucker hadn't come looking for her, then snuck inside.

Ian, Iris, and Blake were all in the cramped room, waiting for her. Did they do everything together?

"We don't have a lot of time. Were you able to figure anything out from the files?" Zoe asked.

"There are a lot of unexplained gaps in your data. Either your department is terrible at data collection, or there's some missing from the files," Ian said.

"That doesn't make any sense. Everything has to be quality checked by the department lead for . . ." Zoe trailed off. Brett was the department lead; if he was working for the Arrows, it would be easy to remove any data they didn't want anyone else to see — or manipulate it to look like there had been a huge unexplained breakthrough.

"Does the name Brett Klein mean anything to you?"

"Yeah, he's my boss. He's the one that took over the department when your uncle left Green Tech. He's also the one who told me that they are releasing the chemical in two weeks."

"From what I can tell in the files, he's been the Arrows' frontman in the lab since he took over. Security was tripled and the team cut in half," Ian said.

"Why, though?"

"Less people to control, less chance of anyone finding out what they were really planning," Iris said.

"What we really need to figure out is exactly what they're going to release so we can see if there's a way to counteract it. The files were annoyingly vague on those details," Blake said, fiddling with a bottle of disinfectant spray.

"I don't know what it is, but I know they're planning on producing it at Green Tech. We're scheduled to start producing large amounts of chemicals tomorrow. That has to be what they're using for Cleansing Rain — or what they're calling it in all the press releases, 'The Antos Solution.'" Zoe wasn't sure if they could see her roll her eyes in the dim light, but she was sure her annoyance was effectively communicated.

"That's nice, your father-in-law wants to place the blame for the end of the world on your shoulders," Iris snorted. "That's a hell of a way to welcome you to the family."

Zoe chose to ignore the comment, mostly because Iris was right and it made her sick to think about it. She had thought the Wilborns loved her like their own children. "I can try to get a sample of the chemical to analyze. I have some basic lab equipment back at my apartment, it could at least tell us where to start. I think it's too risky to run it though any of the equipment at Green Tech."

"That leaves deployment," Ian said.

"Since you're in the thieving mood, see if you can get your hands on one of those drones. That should give me some idea if they're planning an airborne or water-based toxin," Iris said.

"I'll see what I can do." This had to be the strangest planning meeting Zoe had ever been a part of — and probably the most important.

"One last thing." Ian nodded to Blake, who set the disinfectant bottle down and pulled out a phone.

Confused, Zoe took it from him. It was an old-school flip phone like she'd had in high school. "What's this for?"

"That's what we in the criminal world refer to as a burner phone," Blake smiled. "Welcome to the club."

She didn't want to admit it, but he was right. She was a criminal. Normal law-abiding citizens didn't meet with thieves and kidnappers in broom closets to put together a plan to steal confidential information from their fiancé's family.

"All our numbers are in there under aliases." Ian pointed at the phone in her hand. "Delete Blake's number from your other phone. Once the Arrows suspect you're working with us, they'll tap your phone, if they haven't already."

Zoe hadn't even thought of that. She might be entering the criminal world, but it was clear she had a lot to learn.

"Don't let that out of your sight for a second. If they find it, we're all screwed," Iris added.

Zoe nodded and put the phone in her pocket just as the alarm on her watch went off. "I need to get back. Tucker will be coming to check on me soon. I need to work for at least another hour to make this seem like a normal trip. Will you be alright in here until then?"

"We'll manage," Ian said. "Be careful, Zoe."

Zoe nodded again and slipped out of the closet.

«« Chapter 18 »»

Cole had barely set his stuff down in his office when Jackson and Gordon walked in. It was unusual for them both to come see him first thing in the morning. Cole had checked his email when he woke up and hadn't seen any issues with his facilities that would require an early-morning visit from his father. "What happened?"

"It's nothing bad." Jackson leaned on the small table in the corner.

"We're taking the Board to Green Tech in an hour, and I want you to come," his father said from the doorway.

"I don't have anything to do with the operations at Green Tech," Cole said, looking from his dad to his brother.

"I know that, but with everything that's going on with the plastic decomposition project, they are suddenly a lot more interested in the lab. The last thing I want is for a Board member to corner one of the scientists and start asking questions the team at Green Tech shouldn't be answering."

"So you want me there to help babysit the Board?"

"Exactly. We leave in an hour." His father left without another word.

Cole sank down in his chair and pulled up his calendar. He had a few meetings lined up for the day, but nothing that couldn't be rescheduled.

Out of the corner of his eye, he noticed Jackson was still there. "What's this meeting really about?"

Jackson sat down across from Cole. "We're getting some pushback from the larger scientific community about running the field test, and the Board members are getting nervous. Dad wants them to see that Green Tech knows what they're doing, and hopefully that will be enough to put them at ease." Jackson took a sip of his coffee. At least he didn't seem worried.

"The Board won't have any idea what they're looking at. I don't even understand most of it, and I hear about it all time from Zoe." Cole leaned back in his chair, smirking as he thought about William Conner looking over the lab equipment, pretending to know what any of it was. Conner hated looking stupid, and Cole couldn't wait to see him put in his place. It would be nice payback for putting Zoe on the spot at the engagement party.

"Be careful, or I might let it slip to Zoe that you don't listen to her," Jackson said with a wicked smile.

Cole rolled his eyes. "If the Board is concerned about pushback from the scientific community about the plastic decomposition project, why don't we field test a different project instead? Zoe told me the water filtration project has had amazing success and that it's ready for real-world applications. And it would still make Green

Tech look good." How was that for proving he did in fact listen to Zoe when she discussed her work?

"Funny you mention that—I asked Dad the same thing when I started getting calls from angry scientists all around the world."

"What did he say?"

"That the water filtration project is important, but it will really only help a small portion of the global population, whereas cleaning the oceans will save the whole world. You know Dad, he likes being the hero." Jackson raised his cup of coffee in a toast.

"Bigger risk, bigger payoff." Cole recited the motto he had heard from his father his whole life. It had worked out for him so far; it was how he'd built Wilborn Holdings and secured a future for the family.

"We need to go in there, show the Board some fancy science stuff, and have Zoe and Brett confuse everyone with some technobabble so they'll let Dad take this big risk," Jackson said.

"Does Zoe know about this? She doesn't normally give tours." Cole raised an eyebrow.

"Don't worry, Brett will be doing most of the talking. He loves the limelight, probably more than any scientist should. I'm not saying he's on mad-scientist level, but I am surprised he didn't insist we name the project after him." Jackson stood. "I'll see you down at the car."

An hour later, Cole headed down to the parking garage, where his father and Jackson were waiting. The Board members showed up a few minutes later, and they all piled into the company cars that would take them to Green Tech. Cole didn't pay much attention to the conversations around him, which alternated between golf and boating, neither of which he enjoyed.

Something Jackson had said that morning was bothering him. If the scientific community had concerns about the field test, maybe there was more at play than his father's ego. Maybe this was why Zoe had been so distant and distracted the last week. He had assumed it was the aftermath of the kidnapping, but she always tended to retreat inside herself whenever things went wrong at work. The fact that she hadn't mentioned the field test to him was a huge red flag. Did she think it was a bad idea, too?

Cole would have to get her alone and ask her flat out what her thoughts were. This might be the one time he had to force himself into her work.

«‹‹›»»

Three days had passed since the planning meeting in the broom closet, where Zoe had promised to steal for her kidnappers, and it was a promise she hadn't fulfilled yet. She'd thought it would be easy to get a sample of the toxin—it was supposed to be her project, after all—but they kept the production room tightly guarded, and it wasn't like she could ask Brett to let her in without drawing suspicion. As for the drone, she didn't have any idea where to get one of those.

All of it made Zoe feel like a failure. She couldn't do anything right these days. She was lying constantly, afraid that everyone she once trusted was out to destroy her, and the experiment she had spent her whole career working on was a total sham. Now, on top of everything, she couldn't even find a way to steal a few vials of a chemical that was being produced in her name.

"Hey there, beautiful."

Zoe jumped out of her seat and spun to find Cole standing behind her, laughing.

"Don't do that to me!" She punched his arm. Cole rarely stopped by Green Tech, and when he did it was usually for lunch, not first thing in the morning. "What are you doing here?"

"The Board is here for a tour. They want to see what's going on with your project. Dad and Jackson are with them in the lobby, going through all the safety orientation stuff."

"I hope you weren't sent here to convince me to give the tour." She couldn't think of a worse way to spend the day, especially since she suspected all of them were part of The Arrow Equilibrium. They were probably here to check on the progress of their end-of-the-world plot.

"Kind of," Cole admitted sheepishly. "Though I've been assured Brett will do the majority of the talking."

Zoe was about to protest when a thought occurred to her. The Board would surely want to see the chemical production and deployment system; this might be her only chance to get a sample of the toxin. Her mood lifted at once. "If you promise I won't have to do a lot of talking, I'll do it for you." She leaned forward and gave him a quick kiss.

"Thank you." Cole looked around her cube. "Where's your lab coat? You should wear it, makes you look extra-sciencey."

Zoe cocked an eyebrow at him. "It's in the lab where it belongs." She turned off her computer. "And how old are you? *Sciencey*? And they let you oversee operations," she teased as they walked down to the main conference room where the Board members were waiting for them.

Brett met them outside the door, nodding to Cole as Cole entered the conference room — leaving him and Zoe in the hall.

"There's my superstar," Brett beamed, handing her one of the lab coats draped over his arm. Zoe shook her head as she put it on. "Are you ready to put on a show for the suits?"

"Are you? You seemed pretty excited after your last meeting with them. Think you can keep it together this time?" Zoe returned his smile. She had been managing to mimic her normal relationship with Brett, but it was getting harder every day.

He chuckled and opened the door for her. Zoe took a deep breath as she walked inside. She would have been less afraid to enter a room filled with hungry lions. She tried to take a seat in the back, but Brett ushered her to the front with him.

"Thank you all for coming today," he said. "We're excited to share what we've been working on with all of you. My team has been working hard for years to develop a chemical that will quickly and safely decompose the plastics clogging our oceans. It can handle anything from microplastics to large debris. With me today is the lab supervisor and lead scientist on the project, Zoe Antos."

Everyone in the room clapped politely, while Zoe gave an awkward wave. She locked in on Cole, who fingered his jacket and mouthed, "*Sciencey,*" smirking at her. She bit the inside of her cheek to stop herself from laughing; she had to remain professional.

"Zoe is the scientist responsible for the formulation that gave us the amazing results which will allow us to run a field test. We believe that this test will start to put the environment back in balance and correct some of the damage humans have caused to the planet."

Zoe tried to suck back a gasp, but ended up choking herself on the air she inhaled. It was like Brett was reading straight from the Arrows' handbook. If there was any doubt in her mind about what the Arrows were up to, it was gone now.

She almost felt the color drain from her face as the realization washed over her. They were days away from the end of the world, and it was up to her to stop it.

"If you'll follow me, I'll take you on a tour of our operations so you can see for yourself the groundbreaking work we're doing here." Brett moved to the door and left Zoe standing alone in the front of the conference room. Slowly, the Board members filed out, with Zoe bringing up the rear. It wasn't like she had access to where they were going anyway. She tried to catch Cole's eye again, but he had been roped into a conversation with two Board members she didn't recognize. It made her sick seeing him talk to them. She desperately needed to believe that he knew nothing about the Arrows and was simply doing his job, unaware of the actual implications of the work happening at the lab.

Brett fished a key card from his back pocket and used it to unlock the door to the room where the toxin was being produced. Most of the chemical mixing was done by machine, with only one supervisor in the room to oversee the operation. It made sense — they wouldn't want anyone else to realize that they were producing a chemical meant to kill people instead of decomposing plastics.

Once inside, Brett gave an overview of the operation. Zoe positioned herself in the back of the room, near one of the cases holding vials of chemicals. Scanning the room, she spotted a security camera in the corner of the ceiling. It was pointed at the door.

She moved over to make sure she wasn't in the frame. When no one was looking, she slipped two of the vials into her coat pocket. She was halfway there.

"Zoe can answer that better than I can," Brett said from the front of the room.

Everyone turned to look at her, and Zoe froze. She was sure everyone could see the vials in her pocket. "I'm sorry, I got caught up in the impressive operation in here," she said awkwardly. Everyone chuckled.

"I was asking if any of the chemicals have any adverse effects on animal or plant life," one of the Board members repeated. "The last thing we want to do is solve one problem while creating an even bigger one."

Zoe wondered if this was all an elaborate show for her benefit, or was it possible that a few members of the Board weren't part of the Arrows? "All the chemicals we use in the lab have been through rigorous testing to ensure they don't cause any harm to humans or the environment. They can't make it into my lab unless they pass that stage first." It was ridiculous explaining a process that she knew was exactly the opposite of what was being done, but they were all putting on a show, and she needed to play her part to keep herself safe. She had a sinking feeling that the deeper she got into things, the less protection she would get from her association with the Wilborns.

They spent a few more minutes in the chemical production lab before moving on. This was the part Zoe was the most interested in. She had no idea where the deployment system was being built; now she was being led directly there.

Though, she suspected stealing a drone would be a lot harder than slipping a few vials into her pocket.

Brett led them to a large room off one of the shipping docks, and she was shocked to see it stacked to the brim with boxes. There had to be at least a thousand finished drones. A small assembly line was set up along the far wall, where more were being put together every minute.

Zoe started to move forward with the group, but Cole gently grabbed her arm so she would hang back with him. "I wanted to catch you alone," he whispered as the others moved on without them.

"What about?" They had plenty of time to talk alone after work. What was so important he needed to discuss it with her right now?

Cole led her behind a stack of boxes. "About this field test. I want to know how you feel about it. I'm not sure if you're aware, but we're getting a lot of pushback from the scientific community. They think we're acting prematurely."

Zoe heaved a sigh. "I agree with them. There's so much work that needs to be done before we should even start talking about a field test. We haven't had a chance to replicate the results in the lab, much less have them peer reviewed and brought before an ethics committee."

"Why didn't you say something?"

"I did. Repeatedly."

"Not to me." Cole looked hurt, but he didn't have any authority over Green Tech and she hadn't wanted to get him involved. She wouldn't do anything that would put him at risk.

"You're right. I did talk to Brett about it, but he didn't think my concerns were valid. He's been avoiding me ever since. He even locked me out of the lab," Zoe said in a rushed whisper. How long would it be before the others realized they were gone?

"Jackson was afraid Brett would try to take over. It must be killing him that the project is named after you."

"You know I don't care about any of that. I only care about doing what's right, and running a field test right now is possibly the worst thing I've ever been part of." It felt like a huge weight had lifted off her shoulders. She hated keeping things from Cole. At least now he knew why she was so stressed, even if she had left out a lot of important details.

Cole ran his hand through his hair. "I don't have much pull over Green Tech, but I'll see if there's anything I can do to delay the field test."

"You'd really do that for me?"

Cole took her hands. "When will you learn I'll do anything for you?" He brought her hand up to his lips and kissed her knuckles.

"Thank you." Zoe wrapped her arms around his neck, and they brushed against a box behind him. She needed to get into that box without him knowing.

"We better get back to the group. I'm going to have to do a lot of sweet talking if I'm going to pull this off."

"Good idea." Zoe pretended to choke back a few tears, flashing him a weak smile. "I'll be there in a second."

The moment he was gone, she dove at the box, disappointed to find it was sealed. Someone would notice if she opened it.

She looked around frantically. There had to be more. There was one open box along the wall that had the word "scrap" scribbled across it. She looked in and found it was full of parts.

Zoe grabbed what she could and stuck them in her pockets. She had no idea if it was what they needed, but it was the best she could do.

«« Chapter 19 »»

Zoe nearly ran back to her office when she was released from the tour group. The Board were going to spend some time discussing the project before they left the site, but she wasn't important enough to be present for that.

Not that she wanted to be. She was tired of putting on a show.

She made sure no one was watching her, then got her purse out of the cabinet and carefully placed the vials of toxin and the drone parts inside. Zoe tried her best to use the contents of her purse to conceal them. Once that was done, she pulled out the burner phone and ducked into an empty conference room.

She dialed Ian. It only rang once before he picked up. "Yeah?" He wasn't one to waste time with pleasantries.

"I got it."

"Seriously? Everything?" Shock raised his voice, and Zoe wasn't sure if she should be insulted. Honestly, she hadn't been sure she would pull it off, either.

"Can you get to my apartment so we can start working on it?"

"Yeah. How soon can you get there?"

"The executive Board for Wilborn Holdings is here right now, checking up on the project. Once they're gone, I'll sneak out." It would be the first time in her career that she snuck out of work early. She felt guiltier about that than she did about taking the toxin and drone parts.

"Zoe, be careful. There's no telling what they'll do to you if they suspect you're onto them." The concern in his voice stunned her silent for a moment. She guessed she really was part of the team now.

"I will." Zoe hung up the phone and went back to her desk.

She tried to work, but she couldn't focus, checking the clock every few minutes. How much longer would the Board members stay? What more could they have to discuss? She thought about trying to sneak out while they were locked away in a conference room, but it was too risky. Cole would definitely come say goodbye before they left, and if she wasn't there, he would be worried. Zoe didn't want to draw any more attention to herself.

An hour later, someone tapped on the outside of her cube. She looked up to see Cole. "All done?"

"Yeah, but I have some bad news." He sat down in the empty chair next to her desk, and Zoe tried not to let her panic show. Had someone seen her steal the vials while they were on the tour? Had Gordon found out that she had been the one to put up the money for Ian's bail? Had they traced Ian to her apartment?

"What is it?" she asked as calmly as she could.

"I'm not going to make it for date night. My dad is making me go to a business dinner with the rest of the Board, and they always go late."

She had completely forgotten it was Friday. "Oh. That's okay. I think I'm going to head to my apartment after work and start packing up. It's about time I bring the rest of my things to your house."

Cole leaned forward. "*Our* house." He kissed her quickly. "I have to go."

"Try to enjoy yourself tonight. Maybe take a shot every time one of them brings up golf," Zoe joked.

Cole turned back to her. "I wouldn't make it through appetizers if I did that. I love you." He spun around and was gone.

Zoe waited another twenty minutes to make sure they were really gone before gathering her things and heading out. She nearly walked right past Tucker before she remembered that she didn't have a car here.

Tucker jumped to his feet and looked at his watch. "Leaving a little early today?" he asked with a raised eyebrow.

Zoe hadn't factored him into her plan. She had no idea if he was going to turn her in or not. She decided it was best to own what she was doing; if she acted like she wasn't doing something wrong, he wouldn't say anything about it—she hoped. "Actually, yes. It's been a long week."

Tucker nodded and held the door open for her. "Alright, home it is, then."

"No. We're going to my apartment," she said casually as they walked to car together, Tucker scanning the parking lot as they went. "I told Cole I was going to be there most of the evening packing. I believe it's one of my approved locations." She made sure he saw her roll her eyes. Hopefully, since she'd already told Cole where she would be, Tucker wouldn't feel the need to verify it with anyone.

"You're the boss." He held the car door open for her.

"I seriously doubt that," she said as she slid inside. She could have sworn Tucker suppressed a laugh.

On the drive to her apartment, neither of them spoke. Zoe wanted to pull out her phone and let Ian know she was on her way, but she didn't dare do it where Tucker might see. He was growing on her, but she still didn't trust him. She wasn't sure she would ever really trust anyone again. She had to hope that Ian had made it inside already.

Tucker pulled up to her apartment, and to Zoe's shock, he didn't move to get out of the car. "I'll be out here if you need anything."

She wasn't surprised to find Ian, Iris, Blake, and Hamid waiting for her inside. Ian and his uncle were setting up equipment on the kitchen island, while Iris had taken over the table with a drop cloth and toolbox. Blake lounged on the couch, watching TV. He really was just along for the ride.

"You made it alright?" Ian asked once she had shut the door behind her.

"Yeah. Tucker, my bodyguard, is downstairs in the car. I don't think anyone suspected anything." Zoe put her purse on the counter and fished out the two vials of toxin. "This is it." She carefully handed them to Ian, and everyone gathered around to look at the amber liquid inside. Not that they could tell anything about the toxin that way; it might have been apple juice for all they could see at this point. "They've already produced thousands of these vials, with no end in sight."

"You got anything in that bag for me?" Iris nodded toward Zoe's purse.

"As a matter of fact, I do." She dug the parts out of her purse. "I wasn't able to get a complete drone, but hopefully there's enough here that you can piece it together with the drawings from the files."

Iris took the pieces, looking each one over carefully. "I can work with this." She took them all over to the table.

Zoe turned to Ian. "I guess we should get started."

Ian nodded. Zoe took a sample of the toxin, careful not to let any of it touch her skin, and put it on a microscope slide. Ian and Hamid did the same. Under the lens, Zoe studied it carefully. It didn't appear to be biological, which she guessed was good. Biologicals could mutate and become unmanageable.

The only thing she could confirm was that everything they were telling her about the Arrows was true. The chemical in the vial didn't even remotely resemble the plastic decomposition agent she had been working on.

«‹‹›»

The Board headed from Green Tech back downtown. There was a nice restaurant across the street from Wilborn Holdings headquarters where they always went for business dinners. Cole was in a car with Jackson, Gordon, and William Conner. Despite the productive visit to Green Tech, no one said anything on the drive. William shot Gordon a few side glances in the front seat, like he didn't want to talk with the children in the back.

Cole hated that he was missing date night for this, but he had promised to try to get the timing for the field test changed, and he wasn't going to be able to do that if no one was talking. He needed to bring it up organically in conversation and convince the Board members that it was their idea.

Jackson tapped Cole on the arm and pointed out his window. "Why is Mom here?"

Cole turned to look out the other side of the car. He had been so focused on formulating a plan that he hadn't been paying attention to where they were. Sure enough, his mother was standing outside the restaurant, as if this were a planned family dinner and not a business meal.

"No idea." Cole got out of the car and went over to Alana, kissing her cheek. "What are you doing here?"

She looked a little surprised to see Cole and Jackson as well, glancing at their dad for moment before answering, "Your father and I had dinner plans. He forgot to mention that he invited the entire Board to join us."

"Jackson and I can handle the dinner. You guys go have dinner somewhere else." Jackson elbowed him sharply in the side, but Cole didn't care. Without Gordon there, he had a much better chance of convincing the Board to push the field test. He was pretty sure it was his father's ego that had set the date in the first place.

"Don't be silly," William said as he stepped up to greet Alana. "We don't mind if your mother joins us. I'm sure we won't be talking much business anyway."

"In fact, why don't the two of you take off?" Gordon added. "I hate that we're stealing your Friday night."

"It's really not a big deal," Cole said. As much of a family man as his father was, he usually put the company first in these situations. Cole couldn't remember another time his father had allowed them to skip a business dinner.

"No, I insist."

There was clearly something going on here. Why was his mother staying for dinner when she had nothing to do with the business, while Cole and Jackson were being sent away? It didn't make any sense.

"You don't want to spend your Friday night sitting around listening to us old-timers discuss golf and politics," William said with a forced laugh.

"You got us there," Jackson said, stepping in front of Cole.

"I don't mind," Cole argued, gently pushing Jackson out of the way. Jackson gave him a dirty look but didn't say anything.

"We had a good meeting today. I think everyone was impressed by the work being done at Green Tech. Your work is done," Gordon said firmly.

"Dad, is everything okay?" Cole pushed. Again, Jackson elbowed him in the ribs, harder than before. Cole remembered that he'd mentioned having a date tonight—a date he would have to cancel unless he could get out of dinner.

"You boys go enjoy your weekend." Alana stepped forward and kissed their cheeks. "I'm sure your father will fill you in on Monday if anything important comes up."

And just like that, the conversation was over.

"We will. Thanks, Mom." Jackson nearly dragged Cole across the street before he could protest. "Dude, what are you doing?" Jackson said once they were out of earshot. "Do you really want to spend all night making small talk with the Board?"

"Of course not. But doesn't it seem weird for Dad to let us off the hook like that?" Cole glanced back at the restaurant. The sidewalk was already empty.

"Maybe a little, but who cares? I got to go. Tell Zoe I said hi." Jackson turned and jogged into the Wilborn Holdings parking garage.

Cole followed at a much slower pace. For a second, he thought about turning around and imposing himself on the dinner, but he wasn't sure that would win him any points with the Board, and he needed them on his side if he was going to keep his promise to Zoe.

The battle could wait till Monday. A quiet night with Zoe was what he really needed. He would grab some pizza and go help her pack.

«« Chapter 20 »»

Two hours down, and they still didn't have any idea what the toxin was or how it was going to kill people. Hamid had spent some time going through his old research to see if there were any clues in there, but of course there weren't. The Arrows weren't stupid enough to leave the formula for their death serum in research files anyone at Green Tech could access.

"I need a break." Ian turned away from the microscope, light red rings circling his eyes. He was pressing too hard. He went over to the fridge and pulled out a bottle of RiverLife water. "Don't you have anything stronger than this?"

"I didn't have time to shop. Blake's not doing anything; send him on a beer run." Zoe rubbed her eyes. This was useless. How were they supposed to figure this out with a couple of microscopes and a centrifuge with less power than her salad spinner? They needed better equipment.

"I'll have you know that I'm monitoring the news and police scanners for any mention of Ian or The Antos Solution," Blake yelled from the couch.

"And have there been any?" Zoe asked.

"No."

She shook her head and turned toward the table where Iris had carefully laid out all the drone parts. "Have you made any progress?"

"Actually, yes." Iris set her tools down and sat back. "They're planning on aerosolizing the chemical. It's going to be airborne."

Ian walked over to the table and picked up one of the pieces. "Are you sure?"

Iris took the part back from him and set it back down. "I have a degree in mechanical engineering—can't you just trust me on this one?" Ian put his hands up in surrender and walked back to the kitchen island.

"That's something to go on, at least." Zoe turned back to the microscope. If she could identify the liquid carrying the toxin, maybe she could isolate and identify the toxin itself.

A scratching sound came from the outside the front door, and everyone froze. Had Tucker gotten bored waiting and decided to come check on her? No, it couldn't be him. The doorknob was turning. Tucker wouldn't walk in unannounced unless there was an emergency. What if the Arrows had sent someone to stop them?

Ian moved to the front door, his right hand behind his back. The door swung open and Cole walked in, balancing a pizza box in one hand and a six pack of beer in the other.

Zoe's stomach dropped out of her body. This was so much worse than anything she had imagined.

"Zoe?" Cole quickly scanned the room. Ian slid behind him and slammed the door shut, then pulled out a gun and pointed it at Cole.

"You have a gun?" It was probably the worst thing Zoe could have said, but it was the only detail she could focus on at the moment.

"Of course I have a gun. It's only a matter of time before the Arrows try to kill me; I'm not going to make it easy for them," Ian said.

Cole looked wildly between Ian and Zoe. "Are you with him? Who are the Arrows? Zoe, what the hell is going on?"

"It's not what it looks like." Zoe could already feel the tears forming in the corners of her eyes when she stepped forward, but she willed them to stay there. She couldn't break down.

"The kidnapping—it was staged, wasn't it? You two are working together. Have you been playing me this whole time?" Cole waved the pizza box frantically at her. She made a move to take it from him, but stopped abruptly when he recoiled.

"Cole, I love you. The kidnapping was real. Please, just give me a chance to explain," Zoe pleaded.

Cole set the pizza and beer down on the kitchen island. "No. I'm calling the cops, and I'll let them sort this out." He pulled out his phone, but Ian pushed the gun into his back. Zoe remembered how it had felt when he did the same thing to her in the Green Tech parking lot, and shuddered.

"Sorry, buddy, I can't let you do that." Ian grabbed the phone from Cole.

"Alright, just take it easy." Cole held up his hands.

"You don't need to do that." Zoe gestured to the gun still at Cole's back. "We can trust him."

"Really? 'Cause I'm pretty sure he was about to get us all killed," Iris said. "What do you think would happen if one of the cops he called in was an Arrow? None of us would make it to the station alive."

"Arrow?" Cole looked at everyone in the room except Zoe, and it broke her heart.

Hamid got up and went to Ian's side. "Let's all calm down." He put his hand on Ian's arm and lowered the gun. "If Zoe says she can explain it to him, then we need to let her try."

"I'm not listening to anything you have to say." Cole finally looked at her. "I'm leaving."

"That wasn't a request." Ian shoved Cole forward, making him stumble.

"Enough, Ian." The tears had started to roll down Zoe's cheeks, but she didn't care. If she couldn't fix this, it didn't matter for her if the Arrows released their toxin or not. Zoe's world would be over either way. "Please, Cole. It's still me. Give me a chance."

Cole stormed into the bedroom without saying a word. Zoe brushed the tears off her face, allowing herself a brief moment to gather her composure before following him. If she was going to convince Cole that the Arrows were real, she would need to be calm and rational. Otherwise, she would lose him forever.

Ian reached out and gently touched her arm in passing, and Zoe was surprised she didn't jump. She truly wasn't afraid of him anymore. "We'll be out here if you need anything. Just yell."

"I'll be fine." The shift in dynamic sent a chill through her body. When had she gone from needing protection from Ian to him protecting her from Cole?

Zoe entered the bedroom and gently closed the door behind her. Cole was pacing next to the bed like a caged animal. He turned on her the second the door was closed. "Are you going to tell me what the fuck is going on out there? Was the whole kidnapping a set-up?"

"No. Like I said, the kidnapping was real," she said slowly. Cole rarely swore. She had never seen him like this before, and she wasn't sure she would be able to calm him down enough to listen to her. "I had no idea who they were before that."

"So why is Sutton here now, and who are the other people? What are you doing with them? Is this some post-traumatic Stockholm thing?"

Zoe took a deep breath. "While they were holding me, Ian told me what he was really doing at Green Tech that day. There's a powerful underground organization called the Arrow Equilibrium that's trying to end human life as we know it. Ian and the others out there are trying to stop them. That's what we were working on tonight. We're trying to figure out what makes up the toxin they plan on releasing." She chose her works very carefully; as soon as she mentioned Gordon, she would lose him.

"Zoe, do you hear yourself? What you're saying is insane." Cole grabbed her shoulders and looked her straight in the eyes. "If they are forcing you to do this somehow, just tell me. I can have the security detail up here in seconds and we can get you out."

"I'm being serious. Ian was at Green Tech to steal the research surrounding the toxin, but I got in his way. That's why he took me."

Cole released her. "Wait, are you saying this world-ending toxin is being made at Green Tech?"

"Yes."

Cole laughed, a cold, cheerless sound that cut through Zoe's soul. "You know better than anyone that that isn't possible."

"I said the same thing when they first told me, but I was wrong. That chemical we're studying out there—" She pointed toward the door. "That isn't my plastic decomposition formula. It's unlike anything I've ever seen."

"You stole chemicals from Green Tech? For him?"

Zoe looked away. She couldn't stand the way he was looking at her. "It gets worse."

"I'm not sure that's possible."

"This group that's trying to end human life, the Arrow Equilibrium—your father is a founding member, and I suspect the rest of Wilborn Holdings's Board is, too. I'm pretty sure the tour today was a cover to check on their plan."

"This is insane. My *father*? There's no way." Cole started to pace again.

"Think about it for a second. You said yourself that the scientific community has voiced concerns about our field test, and there's a reason for that. Releasing a chemical in the environment after one successful run isn't how experiments work. They need to be repeated over and over before they can be taken as fact, and we're skipping all of that. There has to be a reason."

"And you're saying that the reason is because my father is planning to release some kind of toxin that will kill all human life? Why would he even do that?"

"To restore balance between humans and the environment."

Cole's face went pale. Had something registered with him? Did he believe her? She couldn't even risk hoping for that.

"I want to see everything you have to support this insane theory. Every shred of evidence you have." It was the calmest he had been since entering the apartment.

"Of course." Zoe's heart was beating so fast, she was afraid it would burst. Cole hadn't dismissed her outright. He hadn't tried to run out of the apartment to turn them in. There was hope.

"Not here, though. You and I are going home. We can talk when there isn't a room full of criminals outside the door."

Zoe nodded. It was more than she could have hoped for. "On one condition. You have to promise to tell no one what we are doing here. If anyone finds out we're onto the Arrows' plan, they'll have us killed. Promise me, and I'll tell you everything I know."

"Zoe, that's not fair."

"I know it's not, but it's the way it has to be. Without that, I doubt Ian will let you walk out of this apartment."

"Is that a threat?" Cole growled.

"No." She stayed steady, holding his gaze. After a moment, he relented.

"Fine. I won't say anything. Can we please go now? I can't do this here."

"Sure." Zoe opened the door. The others milled around nearby, not even trying to pretend they weren't listening. "We're leaving."

"I'm not sure that's smart." Ian stepped in front of them, but at least the gun was gone.

"Smart or not, it's what we're doing. I'll be back in the morning, and we can pick up where we left off." Zoe grabbed Cole's hand. He pulled away slightly, then caught himself and tightened his grip on her hand.

"If this doesn't go the way you want, you know how to get in touch with us. We can get you out of there," Ian said, eyeing Cole. Zoe nodded, and Ian finally stepped out of the way, allowing them to leave.

«‹‹›»»

Cole's head spun. The more evidence Zoe showed him, the crazier it all seemed. How could this supposedly huge organization be planning the end of the world and no one knew about it?

Well, almost no one. The man who'd kidnapped Zoe knew about them—but was he really supposed to trust anything Sutton said? He was a criminal.

But this wasn't coming from Sutton, it was coming from Zoe. One of the smartest, most logical people Cole knew. If she believed it, then there must be some truth there.

The hardest part for him to wrap his head around was his father's involvement. He had never once heard Gordon mention The Arrow Equilibrium, but he had been making more and more comments about restoring balance. It couldn't be a coincidence. Cole hated to admit it, but there were a lot of things his dad had been doing recently that didn't add up. There was the hushed conversation with William Conner while Zoe was kidnapped about the research that had been taken; there was the way he'd acted toward the police once Zoe was found, and the way he'd dismissed Cole and Jackson from dinner last night. Was the Board planning on discussing The Arrow Equilibrium?

Cole glanced at the wall clock in the family room. It was two in the morning. He rubbed his eyes as Zoe finished walking him through the timeline she had put together for the third time. He reached over and shut the laptop lid. "I'm sorry, but this it too much to take in at once."

"I know. I'm sorry." Zoe moved the laptop and inched closer to him, and he opened his arm to her. He was still angry, but at least now he knew why she had been so distant. "I never wanted you to find out this way," she said softly.

"How did you want me to find out?"

Zoe sat up straighter. "Honestly, I didn't want you to find out at all. I know that sounds terrible, but I wanted to fix it so you wouldn't have to deal with it. I know how much you love your dad. I didn't want to ruin that."

"I don't need you to protect me."

"I know, and I'm sorry."

"You can't keep things from me anymore. Promise me right now that we will always be completely honest with each other, from this point forward."

"I promise." Zoe put her head on his shoulder, and Cole turned his head to breathe her in. A month ago, they'd sat exactly like this watching a movie. How he longed to go back to that time.

"How did Ian get out of jail?" Cole hated referring to Zoe's kidnapper by name, but he was trying to get past it. If what Zoe was telling him was right, they would need to work together to stop the Arrows.

"I gave Blake the money we got at the engagement party to pay the bail," Zoe admitted.

Well, that explained why she knew with absolute certainty that he wouldn't come after her again. He wondered how his father's people had missed that connection. "When I called you to tell you he had made bail, you were with him, weren't you?"

Zoe nodded against his shoulder.

Cole leaned forward and put his head in his hands. "Are you sure we can trust them? Could this be some kind of crazy set-up?"

"I've asked myself that same question a thousand times."

"And?" He turned his head to look at her through the gaps in his fingers.

"And I don't think it is. I've researched as many of the news articles on the flash drive as I could, and they're all real. They didn't manipulate the files. There was no way they could have swapped out those vials I took from Green Tech today, and that wasn't my formulation. That was the hard evidence I needed."

Cole leaned back on the couch. "What are we supposed to do now? How do I look at my father after all of this?"

"I don't know. I wish I had answers for you, but I don't. All we can do is try to figure out what the toxin is and hope there's a way to stop it."

"Oh, it's that simple," he said with a small, sarcastic laugh.

"Yeah, simple." Zoe gave him a tiny smile, though he could tell her heart wasn't in it. Cole wondered how many times she had run through all the implications of failing that were just now starting to occur to him.

"Then we should get to bed. You'll need to be fresh in the morning." Cole took her hand and led her upstairs. Everything she had told him was crazy, but he believed her. He would always believe Zoe over anyone — even his father.

«« Chapter 21 »»

Zoe woke with her stomach in knots the next morning. The conversation with Cole had gone better than she hoped, but all of that could change after a few hours of sleep. She had gone back and forth so many times when she first started to dig into the Arrows; there were still times she wasn't sure if she was doing the right thing, and she'd had weeks to take it all in.

Cole insisted on going with her to the apartment, and she agreed right away. She didn't want to fight with him, and besides, she liked the idea of having an ally there. They would still be outnumbered if the others decided to turn on them, but she wasn't alone anymore.

They left Tucker outside and headed into the apartment. Zoe had suggested giving him the day off, but Cole argued it was safer to leave him on duty so Gordon didn't get suspicious.

The others were still there, Iris sleeping on the couch and Blake in the armchair. Ian and Hamid were both working; neither looked like they had slept at all, and they eyed Cole warily.

"We can trust him," Zoe answered their unasked question. "I told him everything."

Iris sat up and looked over the back of the couch. "How can we be sure?"

"Because I said so." Zoe took off her coat and slung it over a chair. She didn't have the energy to argue with Iris.

"And that's supposed to be enough? We barely know you, and you're bringing the son of the man that's trying to end the world in here to help? I'm sorry if I find that hard to believe." Iris must have gotten more sleep than Zoe realized if she had energy to fight.

"If I haven't proven myself by now, then maybe you should leave." Zoe pointed to the door. She wasn't their prisoner anymore. She didn't have to sit back and let Iris talk to her like that.

"Zoe," Ian said in a voice much calmer than his twin's. "It took you weeks going over the evidence to believe us. He's had twelve hours. Not to mention, his personal connection to the situation is a lot stronger than yours."

"Zoe's also a lot more stubborn than I am," Cole said, and everyone turned to look at him. "Honestly, I'm not sure what I think of the whole situation, or my father's involvement in it, but that's not what matters at the moment. I believe that the chemical being produced at Green Tech isn't Zoe's, and it's probably meant to hurt people. That's enough for now."

Zoe rarely saw Cole at work, but if this was how he behaved there, it was no wonder Gordon had put him in charge of operations. The way he spoke, making everyone comfortable while staying on point, was inspiring. Zoe smiled at him for a moment, then turned to the others. "Does that work for you?"

Iris tossed her hands up and turned away. Zoe looked to the others, but no one challenged her.

"Did you make any progress last night?" Zoe asked Ian and Hamid.

"No." Ian turned back to the kitchen island, which was covered in scraps of paper and old coffee mugs. "We need better equipment if we're going to have any chance of figuring out what the toxin is."

"What was your plan in first place?" Zoe went over to join him, and Cole followed, claiming one of the island chairs. Clearly he was planning on staying close to her the whole time. He might believe them, but he still didn't trust Ian. Zoe guessed he had a point; Ian's first reaction had been to pull a gun on him yesterday, a gun Zoe hadn't even realized was there. Was she being too reckless by trusting them completely?

"I had a nice set-up at my apartment, where I was planning on analyzing the toxin," Ian said, "but the police cleared the place out when I was arrested."

"Oh." Zoe turned away and put a hand on her head. Cole grabbed her a bottle of water from the refrigerator.

"So is that it?" Cole asked.

"I don't know what else we can do at this point," Ian shrugged.

"We could tell someone."

"Who?" Iris came into the kitchen, poured two cups of coffee, and brought them over to the table where Blake sat, yawning.

"I don't know, the government or something? There has to be someone out there that can help."

"We can't," Zoe said.

"Why not?"

"Because there's no way to know who's an Arrow and who isn't. They're ingrained into every branch of government at this point." Hamid rounded the island and sat down next to Cole. "I'm sure you don't remember, you were only a child, but you and I have met before. I knew your father; we used to be good friends. I was at your baptism, birthday parties, all the fundraisers your parents put on. I was the one who encouraged him to start Green Tech in the first place."

Cole looked at him closely. Zoe could almost see him sorting through a file of faces in his mind to try to place Hamid. "Then why has my father never mentioned your name before this month, when the police found your name in the files?"

"Because Gordon Wilborn and the rest of the Arrows believe that I was killed fifteen years ago in a car accident they arranged."

"I don't believe that. If you really knew my family, there would be some evidence of it. You can't just erase a person from existence."

"Your birthday is July twenty-fourth. When you were five, you broke your left arm when Jackson pushed you out of your tree house. Your second birthday party was farm-themed, and the petting farm gave Victoria an allergic reaction so bad they had to rush her to the hospital. I can keep going if you need me to," Hamid offered.

"No, I get your point." Cole paled, but Zoe wasn't sure how to comfort him, especially while everyone watched him in silence. She had to get the pressure off of him, give him a few minutes alone to process everything—but he wouldn't leave her side to do it.

"Can you go through what you tried last night? Maybe it will spark an idea for what to try next," she said to Ian.

Nodding, he turned to the microscope, put in a slide, and stepped back so she could see. He walked her through everything in painstaking detail; he truly had tried everything he could with the limited resources at hand. They were at a dead end.

Zoe stepped away, her head spinning. "I don't know what else we can try here. Maybe it's worth the risk to run it through some equipment at Green Tech."

"No. No way," Ian said. "You'd never make it out of there alive."

"Well, I'm open to suggestions."

"Is it really that important to figure out exactly what the toxin is?" Cole asked.

"Only if we want to stop the end of the world," Iris scoffed. "You sure he's not here to slow us down?"

Cole rolled his eyes. "I meant that the real goal isn't to figure out what the toxin is, it's finding a way to stop it."

"You're right." A lightbulb switched on in Zoe's brain. "The Arrows might be crazy, but I never got the feeling they were willing to kill themselves to save the planet, just everyone else. And there were at least a few mentions of regrowth in those files." She rubbed her forehead as she tried to remember the exact wording. She really could have used a few more hours of sleep.

"Which means they must have a way to stop the toxin from affecting a select group of people," Iris said. Zoe nodded.

Blake came over to join them. "All we have to do is find it."

"Which has to be easier than trying to figure out what's in that vial." Zoe picked up her bottle of water.

Cole stood and started to pace. "It would have to be something they could control the distribution of. They'd need it to be widespread enough that the final population would be large enough to sustain life, and it would have to be easy to get people to take it, maybe without them even realizing it." He turned to look at Zoe. "If there's something that can stop the toxin, we've probably already had it. You know how my dad is—he wouldn't do something like this unless he could ensure his family was protected."

Zoe wasn't sure she fell into that category anymore. She dropped her gaze, spinning the bottle of RiverLife water in her hand as she pondered.

A phrase on the bottle jumped out at her: *A second chance for the* planet. It was supposed to refer to the completely sustainable manufacturing process, but what if there was more to it than that?

It was the only water the Wilborn family drank; they even made the bottles for Victoria's baby with it. Cole's mom always had a bottle on her and never hesitated to give it to one of them the moment they mentioned they were thirsty.

Cole's parents had been inoculating them against the toxin their entire lives.

She held the water bottle up and looked at it closely. "It's in the water."

The others exchanged wide-eyed glances.

"It's worth a shot." Ian took the bottle from her and poured a small amount into a beaker, then transferred a drop onto the slide with the toxin. After a minute, he stepped aside and motioned for Zoe to look. Taking a deep breath, she peered through the eyepiece.

The toxin was completely destroyed. They had figured it out—they knew how to stop the Arrows.

"It worked." She looked to the others with a huge grin.

Blake lunged at the open bottle of water and downed the rest of it in one gulp.

"What?" he said in response to their amused looks.

"Relax, there's a whole case in the fridge," Zoe laug.hed.

"Great. So, what do we do now? Break into Green Tech and pour bottled water all over the toxin?" Blake asked.

"I'm not sure it's that simple. I can't even get into the room where it's being made without setting off a ton of alarms."

"Besides, that just eliminates the immediate risk. They can always make more," Cole added.

"Then we find another way. We have to." Zoe looked at the bottle still in Blake's hand. It was consumerism at its peak. The Wilborns would save their customer base, and if you weren't loyal to them, you died. Had she not been dating Cole, she would have never bought RiverLife; it was expensive and only sold in certain stores. In fact, there were whole countries that didn't carry it.

Countries that would be completely wiped off the map if they couldn't find a way to get the cure out to everyone.

«‹‹›»

Cole didn't want to believe the others, but the more they said, the more it made sense to him—and he hated it. He couldn't believe his father had done all this.

Then he remembered the sudden production increase of RiverLife with no addition to the distribution chain. Where had that water gone? Was it being stockpiled to protect the Arrows? To protect him and his family? The guilt knowing he would be safe while the rest of the world suffered left him almost breathless.

He watched Zoe hand bottles of RiverLife water to the others. Her kidnappers, the people who had caused so much stress and anxiety—she was now trying to save them. And not just save, but actively help them. He guessed he was too, though the only thing he had really done was not turn them in to his father. Which, from what Hamid had told him, had probably saved their lives. That was another fact Cole was having a hard time wrapping his head around.

He needed some air. He was about to turn toward the small balcony, but the front door caught his eye.

Something was wrong. Smoke was working its way into the apartment from the bottom of the door. Cole reached out to open it, but it was too hot to touch.

"We have a problem," he yelled to the others.

No one answered. Had he just imagined yelling? The sound of wood cracking and popping started to fill his ears. Why weren't the smoke detectors going off? A thin haze of smoke had filled the apartment already.

Protecting his hand with his sleeve, Cole cracked the front door open. The hallway was engulfed in flames. He slammed the door shut. They couldn't get out that way.

"Guys!" Cole yelled again. "The building is on fire!"

This time, they all stopped what they were doing and looked at him, wide-eyed and gaping.

"We need to get out—this is the Arrows," Hamid said.

The smoke in apartment thickened, and sparks started to rained down from the ceiling. Everyone moved toward the front door, but Cole held up a hand to stop them. "We can't get out that way."

"There's no other way out. We're trapped." The panic in Zoe's voice broke his heart.

"The balcony." Blake pointed across the room to where sunlight streamed through the balcony door. Flames had broken through the walls in the kitchen. How much longer before there wasn't any air left to breathe?

"We're three floors up," Zoe yelled over the roaring flames. Did apartment fires normally progress this quickly?

"It's that or burn. Come on." Ian put his hand on the small of Zoe's back, and a rush of anger washed over Cole. He fought to push it down; Ian wasn't the biggest threat at the moment. The fire had broken through the ceiling. They didn't have much time.

They had only taken a few steps toward the balcony when a loud cracking sound filled the room. A large beam engulfed in flames crashed down to the floor where Ian and Zoe had been standing. Cole rushed toward it, afraid he would see them crushed underneath, but they weren't there. They were on the floor two feet away, Ian shielding Zoe from the burning rain of debris. Cole grabbed a jacket off the back of a chair that hadn't caught fire yet and threw it over Ian, whose shirt was covered in charred holes. He helped Ian to his feet, shooting him a grateful look. Cole wished he had time for more thanks, but that would have to wait until they got out of this.

The others had made it to the balcony door, but they weren't going out. Cole didn't know what they were waiting for. The fire was so intense, it wouldn't be much longer before the floor gave out.

"The balcony's gone," Iris said between coughs once Cole, Ian, and Zoe made it over to them.

"What do you mean, it's gone?" He looked out the window, but they were right. There was nothing there. They were trapped.

"Is there some way we can climb down?" Ian moved forward to look with Cole. There wasn't so much as a drainpipe left on this side of the building. When had everything been removed?

"There's a tree next to the bedroom window." Zoe bent over with her hands on her knees, her breathing shallow.

They wasted no time, though it took far longer than it should have to travel the hundred feet to the bedroom door. Everyone was struggling to breathe, and avoiding the flames was nearly impossible. The doorframe to the bedroom was ablaze. They ran through it one at a time, like it was a ring of fire in a circus stunt show. Zoe reached the window first and threw it open, and to Cole's relief, the tree was still there. Part of him expected it to have disappeared like the balcony. It was a bit of a jump to get to a branch large enough to support their weight, but it was nothing compared to the alternative.

Blake climbed out first and turned to help Hamid and Iris. Zoe went next at Cole's insistence, her breathing so labored he was afraid she would pass out.

"You next," Cole said to Ian once Zoe had started to climb down. Ian looked like he was going to argue, but with a glare, Cole helped him out the window, noticing how badly he was burned.

"We can't be here when the cops arrive," Hamid said once they were all on the ground.

"You need medical attention," Cole said, looking them over.

"We can't," Ian coughed violently. "Half the doctors in this area are part of the Arrows. We'll never make it out alive."

"Then you guys need to go. Zoe and I will stay and cover for you." Cole put his arm around Zoe's waist, careful not to touch anywhere that might be burned.

"You're in as much danger as we are. You should come with us," Ian looked at Zoe. "Both of you."

"My father won't hurt me, and I can protect Zoe."

"Really? 'Cause I'm pretty sure he just tried to have her burned alive." Blake gestured toward the building burning next to them.

"We'll be alright," Zoe said. "We can't run yet, or they'll know we figured everything out. Now go."

They nodded and took off as the sound of sirens grew louder in the distance. Cole and Zoe slowly walked to the front of the building, where he hoped an ambulance would be waiting.

«‹›»

Zoe allowed the paramedics to give her oxygen and wrap her in a blanket, though she wondered if they were Arrows and would kill her once they got her alone in the ambulance. Thankfully, they didn't seem that interested in her, and they moved on quickly. There were people with far worse injuries than she and Cole had. They sat together on the curb silently, watching the building burn to the ground. Everything she owned was gone, along with all the evidence they had gathered. How were they going to convince anyone to help them now?

Out of the corner of her eye, Zoe saw a familiar Cadillac pull up. She nudged Cole with her shoulder. "Your parents are here."

"How could they even know about the fire? The media isn't here yet." Cole watched his parents rush over to them, and Zoe rolled her eyes. She wanted to say it was because they'd started the fire, but she didn't. She had put Cole through enough in the last twenty-four hours.

"Are you two alright?" Alana asked as soon as she reached them. She bent down in front of Cole to inspect him for injuries before turning to do the same to Zoe.

"We came as soon as we heard. Cole, I thought you were supposed to be golfing with Jackson this morning," Gordon said.

Zoe shot Cole a look. Gordon hadn't known Cole was at the apartment, then; the fire was only meant to kill her and the others. "How did you hear about the fire?" she asked.

"Detective Pearson called me once he realized it was your apartment and it might be related to your case. This was what I was afraid of," Gordon said.

Zoe fought back the urge to laugh. So, he was going to blame this on Ian.

"Good thing I had a bodyguard to prevent anything from happening," Zoe said before she could stop herself. It felt good to push back.

"Where is Tucker?" Cole looked around the parking lot.

"I haven't seen him since we got here," Zoe said. Maybe he was the one who started the fire. It would have been easy for him to do it once they were all inside. They had been working for hours, giving him more than enough time. He would probably be in trouble for doing it with Cole in the building, though.

"I'm going to talk to the fire chief and see if I can get some answers," Gordon said, striding away.

A coughing fit overtook Zoe, and she reached for the oxygen mask again, breathing deeply until it passed.

"Here, dear, drink this. It will help." Alana pulled two bottles of RiverLife from her purse and handed one to each of them. Zoe gingerly accepted hers and took a small sip. Did Alana even know what she was carrying around?

An unmarked cop car pulled into the lot, and Pearson emerged, standing with the driver's-side door open, watching them. She needed to talk to him without Gordon knowing. She was pretty sure Pearson wasn't an Arrow; he had stood up to Gordon and Frank. She didn't think he would do that if he was one of them. Zoe needed to trust someone, and he seemed like the best option.

Alana stepped away to make a quick call. It was now or never.

"Cole," Zoe whispered. "I need you to distract your parents while I go talk to Pearson." He nodded.

Zoe had Pearson's attention the moment she was on her feet. She nodded toward a small group of trees in a median at the back of the parking lot. Pearson closed his car door and made his way over there. Zoe looked over her shoulder to make sure the Wilborns weren't watching, then joined him.

"Ms. Antos," Pearson said by way of a greeting.

"Detective," Zoe said, unsure how to start this. It wasn't safe to go into details here, but she needed to tell him something. "I need your help."

"Do you think Ian Sutton started the fire?" Pearson raised an eyebrow.

"I know for a fact that he didn't, but I have a pretty good idea who did." Zoe looked back to where Cole and his parents were standing. They didn't seem to notice she was gone, but she doubted she had a lot of time.

"Please, enlighten me." She could tell from his tone that Pearson was skeptical; she wasn't sure how to make him see that she wasn't just another Wilborn who thought the cops worked for her.

"I'll tell you everything I know" — she glanced over at Gordon, still harassing the fire chief — "but not here. It's not safe. Can I meet you somewhere tomorrow morning?"

"You can come to the police station."

"No." Zoe shook her head. "They'll know. It needs to be somewhere private, somewhere safe. There's a lot more going on than you probably realize. I'm not sure who can be trusted."

"But you think you can trust me." Pearson smirked. Maybe she had been wrong? Maybe Pearson and Frank had been putting on a show for her benefit at the police station?

"My gut tells me I can, and I really hope I'm right. If not, then I doubt I'll make it 'til tomorrow morning." Zoe looked back at the fire that she knew was meant to kill her while Cole was out golfing with his brother. If Gordon had known his son was with her, would he have tried to kill her in some other way, where he could be sure Cole wasn't caught in the middle?

"Has someone threatened you? If you're in danger, I can protect you," Pearson said with more intensity than before.

"Not directly. I don't need you to protect me — I'm not sure you can. What I need is for you to meet me somewhere tomorrow morning and for you to believe me."

Pearson sighed. "There's a small diner two blocks from here. My parents own it. I'll be there for breakfast tomorrow at six." He pulled out a small notepad, jotted down an address, and handed it to her. Zoe shoved the paper in pocket without looking at it. She turned to go back, but looked at the bottle of water in her hand.

"There's something else," she said, turning back to Pearson. "I know this is going to sound crazy, but I need you to trust me." Pearson folded his arms and didn't say anything. Zoe took a deep breath, wondering if this would be the strangest request he had ever gotten. "Go buy a couple cases of RiverLife water, and make sure your whole family drinks it as soon as they can. Start with this."

After handing her bottle to him, she made her way back to Cole.

«« Chapter 22 »»

The diner was surprisingly busy given the early hour. Zoe had asked Pearson to meet her somewhere private, and this was where he chose? Any one of these people could be part of The Arrow Equilibrium. She thought about leaving—Pearson hadn't seen her yet—but after what she had told him yesterday, he would likely hunt her down if she didn't show up. She just needed to be sure it was safe, so she sat in her car and watched the front door, a luxury she hadn't had yesterday when Tucker was monitoring her every move. He still hadn't turned up, confirming her suspicion that he was working for the Arrows. She'd expected a new bodyguard to be at the house when she woke up this morning, but no one came.

Gordon must've decided she wasn't worth protecting anymore.

It was 6:10 now, and Zoe hadn't seen anything unusual—not that she knew what she was looking for.

She would have to take her chances. The Arrows would probably come after her again sooner or later, but she wouldn't let them scare her into not talking.

Pearson was sitting alone at a booth in the back corner of the restaurant, eating breakfast. He didn't look up when she entered. Either he was really enjoying his breakfast, or he was much more comfortable with covert meetings than she was. She walked over to him, but stopped in her tracks when she saw the second plate of food sitting across from him. Was someone else here?

"Sit down and eat." Pearson motioned toward the second plate with his knife. "It might be a little cold since you're late."

Zoe plopped down in the booth. Why was she so scared? Pearson was supposed to be one of the good guys, the person she had decided to trust despite the risk. "Thank you," she said, but didn't touch the food in front of her.

"Alright, Ms. Antos, you got me here. What is it that you couldn't tell me yesterday?" Pearson looked up at her.

"I'll be putting you in danger if I tell you." If anything happened to Pearson, it would be her fault; but if she didn't tell him and they weren't able to stop the Arrows on their own, he would be dead in week anyway.

"I think I can handle it. You should try the sausage gravy — it's my mom's secret recipe. Best in the state." He pointed at it before taking a bite. Zoe wasn't sure if he was trying to make her feel more comfortable or if he really didn't grasp the seriousness of what she had come to tell him.

Zoe took a bite of the sausage gravy to buy herself a few moments to think. "Have you ever heard of The

Arrow Equilibrium?" Pearson shook his head while he continued to eat. "They're a powerful underground eco-terrorist organization, most likely founded by Gordon Wilborn." She stopped to see if that got any kind of reaction out of him.

"Keep going," he said, twirling his fork at her.

Zoe took it as a good sign that he didn't dismiss her. "Their goal is to restore balance between humans and nature, and they plan on doing that by releasing a toxin that will kill everyone on planet who isn't immune."

She expected Pearson to look at her like she was insane. To get up and leave, berate her for wasting his time, maybe even take her in for a psyche evaluation, but he didn't. He set down his fork and looked her straight in the eye. "Who's immune?"

"There's some kind of vaccine in RiverLife water. It'll protect you from the toxin. Please tell me you had your family start drinking it last night—I don't know how much it takes to build up the resistance in the body." Tears burned in the corners of her eyes. This was all too much.

"I did, actually," Pearson said with a small smile that instantly made Zoe feel better. "My girls thought it was a special treat. We don't do bottled water; it's bad for the environment."

Zoe felt like a huge weight had been lifted from her chest. At least a few more people would live now. She picked up her fork and took a few bites. It really was the best sausage gravy she had ever tasted.

"Do you have any evidence to prove the Arrow Equilibrium is real and that they have this toxin?"

Zoe took Blake's flash drive out of her pocket and slid it across the table to him. Thank God they had left it at Cole's house. "This is a bunch of articles, emails, things like that. I'm not sure if you can use any of it."

Pearson took the flash drive. "Anything concrete?"

"I had samples of the toxin, but they were in my apartment yesterday. It's being produced at Green Tech."

"Did you put this together all on your own?"

Zoe shook her head. "I've been helping Ian and Iris Sutton, Blake Cooper, and Hamid Sami—who's still alive, by the way. They've been working to stop the Arrows for years. I only found out about them when I was being held. I didn't start to believe them until after I was home and Blake reached out to give me that flash drive."

"Which is how you know that Ian didn't start the fire."

"He was in the apartment with me when the fire started. They all were. The Arrows set the fire to stop us."

Pearson rubbed his mouth. "So you're saying Gordon Wilborn, the founder of this Arrow Equilibrium, set your apartment on fire to stop you from telling anyone about his plan to release a toxin that will kill everyone who doesn't drink his brand of bottled water."

"I know it sounds insane." Zoe closed her eyes and let out a breath.

"Not as insane as you think."

She blinked at Pearson in shock. He shrugged. "I've suspected from the beginning that there was more going on here than meets the eye. Every time I tried to dig into it, someone at the station would stop me. I couldn't get warrants or the resources I needed to properly investigate Green Tech or Gordon Wilborn. Then there's your bodyguard, Mathew Tucker. The coroner's report lists the cause of death as smoke inhalation, but I saw his body. Someone put a bullet in his head. Ian Sutton doesn't have the power to cover something like that up. Gordon Wilborn, on the other hand, does."

"Tucker's dead?" Zoe rasped. He wasn't an Arrow. "I didn't even know his first name."

"You're mixed in with some very dangerous people," Pearson warned. "I think it's time for you to walk away."

"I can't walk away. I have to do something, I'm just not sure what that is."

"You've done it." Pearson smiled warmly. "You've given me what I need to go after Gordon Wilborn. I won't stop until I find a judge willing to give me a warrant to search everything connected to him."

"I don't think that will be enough," Zoe said desperately.

"You came here for my help. Now you need to step back and let me do my job."

Reluctantly, Zoe nodded. There wasn't much else she could do. "Thanks for breakfast." She got up and left the diner, not sure if she had gained an ally or signed her own death certificate.

«‹«›»›»

Zoe didn't want to head back to Cole's house after leaving Pearson. She was afraid Gordon would there, and she wasn't sure how she was supposed to sit in a room with him knowing everything he had done. It wasn't even the fact that he'd tried to kill her that made her so angry. It was what he was planning to do to the rest of the world that would make it impossible for her to exchange pleasantries with him.

She hadn't heard from Ian, Blake, or Iris since they separated yesterday. She wasn't sure if she ever would again. If they wanted to be rid of her, this was the perfect opportunity. It wasn't like she was of use to them anymore.

Zoe pulled out the burner phone Blake had given her while she tried to decide what to do. It couldn't hurt to check on them, just to make sure everyone really was alright. Ian had been burned in the fire, after all, and she had no idea how bad it was.

She flipped the phone open to see a text message waiting there from Ian. It just had an address. Zoe plugged it into her GPS and found it wasn't far.

Minutes later, she pulled up in front of a nice house in an older neighborhood — not what she was expecting. She double-checked the address, then parked her car a few houses away and made her way back. She knocked on the door and waited, looking over her shoulder every few seconds.

Finally, Iris opened the door and stood back to let her in without saying a word.

"Is everyone alright?" Zoe asked as they moved through the house to a family room in the back.

"We'll all survive," Iris said. "Where's Cole?"

"He's at home. I left before he got up this morning."

The others were sitting in the family room, watching the morning news. A few family pictures were scattered around on tabletops with younger versions of Ian and Iris. This must have been their childhood home.

Ian winced as he sat up and turned to look at her, a white bandage peeking through the collar of his shirt. "Why?"

"I met with Detective Pearson this morning. He's the lead investigator on my case." Zoe hesitated. "I told him everything." She sat down on the edge of an empty chair. She figured it was better to get it all out in the open.

"Why would you do that?" Blake snapped.

"Because we're in over our heads, and we need help. He seemed to believe me. I think we can trust him." Zoe was too tired to care that Blake was upset with her. She just wanted this whole thing to be over.

"You better be right. If not, you put all our lives in danger." Iris said without her normal feisty bark. The fire had taken a toll on all of them.

"Our lives are already in danger." Ian gave Zoe a weak smile. "The Arrows know what we're trying to do. That fire was meant to kill us. It's only a matter of time before they realize it didn't and come after us again."

"They're going to pin that on you, by the way." Zoe nodded to the TV, where the headline read *Five Dead in Apartment Fire.*

"Figures," Ian shook his head. "How did you manage to get here without a bodyguard? Especially since I'm going around lighting buildings on fire."

"Tucker is one of the five. He hasn't been replaced." The deaths of those people weighed heavy on her. Their only sin was having the misfortune of living in the same apartment building as her. They probably hadn't even known who she was, since she preferred to keep to herself. Now they were dead because of her.

Zoe looked from Ian, to Iris, to Blake, waiting for one of them to tell her what the plan was. They all looked completely defeated. "Where do we go from here?"

"South." Ian leaned back down on the couch. Pain tightened his features.

"What does that mean?"

"It means we're leaving. Going to try to disappear for a while. We're leaving in two days. You should come with us—it'll be safer than staying here," Iris said.

Zoe gaped at them. "You're running away?"

"What else can we do?" Blake said.

"What were you going to do to stop the Arrows before I got involved? You had to have had a plan!"

Ian looked from Iris to Blake. She might have been on their side now, but she still wasn't privileged to their silent language. Ian finally sighed and turn to her. "We were going to leak what we found to some friends in the medical field who can be trusted. The idea was that we'd get the information out slowly and let it spread organically. That way, people would know what the Arrows were planning and it would be almost impossible to trace it back to any one person."

"Then let's do that!"

"We don't have that kind of time. We thought we'd have months, even years maybe, to spread the information. Not days," Iris said.

Zoe jumped to her feet. "There has to be more we can do. We can't sit back and wait for the end of the world."

"What do you suggest we do?" Ian said. "All of our evidence is gone. We have no power. The Arrows won."

"I can't accept that. We need to warn people. We know how to stop the toxin. It's our duty to try save as many lives as we can."

"How? It's not like we can go to the news with the story. They'll think we're insane," Iris said.

"Not to mention the Arrows probably have control over what gets broadcast. The story will never be reported," Blake added.

"Pearson said he would get a warrant to search Green Tech and Gordon. He'll find something, and then they'll have to report it." Zoe was grasping at straws, unwilling to accept defeat. They had dragged her into this, and she was determined to see it through to the end, even if that meant she would have to do it alone.

"You're kidding yourself if you think that will happen." Iris went into the kitchen and returned a few minutes later with a glass of water and a handful of pills, which she gave to Ian.

"Fine. You might be willing to give up, but I'm not. I'll go into Green Tech early tomorrow and steal more toxin. I'll take it to every news outlet there is until I find someone to report it." Zoe pointed to Blake. "I need you to come with me, now."

She stormed from the room and waited at the front door. She heard them talking in the other room, but she couldn't make out what they were saying. That was fine. She didn't need them. She would figure out a way to stop the Arrows on her own.

"How can I be of assistance?" Blake joined her in the front hallway.

"I need a gun."

"Why?" He leaned against the staircase and watched her carefully.

"Dangerous people are hunting me — I need to be able to protect myself," she said, using his words. "Cole thinks he can protect me from his father, but I know he's wrong. They already tried to kill me once, and we both know they'll try again."

"Then come with us. We have a lot of experience hiding people from the Arrows."

"I can't."

Blake sighed and walked over to the hall closet. He pulled down a small safe, opened it, and handed Zoe a handgun. "Do you know how to use that?"

Zoe shook her head. She had never held a gun before. She had never thought she would need one. The weight alone surprised her.

Blake showed her how to load it, where the safety was, and how to fire it. "Thank you." She put the gun in her purse and left, unsure if she would ever see them again.

«‹«›»»

Cole had never been nervous in his father's presence before, but as he sat in his living room with his mom and dad, he couldn't stop his palms from sweating. When he had told Zoe he would try to get the field test pushed back, he hadn't known anything about the Arrows or what was really at stake. Now that he had all the information, he couldn't bring it up. If he did, he would be putting Zoe at risk, and he wasn't willing to do that.

Alana had just finished telling him how Victoria and the kids had decided to extend their stay a few weeks, even though her husband had gone back to London, but Cole wasn't really listening. He couldn't stop thinking about the Arrows and how his father was connected to them. The same man who'd taught him to do whatever he could to help others was planning on killing everyone who didn't buy into his expensive, hidden vaccine.

The front door opened, and Zoe walked in. Cole let out a sigh of relief that he hoped his parents didn't notice. Zoe had left a note saying she was going out and would be back soon, but didn't mention where she was going. Cole wasn't sure he wanted to know, honestly. Still, he worried that she would do something to put herself in danger again; it was a relief to see that she was home safe.

Zoe hesitated as she came into the living room, and Cole couldn't blame her. He hadn't been sure how to act when his parents showed up unannounced this morning. "Hey Zoe, how were your parents?" He hated lying, but what else could he do? It seemed his father had been lying to him his entire life, so turnabout was fair play.

That didn't stop his guilt from taking up residence in the pit of his stomach.

"Umm, they're good." Zoe slowly made her way to the couch and sat down next to Cole, putting as much space between herself and Gordon as she could. "They were really worried after the fire, so I thought it would be nice to have breakfast with them. I haven't been spending enough time with them recently."

"I'm sure they understand," Alana said with a small smile. "You've had a lot to deal with the last few weeks. By the way, have you had a chance to go over any of the wedding samples Rachel sent over?"

"No, I haven't, sorry." Zoe grabbed Cole's hand and squeezed. It felt absurd to be discussing wedding details right now.

"How are you doing after yesterday?" If Cole didn't know any better, he would have thought Gordon was really concerned about Zoe.

She looked at Cole for help, but he was at a loss for what to say. "I don't really know how I feel about it," she said awkwardly.

"That's understandable. I'm sure you thought you were safe with the bodyguard, and then to have something like that happen . . ." Gordon shook his head. "Sutton should have never been able to get that close to you. You'll be happy to know I'm pulling the private security team. They don't seem to be worth the money I'm paying them."

"You know Tucker is dead, right?" Zoe snapped.

Cole turned to look at her. "He is?"

Zoe nodded. "The cops found his remains in the fire." She turned away from him and looked directly at his father. "There was a bullet hole in his skull."

Alana shifted in her chair. "How do you know that?"

"I overheard the police talking about it yesterday," Zoe said a little too quickly. This had to be the fakest conversation Cole had ever been a part of. No one was telling the truth, and he was pretty sure everyone knew it.

"That's a shame," his father said. "I would have thought the security firm would have better-qualified people. It goes to show how unhinged Sutton is. I'm sure the police will have him back behind bars soon."

Zoe scoffed, then covered it with a coughing fit. Cole gently patted her on the back, hoping it would help sell it to his parents.

"I'm sorry," Zoe said. "I'm not feeling very well. I think I'm going to go lie down a for a bit."

"Do you want me to call the family doctor to come over and check you out?" Alana offered when Zoe stood. "It can't hurt to make sure there isn't any lasting damage from the fire."

"No!" Cole and Zoe said together. If this doctor was an Arrow, Cole feared Zoe would never wake up from her nap.

"I'm sure a little rest is all I need." Zoe's voice lacked any emotion. "If it gets worse, I'll be sure to go get checked out." She left without another word.

Gordon watched her go, and then turned to Cole. "I'm worried about her. She hasn't been herself since the kidnaping."

"Can you blame her? She's been through more than any person should have to deal with. She just needs time."

But Cole feared they would run out of it long before he ever got up the courage to confront his father about the Arrows.

«« Chapter 23 »»

Zoe headed to Green Tech with a renewed sense of determination. The others might have felt like they had already lost, but she wasn't willing to throw in the cards yet. She would find a way to get back into the lab where the toxin was being made and destroy it. Or at the very least, she would find a way to steal another sample and go public with it. How hard could it be to get in there? Her name was on the project; she was pretty sure she could use that to get someone to let her in.

The lab was unusually busy given the early hour, with several trucks lined up at the loading docks when she pulled in.

Her insides turned to ice.

Zoe ran inside and threw her things down on her desk, then tried to walk at a normal pace to the lab where the toxin was being produced, but she found her stride quickening every few steps.

The lab door was open when she arrived, and Zoe rushed inside. It was almost empty. There was only one pallet left in the corner, filled with boxes of toxin, shrink-wrapped and neatly packaged. There was no way she could get a sample from there without anyone noticing, but at this point, Zoe wasn't sure she cared. It wasn't like the Arrows didn't know what she was doing. She studied the pallet closely, trying to figure out the best way inside.

"Good morning, Zoe," Brett said from the open doorway. Zoe spun around, clutching her heart. She hadn't ever been that startled, even when Ian first pushed the gun into her back in the parking lot. "What are you doing in here?" Brett moved closer, and Zoe fought the urge to run. A guy with a pallet jack entered the room behind Brett, went directly to the pallet full of toxin, and rolled it out of the room.

Zoe watched it go with a heavy heart. Had she really lost that easily? She hadn't even had a chance to put any kind of resistance.

Brett was watching her closely. He expected an answer; she would have to play the game a little longer. Maybe she could convince him to tell her where the toxins were going, and she could try to destroy them there.

"I realized during the tour that I didn't know how the chemicals were being mass-produced, so I came down here hoping someone could walk me through the process." That seemed like a totally reasonable and safe excuse. Hopefully Brett would buy it. "But it seems like I'm too late." Zoe spread her arms out to the empty room and smiled. She needed to come off as the same eager student who first came to Green Tech.

"They finished production yesterday morning. I could have one of the operators come back in tomorrow and walk you through the process if you're really interested." Brett leaned against the table in the back of the room, completely relaxed. Maybe he didn't realize Zoe was trying to stop the Arrows. It was possible, given her connection to the Wilborns, that he thought she was part of The Arrow Equilibrium. She could use that to her advantage.

"I don't want to waste anyone's time. You know me. I was just curious." Zoe forced out a small laugh. "Where are they taking all of this, anyway?"

"I'm not sure exactly where all the drones are going. The plan is to spread them out along the coast lines to get the best coverage. The London office is handling the logistics in Europe and Asia."

As the project lead, shouldn't he know exactly where they were releasing the chemical?

Shouldn't a great deal of research and planning have gone into that decision? The words were screaming in Zoe's mind, but she held back. "I didn't realize the field test was going to cover that much area. Are we going to have ground teams at each of the sites to coordinate the release?" How would she make it across around the world to destroy the toxin before it was released?

"No. The launch is being coordinated from a command center at Wilborn Holdings Headquarters Friday morning. That way we can ensure it's all perfectly timed. I can see if you can join me there, if you want."

That was the answer. Zoe needed to get into that control room. From there, she could stop the launch. "If you think I'll be needed, then sure. Otherwise, I'd like to monitor the test from here. I want to see the results in real time as they're coming in. Besides, you know Cole and I try to maintain separate professional lives as much as we can."

"Of course, makes perfect sense. I'll be there to represent this team's amazing work." Brett beamed at her and walked out of the lab. Zoe had no idea if he'd bought her story or not, but it didn't matter. A plan was forming in her mind. For the first time, she felt like she might actually be able to stop the Arrows.

«‹›»

Cole collapsed on the couch as soon as he got home from work. It has been a lot harder pretending not to know what was going on than he'd thought it would be. He wasn't sure how much longer he could keep it up. If things really happened the way he believed they would, he would never be able to look at his father again. And if they didn't, then Ian had either tricked Zoe into following his crazy theory or she'd been in on it from the beginning. Though, Cole didn't know what they would get out of playing him like that. If this was some kind of elaborate scam, wouldn't they have asked for money or something like that? Not to mention ten years was a long time for Zoe to invest in him if their relationship wasn't real.

He pushed the thought from his mind, leaned his head back on the couch, and closed his eyes. He loved Zoe, and she loved him. He was sure of that much.

The front door opened and slammed shut. Cole didn't open his eyes until Zoe plopped down on the couch next to him. She set a large cheese pizza down on the coffee table and grabbed a slice.

"Bad day?" Cole asked, reaching for a slice himself.

"They moved the toxin out of the lab before I got there this morning. I couldn't steal another sample to prove what the Arrows are up to," Zoe said between bites.

"Maybe we should leave. Get out of here before everything goes down, somewhere no one can find us." Cole had been thinking about it all day. They might not be able to save everyone, but maybe there was someplace they could go that the toxin wouldn't reach and they could live a simple life. Zoe was always teasing him about not knowing what normal was. This would be their chance to live that kind of life—the life she wanted.

"Why is everyone so willing to give up and run away?" Zoe threw down her slice of pizza and glared at him.

"What else can we do? It's not like we're superheroes. We are in way over our heads. We tried to do something, and were almost burned alive because of it!"

"Do you really think there's somewhere we can go that the toxin won't reach?" Her tone was almost patronizing. "They are going to release it into the atmosphere. It will make it to every corner of the globe."

"Then what do you suggest we do? It's not like I can confront my father without putting you in danger, and I'm not willing to do that."

"I actually have an idea." Zoe avoided his gaze.

"What's that?" Cole set down his pizza so he could give her his full attention.

Zoe took a deep breath. "Brett told me that they're going to control the release from a command center at Wilborn Holdings. If we can get in there, maybe we can stop it. Blake's good with computers—I saw him hack into the police system to check on my case while they were holding me. I bet he could plant a virus or something that would make it impossible for them to launch the drones." The longer she talked, the faster the words came out.

Zoe was clearly excited. She really thought this plan would work.

"There's no way. What am I supposed to do, get Ian, Iris, and Blake visitor badges and let them loose on our network? Once they're in, what's to stop them from stealing all the company's confidential information? There's no telling what kind of damage they could do. Maybe this is what they've really been after all along. Maybe *they're* the Arrow Equilibrium and they want to try to take down the company and destroy my family." There was the payoff he had been looking for, and it was one that made a lot more sense than his father trying to end the world.

Zoe scoffed and folded her arms. "First of all, they don't know anything about this plan. I came to you first. I told you I wouldn't keep anything from you. So, if you're saying this was a setup to steal from your family's company, then what you're really saying is that you don't trust *me*. You think I orchestrated this whole thing to destroy your family. That my love for you is all part of some crazy con."

"Zoe, that's not what I meant." Cole sighed and leaned back into the couch. "You know I won't be able to get them past the entrance. I'm sure my father has security on high alert at this point."

"Maybe you can just get me in, then?"

"I could probably get you up to my office without any issue, but there's no way I can get you to the top floor where the command center is. It's heavily protected, and only a handful of people have access."

"But there *is* a command center, and you have access to it, don't you?"

Cole didn't like where this was going. Zoe was not a risk-taker, but here she was trying to plan a way to break into the secured floor of his company. "There are armed guards up there, Zoe. It's too dangerous."

"And if we don't try, then everyone on the planet, except for the people who drink RiverLife, will be dead. Do you really think you can live with that? Knowing that you had the means to stop it and did nothing?"

Cole jumped to his feet. "I'm not letting you go up there. You'll get yourself killed."

"Cole," Zoe started, but he cut her off.

"No. I'm serious. It's too dangerous. Even if you could get up there, how are you going to shut it down? I had to get you back into your email after you got yourself locked out." It was a low blow, but he didn't care. He needed to make her see reason.

"I'll figure something out." She looked up at him defiantly.

Cole sat back down and took her hands. "Let me see what I can do first, okay? We still have a few days to figure it out. Don't go doing anything rash and getting yourself hurt." Cole wondered how hard it would be to tell her they were heading to Wilborn Holdings and just drive in the other direction.

"Fine."

"No, that's not enough. Promise me."

"Alright, I promise." Zoe leaned forward and kissed him. Cole couldn't help but feel like it was a goodbye kiss.

«« Chapter 24 »»

Zoe barely slept that night. She hated lying to Cole, but she had made up her mind on what she needed to do before she made that promise to him. She couldn't sit back and wait; she needed to act now.

Cole had been right about one thing, though — it would be dangerous. Which was why she had decided to go alone. She wouldn't put Cole or the others at risk.

Zoe slipped out of bed long before their alarms were set to go off and quickly made her way to the other side of the room, where Cole had laid out his things for work, just as he did every day. She picked up his wallet and found his access card for Wilborn Holdings. He hadn't confirmed it, but she suspected this would get her into the command center.

She looked back at the bed where Cole was still sleeping soundly. Zoe needed to do this for him. It wasn't fair to ask him to betray his family. She would confront them so he didn't have to.

"I'm sorry, Cole. I love you," she whispered, her final goodbye. He stirred in his sleep, and for a second, she thought about climbing back into bed, but she couldn't. This was the way it had to be.

She left the room, grabbing the clothes she had left out for herself, then changed in the hallway and headed to her car. The gun was waiting in the glovebox, and she took a moment to make sure that it was loaded before tucking it into the back of her waistband. It pushed into her back, but she didn't mind. The dull pain helped keep her focused.

The parking garage only housed a few cars when she arrived. It would be several more hours before people started to show up for work. She planned to be long gone by that point.

Zoe took a few deep breaths before heading inside.

There was a security guard stationed at the front desk. Zoe had hoped she would be able to slip by him unnoticed, but his eyes locked on her the moment she entered the lobby. Putting on a confident face, she walked over to him.

"Good morning," she said as brightly as she could, despite the fact that she felt moments away from breaking down in tears. She needed to hold it together.

"What can I do for you?" the guard asked.

"I'm Zoe Antos, Cole Wilborn's fiancée." She held out her hand.

"I know who you are." The guard didn't shake her hand.

"Great." Zoe lowered it. Could this be any more awkward? "Cole's pretty sick, and he sent me to get some things from his office."

She took a step toward the door leading into the building, but the security guard put his hand up to stop her. "I'll call someone to escort you up there."

"That won't be necessary. I know where I'm going, and Cole gave me his card to get in." Zoe held up the keycard, praying that would be enough.

"I'm sorry, but that's not how this works. You'll have to wait here for someone to take you up."

Zoe was done messing around. If she had to wait, she would likely lose the shred of courage she had.

"I can call Gordon Wilborn and get him to approve it" She pulled out her cell phone. "But he hates being woken up this early, especially over something as trivial as this. In a few months, I'll be a Wilborn, and part of this company will be mine. I'd hate for anything to happen to your job because you were difficult to work with."

The guard rolled his eyes. She was sure the Wilborns weren't paying him enough to deal with what she was putting him through. "I'll need to check your bag," the guard said in a last-ditch effort to maintain some authority.

"If you must." Zoe tossed it at him, thankful that she had put the gun in her waistband. She tapped her foot as she watched the guard go through her purse. He pulled out her wallet and checked her ID before putting everything back. "Can I go now?" Zoe grabbed her purse off the table and slung it over her shoulder.

"Yes, you're free to go."

"Thank you." Zoe swiped Cole's badge at the turnstile and entered the building, making a beeline for the elevators and praying that no one would be there. She really didn't want to have to make a detour to Cole's office before going up to the command center. Every minute she spent inside the building put her at greater risk.

Thankfully, the elevator was empty. Zoe pushed the button for the top floor, but nothing happened. She remembered that Cole had said access was limited. She swiped his badge on the elevator's card reader, and her heart jumped out of her chest as it sprang upward at an alarming speed.

She didn't realize she was holding her breath until the doors opened on the top floor. Cole had mentioned armed guards, but the hallway was empty. Now that she was here, Zoe wasn't sure what to do. Peeking into a few rooms, she didn't see anything that looked like it would be a control room.

Panic choked her. She was running out of time; people would start showing up for work soon. Zoe wandered the hallway aimlessly until she finally heard a humming sound from one of the rooms — the same sound the computers in her lab made. She ran toward the door and threw it open, entering a room full of control panels and large screens.

This had to be it.

She went to the station closest to her, but now that she was here, she had no idea what to do. She didn't even know how to turn the thing on, let alone how to stop the toxin's release. If she wasn't careful, she might end up accidently releasing it herself.

Zoe looked around the room for help, and her eyes landed on a water jug in the corner. It was only a third full. She might not know much about computers, but she knew they didn't get along with water.

She grabbed the bottle and dumped it on the first station. The computers hissed and then flashed out. One down; only three more stations to go.

Zoe searched the room for another bottle of water, but there was none. She would need to figure something else out.

With a sigh, she pulled out the gun. She had no idea if this would work, but she was desperate. Praying the room had some kind soundproofing, she walked over to the second station and aimed the gun at the center, firing two shots. The lights flashed, but she had no idea if she had hit anything important.

Zoe was debating if she should fire again or move on to the next one when the door flew open. Definitely not soundproofed.

Zoe spun around as the two guards rushed her. One slammed into her, sending her to the ground and knocking the wind out of her. She coughed and gagged as she tried to refill her lungs, then realized the gun was missing from her hand. Zoe scrambled to her feet, looking for it as she went.

It was too late. The gun was already under Alana Wilborn's shoe.

Cole's mother bent down, picked the weapon up, and pointed it at Zoe. "You silly, stupid girl. You couldn't leave well enough alone, could you?"

Zoe was having a hard time processing what she was seeing. Alana didn't belong here. She didn't have anything to do with Wilborn Holdings or the Arrows. It should have been Gordon pointing the gun at her.
"You're the one behind this?" Zoe choked out the words, forcing herself to believe what was right in front of her.

Alana was an Arrow.

"Yes," Alana beamed. "The Arrow Equilibrium is my organization."

"How did you know I was here?"

"I was alerted the moment you drove into the parking garage. The only reason security didn't stop you was because I wanted to see how far you'd get. I always knew you were smart, Zoe, but I must admit I didn't think you'd have the courage to try something like this."

"I know what you're planning, and I won't let you go through with it." Zoe tried to ignore the gun pointed at her chest. She would show Alana how much courage she had. Not to gain her approval, but to defy her—a woman she had loved like her own mother for years, and a woman she'd thought loved her back.

"You really believe shooting our control panel would stop us?" Alana's laugh echoed through Zoe. "We have layers and layers of redundancies built in. You can't stop us."

Alana lowered the gun and walked over to the row of control panels. Zoe glanced to the door, thinking maybe she could make a break for it while the woman was distracted, but the guard who tackled her was blocking it. She was trapped.

Her gaze went back to the gun in Alana's hand. Several people had pointed weapons at her over the last few weeks, but this was the only time Zoe was absolutely certain the owner wouldn't hesitate to pull the trigger.

"Why are you doing this?" Engaging with Ian and Blake when they'd held her captive had given her a chance to free herself; maybe it would work again. At least it might buy her more time to think.

"The planet is dying. Humans have taken and taken without any regard to the consequences. The only way we can save Earth is to restore the balance. And you could have been a part of it, made a better future for your children. You're an environmentalist at heart,"

Alana said as she looked over the control panel. "I would have thought you of all people would understand. I had such high hopes for you, Zoe. We could have remade the world together, if only you had stepped aside and let me do the hard part."

"Not if that means killing billions of people." Zoe's eyes darted around the room, searching for something to protect herself.

"The planet is overpopulated. It's not sustainable. If we don't do something drastic, everyone will die anyway, and it will be a much more painful death than what I'm giving them. Disease, hurricanes, floods, earthquakes—these are the planet's way of bringing itself back into balance. The Arrow Equilibrium is simply aiding that process." There was so much conviction in Alana's voice. She clearly believed this was her purpose in life—and it terrified Zoe.

"I've told Cole everything. He'll find a way to stop you." Tears coursed down her cheeks.

"That is unfortunate. I didn't want him to find out this way. It would have been easier for him to accept after the fact." Alana tapped a few keys on the panel. "But he won't get the chance to stop us. No one will. All you've done is move up our timetable a few days." She clicked a few more buttons and turned back to Zoe. The screens filled with the words, *Launch Successful.*

It was too late. The toxin was being released, and there was nothing Zoe could do to stop it. She had failed.

"Now, what are we going to do about you?" Alana pointed the gun at her again.

"Just kill me." Zoe didn't bother to hold back the sobs. "I know you want to." She couldn't believe this was happening. So many people were about to die, and they had no idea.

"I would love to, but my son loves you, and he would never forgive me if I killed you," Alana said—as if Cole would have no problem forgiving her for killing off the rest of the planet. "Still, I can't let you walk out of here and tell everyone what happened." She lowered the gun slightly and pulled the trigger. A searing pain cut through Zoe's thigh. Screaming, she collapsed.

Alana crouched down in front of her. "By the time that heals, you'll see things our way."

In that moment, Zoe wished the bullet had hit her heart.

««»»

Cole woke slowly and stretched out in bed, only to find the other side was cold.

He shot up. Zoe was gone.

He grabbed his phone off the nightstand, and dread washed over him. It was too early for her to have gone into work. She had gone to Wilborn Holdings alone to try to stop the release of the toxin.

Cole jumped out of bed and ran over to the dresser, where his wallet lay open. His keycard was gone. "Damn it, Zoe!"

He quickly threw on a pair of pants and a shirt. Out of the corner of his eye, he noticed an unfamiliar flip-phone lying on the floor. Zoe must have dropped it. Cole picked it up and turned it on. There was only one number in the call history. He hit dial as he ran down the stairs.

"Hello," Ian's groggy voice came after the second ring.

"Please tell me Zoe is with you," Cole said as he threw on some shoes and grabbed his keys from the table by the front door.

"Why would she be with me? What happened?" Ian sounded more alert now. Was that concern for Zoe's safety in his voice, or for his own? Cole had assumed Ian only saw Zoe as a tool to get the information he wanted. He hadn't considered that Ian might actually care about her.

"I think she went to Wilborn Holding to try to stop the Arrows on her own. I'm heading there now." Cole wedged the phone between his shoulder and ear as he got into his car.

"We'll meet you there." The line went dead.

Cole started his car and pulled out. He didn't pay any attention to what he was doing as he drove to the city. Why had he chosen to live so far away? Zoe was in trouble, and Cole wasn't sure he would get there in time to help her. He honked his horn at a car driving five miles under the speed limit as he weaved through traffic.

Ian, Iris, and Blake were waiting for him when he pulled his car into the parking garage. Cole drove directly to them and jumped out, leaving the car parked in the lane. "Let's go. She's in there with no way to protect herself."

"Not exactly," Blake said.

Everyone turned to look at him. "What do you mean?" Ian asked.

"When she was at the house the other day, she asked me for a gun. I gave her mine."

"Why would you do that?" Ian snapped.

Blake shrugged. "She wanted to be able to protect herself."

Cole couldn't decide if Zoe having a gun made the situation better or worse. Ian clearly thought it was a bad thing. "It doesn't matter," he finally said. "We need to get to her. Come on." Cole led the way across the lobby to the security desk. "Let us in," he barked while they were still several feet away from the desk.

The guard fumbled at the computer. Shift changed had just happened, and he wondered if the guard was even logged in yet. "I'm sorry, Mr. Wilborn—it looks like you've already badged in for the day," the guard said, confirming his fears. Zoe had stolen his keycard to break into the building and was probably going to end up getting herself killed. "I'm going to need to call my manager," the guard added, her voice trembling as she reached for the phone.

"Pick up that phone and you're fired. I said let us in—and give me your keycard." Cole nodded to the card attached to her waist. The guard hesitated. "Now!"

She quickly removed the badge and handed it to Cole, who opened the door for the others to pass through before quickly following. "This way. She's on the top floor."

They ran to the elevators. The door to one was in the process of closing when Blake lunged forward and thrust his arm in before it could shut completely.

"We need this," Blake said. The people on the elevator didn't move.

"Everyone out!" Cole barked as he pushed the door open. At the sound of his voice, everyone piled off. He wasn't the most powerful Wilborn in the building, not by a long shot, but he had enough power for this. He pushed the button to close the door, then swiped the guard's card to get them access to the top floor.

The elevator rose though the building more slowly than Cole remembered. He was pretty sure it was be broken.

The doors had just started to open on the top floor when he heard the echo of a gunshot. Time froze as the sound echoed in the tiny metal box, vibrating across every nerve in his body vibrate. "Oh my God."

Cole pushed the doors open the rest of the way and took off running toward the control room at the end of the hall. There was a body blocking the entrance — someone from security. Cole shoved them out of the way with a strength he didn't know he had. Zoe was sprawled out on the floor with tears streaming down her face. She turned to look at him with pain and fear in her eyes, her left leg soaked in blood.

The part that Cole couldn't believe was his mom, crouched down in front of Zoe with a gun in her hand.

"Mom?" His voice shook as he croaked the word.

Alana shot to her feet. "Cole, darling, you shouldn't be here."

He rushed to Zoe, dropping to his knees next to her. She clutched his hand as she pulled herself closer to him, her face streaked in tears and blood.

"What did you do?" He glared at his mom as someone gasped behind him. The others had finally caught up.

"Leave her alone, Cole," Alana ordered.

"No."

"I said, get up. Zoe will be fine if everyone does what I say." His mom pointed the gun at Zoe again. Cole didn't doubt she would follow through on her threat. He put his hands up and slowly rose to his feet.

"She released the toxin," Zoe said as she slowly pulled herself across the floor. "We failed. You need to get out of here. Go, before she does something to you." Cole saw her wince with every move she took.

"We aren't leaving without you." Ian took a step toward Zoe, and Alana aimed the gun at him instead. Ian stopped dead.

"No one is going anywhere," Alana said. Zoe had made it halfway to the door, leaving a trail of blood behind her. Cole wanted to go to her, but he wasn't sure what his mother would do if he tried. He had never seen this side of her before. "I would stop moving, unless you want a bullet in the other leg as well."

"Why are you doing this?" Cole had almost come to accept that his dad was an Arrow, but this was too much. How could his mom have shot Zoe?

"It's the only way to ensure the planet has a future. I don't expect you to understand now, but you will eventually." She looked at him like he was a child. Nausea burned in Cole's throat.

"No, I won't." He took a small step back, wanting to put some distance between him and the woman who gave birth to him.

"You're my son, and I love you, Cole, but this is bigger than you. It's bigger than all of us." Alana turned to the security guard beside her. "Kill them," she nodded to Ian, Blake, and Iris, "then take Zoe and my son to a safehouse. Keep them there until I arrive."

The guard pulled out a gun, and a hand wrapped around Cole's arm. The next thing he knew, there was a gun pressed to his temple. "That's not going to happen," Ian growled behind Cole.

"Let go of my son." Alana's words were carefully measured to mask her anger. Cole had heard that tone from her growing up; she was moments away from snapping. Would she sacrifice him for the Arrows? Cole had no idea if Ian would pull the trigger or not, but at the moment, he was more afraid of his mom.

"Drop your weapons," Ian said. No one moved. Ian twisted Cole's arm into his back, and he cried out in pain, exaggerating for effect.

"Mom, help," Cole begged. The only way the others would get out of the building alive was if he could reach the part of his mom that wasn't an Arrow. The part that had kissed his skinned knees and chased away the monsters under his bed. The part that loved him.

"Alright," Alana said, putting her hand up carefully and setting her gun down on floor. The security guard followed suit. "Now what? It's too late for you to stop us."

"Now you're going to let us walk out of here. All of us. And once I'm sure we're safe, I'll release him. Try and stop us, and I put a bullet in his head. Blake, Iris, grab Zoe and get her back to the car," Ian said.

Cole watched as Iris and Blake helped Zoe to her feet. She let out a choked scream as she tried to put pressure on her injured leg. God, that was a lot of blood. Blake wrapped his arm around her waist to support her, and the three of them slowly made their way from the room. Ian didn't budge; Cole guessed he wanted to give them a head start. Zoe wasn't moving anywhere fast.

"Alright, stay here. If you don't follow us, I'll release your son in the parking garage. Try and stop us from leaving, and he's dead." Ian slowly backed from room. He eased up his grip on Cole's arm as they moved down the hall and into the elevator, but he never let go. Cole wasn't sure if this was an act or not, and he didn't really care as long as Zoe got out safe. She needed medical attention, and soon, or it wouldn't matter that his mom had only shot her in the leg.

His father was waiting for them in parking garage with a group of security guards and Jackson. "What the hell is going on?" Cole's brother jerked toward him, but their father put out an arm to stop him.

Blake and Iris were standing next to their car, where Cole could just make out Zoe lying in the back seat. Ian waited until he was next to the car to let go of Cole's arm. Cole turned to face him. "Take care of her for me."

Ian nodded and got into the car. Cole didn't move as he watched them speed out of the parking lot.

He didn't know if the toxin his mom had released would really bring about the end of the world, but he knew as he watched Ian's car disappear around the corner that the world he knew, at least was over forever.

«‹◊›»

Pain—that was all Zoe had left. The wound in her thigh wasn't the worst part, though that was growing more intense with every passing moment. It wasn't even the pain that came with knowing that she had failed and billions of people were going to die. That pain was too big to really be felt. It was abstract. No, what hurt the most was knowing that she had lost Cole, probably forever.

That was what she focused on now as she lay in the back seat of Ian's car with her head in Iris's lap. The woman was trying to comfort her, slowly brushing her hair out of her tearstained face, but Zoe didn't want to be comforted. This pain was all she had left.

"Ian, there's so much blood," Iris said.

"I know." Ian was kneeling backward on the front passenger seat, while Blake drove them away from

Wilborn Holdings Headquarters. "We need to get pressure on it, try to slow the bleeding down."

"Just let me die," Zoe groaned.

"I promised Cole I'd take care of you, and I intend on following through on that promise." Ian fumbled with a first aid kit, managing to pull out a roll of gauze before dropping the rest of it on the car's floor. He wedged himself in between the driver and passenger seat, then started to wrap the gauze around the bullet wound. Zoe winced every time he touched her.

"Everyone hang on," Blake called over his shoulder. The car jerked across three lanes of traffic and headed toward the off-ramp. Zoe screamed. It sounded surreal in the confined space of the car.

"What the hell, Blake," Iris yelled.

"I need to make sure we aren't being followed."

Zoe was dizzy. She could hear the others in the car, but it was like she was watching a movie that kept fading in and out. She desperately wanted to let go.

"A gunshot wound to the leg." Ian had a phone wedged between his ear and shoulder as he continued to put pressure on Zoe's wound. "Can you meet us? I'm going to need help on this one. I'll text you the address."

"Who was that?" Zoe's said in between short breaths.

"A friend."

They bounced in the back seat as the car hit a pothole. "I'm going to be sick," Zoe said as a fresh wave of pain washed over her.

Iris grabbed a plastic shopping bag from the floor of the car and held it open for Zoe. "In here." Zoe turned her head just enough to vomit into the bag.

"Shit," she heard Ian say, though she could barely focus on him. "She's going into shock. We need to elevate her feet." Ian grabbed a duffle bag from the front seat and shoved it under her legs. The sudden movement bought about another wave a vomit.

"Just hang in there, Zoe—we're almost there," Blake called, taking another sharp turn.

Zoe didn't want to hang in there. She wanted to let go. It was getting harder to breathe, and she felt so weak. She just wanted it all to be over. Zoe felt her eyes close, her mind slowly going blank. What was the point of fighting anymore? The end of the world was here.

«« Acknowledgements »»

Cleansing Rain was the just for fun side project that took hold of my mind and heart and demanded to be shared. The inspiration for this story came from so many unexpected places that I'm still surprised it all came together. There are so many amazing people that helped me to bring this story to life and keep me going on the days that I wanted to give up.

As always, the first person I need to thank is my incredible husband Mike who does everything in his power to make sure I get the time and space I need to write. This means keeping the tiny people that reside with us occupied while I try to slip away for an hour on the weekends and handling the bath and bedtime routine every night so I can focus on writing. Without him, none of this would be possible.

A huge thank you to all of my Beta readers for the incredible feedback that helped me to shape the story to what it is today. Especially Jerusha who not only provided amazing feedback but has become one of my closet writing friends and a huge cheerleader for me over the years. I'd be so lost without your support and friendship. And Alex who took a chance when a complete stranger emailed him out of the blue for a beta swap. Your notes helped me to completely reshape Zoe's rescue and added so much depth to the story. You also gave me one of the best compliments I've ever received when you told me you were busy and it would be awhile before you were able to finish reading the second half of the book, only to wake up the next day to find you had finished the whole thing overnight.

I also owe a huge thank you to my mom who always gets to read the awful first drafts and still tells me they are good.

This book wouldn't be possible without the amazing team of people who help me polish and present the story. My incredible editors Renee Dugan and Dylan Garity who took my words and elevated them to a level I would never be able to reach on my own. And my amazing cover designer Maja Kopunovic who takes my often poorly written descriptions of the story and turns it into the most incredible cover designs for the book. Not to mention the RiverLife logo she designed for this story.

Lastly, thank you to all of my readers. Your comments, reviews, and support keep me going on the darkest days when I feel like I'm wasting my time.

CPSIA information can be obtained
at www.ICGtesting.com
Printed in the USA
BVHW080032240921
617451BV00002B/113